INTENDED

CONTENTION

SHERRYL D. HANCOCK

Published by Vulpine Press in the United Kingdom in 2020

ISBN 978-1-83919-322-4

Cover by Claire Wood

www.vulpine-press.com

Also in the *MidKnight Blue* series:

CHAPTER 1

Elizabeth Endicott walked into Cat's apartment. She'd gotten used to dropping in on her, thrilled to finally have someone she could call a true friend. She found Cat on her bed. She was lying on her stomach, and Elizabeth couldn't miss the bruises already starting on her back, along with the scrapes. Her involuntary shocked gasp had Cat craning her neck to look at her. Elizabeth hadn't known Cat had been hurt.

"You cut your hair," Cat commented, not having seen Elizabeth since she'd been back from Vegas.

"Yes," Elizabeth said, grinning. "I thought I needed a change. What happened?" she asked, indicating Cat's back as she walked over to the bed, sitting down and touching the bruises.

Her touch was extremely gentle—Cat flinched all the same.

"I'm sorry," Elizabeth said, grimacing, truly sorry if she'd hurt the other woman.

"It's okay, Bet," Cat said, moving to turn on her side.

Elizabeth saw the marks on her throat then.

"Oh my God!" she exclaimed, her eyes widening dramatically.

"Relax," Cat said, holding up her hand to calm her. It didn't help a lot; Elizabeth was ever shocked by the violence Catalina dealt with on what seemed like a regular basis.

Elizabeth sat down on the bed. "So what did happen?"

Cat shrugged. "Perp got a little too excited, ya know?"

1

Elizabeth grimaced, nodding. She couldn't fathom doing the dangerous job that most of her friends and family did. They were forever getting hurt, shot, stabbed. It was downright crazy, as far as she was concerned.

"How did you get away?" Elizabeth asked, curious in spite of herself.

"Oh, Blue and Mace took care of that part," Cat said, grinning. "The perks to having backup."

"Do you work with Blue regularly?" Elizabeth was curious now, always trying to correlate what her family and friends did with Cat.

"Often enough," Cat said. "Why?"

Elizabeth shrugged. "I've known him a long time," she said noncommittally, not wanting to say too much lest she be telling secrets she shouldn't.

Cat nodded. "And he used to date your sister, and you tried to date him while she was dating him."

Elizabeth was shocked by the statement, not sure how Cat knew that and worried at the same time—what did Cat think of her for that? "How do you know?"

"Blue told me," Cat said, shrugging. "No big deal, Bet. It sounds to me like he was just as guilty as you were."

Elizabeth shook her head, feeling ashamed of her behavior. "It was just another chance to scandalize everyone."

Cat nodded. "Although, he is rather irresistible."

"Oh, yes he is!" Elizabeth agreed wholeheartedly. Christian had always been a source of interest, simply because not only was he incredible-looking but he had that bad boy vibe that drew women to him.

"But definitely worth the trouble," Cat said.

Elizabeth looked back at her for a long moment, shocked by the implication. "You didn't!" she exclaimed.

"I did," Cat assured her, grinning.

"Stevie will kill you if she ever finds out, you know," Elizabeth said, suddenly worried for her friend.

"She knows."

Elizabeth stared back at her. There was no way that Stevie O'Neil knew her husband had slept with Cat and Cat was still alive. No way at all.

"You told her? And you're still breathing?"

"She was there, babe," Cat said, winking.

"You mean, you and she…" Elizabeth began, her eyes wide, now completely shocked by this revelation.

"And Blue," Cat finished, nodding.

"Oh my Lord!" Liz exclaimed, shaking her head. She was having a hard time wrapping her head around the idea. "You must be nothing short of phenomenal, sexually, to have achieved that."

Cat shrugged. "They had fun, I had fun—that's what counts."

Elizabeth shook her head again, still trying to reconcile the picture it painted. "But you're with Kana, aren't you?" she asked, having heard that along the way recently.

Cat nodded. "I am now, but I wasn't then."

Elizabeth nodded, then canted her head to the side. "It's funny, but you don't look like a lesbian to me."

Cat laughed softly. "Well, I'm not. I'm bi—there's a difference."

"So you do both?" Elizabeth asked, intrigued. She had friends that claimed to be bisexual, but it just wasn't something she could grasp.

Cat nodded.

"Hence, Blue," Elizabeth said, nodding to herself, her mind racing as she contemplated the idea.

3

"Right."

"So," Elizabeth said, her eyes narrowed in askance, "would you say sex is better with men or women?" She was asking the question that had come to mind immediately—she wasn't sure why, but she did want to know.

Cat thought about it for a moment. "I'd have to say women."

"Really?" Elizabeth said, surprised. "Why?"

Cat leaned back against her headboard. "Well, personally, I like to kiss. And I think women are so much better at it than men are."

"Hmm," Elizabeth said, looking thoughtful, her curiosity further piqued. "What's different about the way women kiss?"

"Think about the last time a guy kissed you. Didn't you sit there thinking, 'If he'd just do this or that it would be so much better'?"

Elizabeth thought about it, shaking her head. "I don't recall thinking that, but you're right, there are a lot of times when men's kissing leaves a lot to be desired." She shrugged. "I just figured that goes along with good sex, versus bad sex."

"True," Cat said. "But the thing about women is they tend to do those things that we women always want men to do. Since we're the ones that are more involved in the actual foreplay aspect of sex, we know what it takes to excite us. So women tend to do what women desire." She shrugged. "Women know what women want."

Again Elizabeth was contemplative. It did make sense that a woman would know what another woman would want, but was it truly that simple? Not in her experience!

"Well, I've been kissed by a couple of my girlfriends in London. And they did absolutely nothing for me."

"Okay," Cat said, nodding. "But were they family? Or were they just being outrageous?"

"Family?" Elizabeth asked, confused by the term. Certainly Cat didn't mean it the way it sounded—she knew she was missing something.

"Gay."

"Oh," Elizabeth said, surprised by the take on the term. She shook her head. "No, they weren't."

"That's the difference, honey. They weren't doing it to excite you, they were doing it to shock either you or people around you. It's not quite the same thing."

Elizabeth nodded, agreeing with that. Her friends were much like her, always striving to shock people into noticing them.

"I still don't know that a woman could excite me with a kiss, though," Elizabeth said. She was pretty sure it would just be strange. "I mean, women are still women, right? It's that whole same-sex barrier."

Cat shrugged, not looking concerned. "I tend to believe that all women are capable of being at least bisexual."

Now Elizabeth was shocked. Surely she couldn't mean that! "Why do you say that?"

"Women need so much more than men require. And what women need, a lot of men can't provide, because it's not in them to do it."

"In terms of what?" Elizabeth asked, settling comfortably against the footrest of the bed. She was really enjoying this conversation. Cat had a way of thinking that was so unlike anyone she'd ever met before. It was endlessly interesting to learn her points of view, and Cat was always patient in explaining them.

"Women need emotional support—we need to be touched, whether it be emotionally or physically. Many of us need to be intellectually stimulated, and mentally stimulated in order to enjoy sex,"

5

she said, breaking into a wide grin. "Women need a reason to have sex—men just need a place."

Elizabeth laughed. It was true enough, in her experiences anyway.

"There are exceptions to that, though," she pointed out, thinking of men like her uncle Rick and Joe, and Christian.

"There are exceptions to every rule, babe," Cat said. "That's human nature."

Elizabeth nodded, agreeing with that, and noticing that she'd felt a bit of a shiver when Cat called her "babe"—she wasn't sure exactly why.

"So you think that because women need more, they're capable of getting that from other women?"

"I think it's all in how they've gotten it in the past and from who. But think about it, babe. Women get it from each other all the time— that's why you have girlfriends," Cat said, shrugging. "Sometimes it just becomes sexual too."

"Well, what about you?" Elizabeth said, very curious now. "Why do you feel that you turned to women?"

"I didn't turn to women," Cat said. "I've always been attracted to women, since I was fifteen and had my first sexual experience with another girl."

"Oh," Elizabeth said. And then another thought occurred to her. "But do you think that women who are, say, abused by men tend to turn to women?"

"Oh, definitely," Cat said. "They don't find women as threatening. They also get the love and support they've always craved."

Elizabeth nodded again, making a new deduction. "So it's not really about sex at all, is it?"

"Most healthy relationships aren't, Bet."

Elizabeth looked back at her, surprised to realize that she'd never thought about it that way. To her it was always about sex, feeling good, or getting to shock people she had sex with, and where. It was never about feelings or comfort.

"So are all your relationships healthy?" Elizabeth asked, wanting to know if Cat practiced what she preached.

Cat laughed softly. "No, not all of them."

"What about this relationship with Kana?"

Cat thought about it, and nodded. "Yeah, I think it is."

"Do you love her?" Elizabeth asked, not sure why she wanted to know, but suddenly she found that she was holding her breath waiting for the answer.

Cat looked contemplative for a moment, then shook her head. "I care a lot about her. But I happen to know she's still in love with her ex-girlfriend. I can't love someone that doesn't love me."

"Can't?"

"Won't."

Elizabeth nodded, thinking Cat really did have a handle on her love life. She seemed to know her boundaries, her needs, what she could give and what she'd accept in return. Elizabeth wondered if she'd ever have it all together like that.

"Have you ever been in love?" Elizabeth asked then.

Cat shook her head. "Nope. I care about people I see regularly, but I can't say I've ever been in love. You?"

"No," Elizabeth said, shaking her head. "Never anything like what my aunt and uncle have, or even what Susan seems to have found with Dave," she added, feeling sad suddenly.

"It'll happen," Cat said wisely. "It just has to be the right time, the right person, and the right situation."

"That's a lot of things that need to align," Elizabeth pointed out cynically.

"True," Cat said, laughing. "That's why it doesn't happen a lot."

Elizabeth laughed softly. Then she gave Cat a pointed look.

"Now, back to this kissing thing," she said with a wicked grin.

Cat laughed out loud at that. "Still not convinced, huh?"

"Nope," Elizabeth said, shaking her head and feeling a little excited by the conversation, wondering at that feeling in the pit of her stomach, like butterflies trying to escape.

"Want me to prove it to you?" Cat asked, her look challenging.

Elizabeth's eyes widened, even as she felt her pulse quicken at the thought.

"I'm always game for a challenge," she said, feeling self-assured at that moment. There was no way she was going to be attracted to another woman, but part of her was excited to find out.

Cat grinned, moving down to sit right in front of Elizabeth.

"Okay," she said, staring into her eyes. "I want you to think about the last time you got kissed. Think about it, and remember exactly what he did when he kissed you."

Elizabeth nodded, narrowing her eyes in thought. A guy in a club had kissed her the night before—she thought about that.

"Was he a good kisser?" Cat asked.

Elizabeth shrugged, making a gesture with her hand to say "so-so."

"Okay, think of what he did with his hands, how his lips felt, everything."

Elizabeth closed her eyes. He had put his hands to her waist. His lips were strong, but more in a firm way, not so much in the way he kissed.

Before she knew what was happening, Cat's lips touched hers. The first thought was that Cat's lips were so much softer and more sensual than she'd expected. Cat's hand touched her cheek, her fingertips where her jawline and ear met, pulling her closer. Cat's other hand slid through her hair, guiding her head as the kiss intensified. Her lips became more insistent, sucking just enough, parting to kiss over and over again. Within moments, Elizabeth found herself wrapping her arms around Cat's neck, wanting the kiss to continue. Her body was tingling everywhere, and her pulse was racing.

When Cat pulled back to look down at her, Elizabeth found she was out of breath and quite excited. Her eyes widened. The idea that this was a woman that was kissing her had never even gone through her head!

"Oh my Lord…" she said, truly shocked.

Cat grinned. "See?"

Elizabeth nodded mutely. She did indeed see. And all she could think was, *Oh my Lord!*

"You win," Elizabeth said, grinning now too.

"I usually do," Cat said, laughing.

Elizabeth laughed as well. She had to hand it to Cat—the woman did not disappoint when she set out to make a point.

"You usually do what?" asked a voice from the doorway.

Cat and Elizabeth both turned to see Kana standing there.

"Win," Cat said, grinning. She stood up to greet Kana.

"Hey, Liz," Kana said as she walked over to Cat.

"Hey, Kana," Elizabeth replied, looking up at her and for once seeing her as the strong woman that she was, and what likely attracted Cat to her. Kana had a presence that couldn't be denied—she was a take-charge kind of person.

Elizabeth watched as Kana's eyes scanned Cat. She lifted her hand to touch Cat's throat gently, then reached out, turning Cat around so she could look at her back. It was done with the utmost care, and Elizabeth could see the concern etched on Kana's dark features.

"I know," Cat was saying, seeing Kana's grimace and nodding. "They look bad."

"Yes, they do," Kana confirmed, touching Cat's cheek. "Are you okay?"

"I'm okay."

Elizabeth watched as Kana kissed Cat so softly—now Elizabeth could understand the intensity there. She reached up, touching her own lips, remembering Cat's lips on hers moments before. It was definitely interesting to watch with the new perspective she'd just gained. But suddenly she felt like she was a voyeur, and an uncomfortable prickle of jealousy moved through her. She didn't understand it, so she wanted to escape it quickly. "Well, I better get myself out of here," she said, standing up.

"You don't have to leave," Cat said, glancing up at Kana.

"No," Elizabeth said hurriedly, wanting to get out of there now. She smiled. "I have some things to do. I'll leave you two alone."

"You ever look into that restaurant and club idea?" Cat asked.

Elizabeth glanced back at her. "Actually, yes I did," she said, surprised that Cat remembered.

They'd had a short conversation right before she'd left Cat's house that first time. Cat had told her that she needed to find herself something to do to keep her occupied so she didn't think about wanting to use anymore. Elizabeth hadn't been sure of what to do, other than shop. Cat had asked her if she'd ever had a dream. Elizabeth had reluctantly admitted to wanting to open her own restaurant and night club. Cat had told her to go for it.

"And?" Cat asked, giving her a pointed look.

"And," Elizabeth said, "I'm putting the few business courses I took in school to good use and looking for a location." She was inordinately happy that Cat cared enough about her to even ask. It felt so good to finally have a friend that cared about her, not about how much money she had or who her parents were.

"Fantastic," Cat said, smiling brilliantly. "Let me know what you come up with."

"I'll do that," Elizabeth said, laughing softly. "See you soon."

"See ya," Cat said, grinning.

Elizabeth left the apartment with a lot on her mind. She had to admit that visiting with Cat always made her feel like she was really getting her life together. She finally had a friend who wasn't into the bar scene in a big way, didn't use drugs, wasn't always jetting off somewhere to attend the latest greatest party. Cat was a stable, caring, and very trusted friend. Elizabeth honestly felt like she could tell her anything.

"So, what did you win?" Kana asked Cat, moving to sit on the bed and leaning against the headboard.

Cat grinned. "We were having a discussion on why women are better sexually than men."

Kana looked back at her openmouthed. "And why are women better?" she asked, curious.

"Because we kiss better," Cat replied, smiling as she sat down on the bed, leaning back against Kana, careful not to bump her bruised back.

"So *how* did you win?" Kana asked. She knew that Cat had a very different way of looking at things, and she also had her very own way of proving her point sometimes. It was a source of amusement for

Kana, but she was never sure what Cat would do at any given point in time, especially when it came to competition.

Cat grinned mischievously.

"Oh, no, you didn't," Kana said, shaking her head and rolling her eyes.

"Uh-huh," Cat said, chuckling evilly.

Kana gave her a dismayed look. "Girl, you are crazy, do you know that?"

Cat raised her eyebrows, grinning.

"You kissed the chief's niece to prove that women kiss better than men?" Kana clarified, ever shocked at the lengths the woman would go to.

"Right," Cat said. "Although, I'm fairly sure that Bet's not going to go running to her aunt to report that fact, honey."

Kana gave a short, appalled laugh and shook her head again. "You're so bad. I should be jealous."

"Are you?" Cat asked with a knowing grin.

"Did you do anything but kiss her?"

"Nope."

"I'm getting the better end of the deal, so no, I'm not jealous," Kana said, leaning down to kiss the side of her head.

"Uh-huh," Cat said, smiling.

"So what was all that about a restaurant?"

Cat shrugged. "We were talking about healthy hobbies for her to have, and she told me she had wanted to open a restaurant and club at one point. I told her to go for it."

"You did," Kana said, thinking that maybe Cat was buying more trouble with Liz than she realized. The English woman was trouble for anyone that was around her for long.

"Why not?" Cat asked. "She's got a style all her own, and I'm sure she's been in enough restaurants and clubs to know what's been done, done, and overdone. Why shouldn't she give it a shot?" she asked, leaning back against Kana's shoulder and looking up at her.

Kana stared back at her for a long moment, then shook her head.

"You're going to fix the world, aren't you, babe?" she asked, ever surprised by Cat's desire to help people.

"One person at a time," Cat replied, winking.

***

Stacy received notice in jail that Kevin and Erin Elmasian were suing for full custody of Emily Elmasian. She was furious. First of all because what was this Erin Elmasian shit? Second of all, she couldn't afford to lose the income from Kevin; it made it so she never had to work. Goddamn it! She screamed, yelled, cussed, threw things, and raged for three days before she was even able to think clearly. Then she devised a plan. There was no way she was losing this fight. Kevin was an alcoholic! He was a cop that was never home! He was a narc, a scummy narc of all things. And this tramp he was dating, or married to, whatever—what did she know about parenting?

Stacy Mallory conveniently forgot what a lousy mother she was. In fact, she considered herself an excellent mother. Emily always had a roof over her head, clothes on her back, and at least something to eat regularly. Stacy herself hadn't had it so good. She had grown up with a drunk for a mother and an abusive father who had beaten her and her mother regularly. When Sandy Mallory, Stacy's mother, finally left, she didn't take Stacy with her. Even though she'd been an alcoholic, Sandy had been the breadwinner in the house. David Mallory had never kept a stable job; his temper always got him fired. So the next thing ten-year-old Stacy knew, she and Daddy were out on the street. They lived in the family's beat-up van for a while, then in various homeless shelters.

David Mallory had left her at one of those shelters when she was fourteen, and never came back. A blossoming Stacy realized quickly that she'd better do something, so she started with stealing. She'd steal money, food, or small things to sell for money. After being caught twice, she was finally arrested and booked into Juvenile Hall. After that, she'd gone through a couple of foster homes, and she came to realize that she had a gift. She had a way of getting whatever she wanted out of men. She batted her eyelashes, flipped her long hair over her shoulder, showed them a bit of cleavage, and they'd do anything for her. She used it.

She'd caught Kevin Elmasian by using it. And when he'd tried to break it off with her, she'd gotten pregnant. No one left her until she wanted them to. She'd thoroughly enjoyed being with Kevin; he'd fed her need for drama. His buttons were always so easy to push. She'd push, he'd react, they'd have some spectacular fights, it was great! But then he'd had the accident, and that was something she couldn't handle. On top of that, they told him he was an alcoholic, like her piece-of-shit mother had been, and that he'd need his family's "love and support" to help him recover. He'd looked to her, and she'd run like hell. She had no intention of going through that kind of crap, not for him, or any other guy for that matter. Hell no.

She had his kid—that's what she had over him, and he wasn't taking that away, ever. She contacted a friend of a friend that owed her friend a favor, and got herself a lawyer. Then she set the whole story out before him—of course, her version.

"He's not stable," she said, chain-smoking in the jail visitation room. "He's an alcoholic, and he's got ADD. If he doesn't take his meds, he gets really mean."

"Mean?" the mousy-looking lawyer with the bifocals asked. "Did he ever hit you or Emily?"

"Oh, lots of times," Stacy lied easily. "I never reported it, 'cause he was a cop and all."

Fred Keegan, the lawyer, nodded and wrote that down.

"Do you know anything about this woman he's married to?"

"He really is married?"

"There was a marriage certificate included in the package that went to the judge," Fred said.

Stacy made a disgusted face. He'd married the bitch?

"It's just a play to get Emily. That's the only reason he married her."

Fred nodded, not saying anything, seeing the anger in Stacy's eyes and knowing she was jealous. He'd seen it enough times—the ex-girl-friend doesn't want to lose the man for good, he gets married, she gets mad.

"He's an undercover cop," Stacy said. "A narcotics officer, so he's always gone. Who's going to take care of Emily when he's gone? Some woman my daughter doesn't even know? How do I know she even likes kids? How do I know she's not just letting Kevin try to take her away because she doesn't want to lose him? She could be a nut, she could be some kind of tramp—I don't know her at all."

Again Fred nodded, already planning to check into Erin Elmasian-Shandley's background for fitness as a parent.

Stacy stared directly into Fred's eyes, her look promising. "I can't lose my daughter, Freddie. She's my life, the only one I have."

Fred nodded, wondering if what his friend had told him was true. Would Stacy do anything to keep her daughter? She had no money to pay for his services, so he was hoping they could work out some other form of payment.

"I'll do the best that I can," he said, putting his hand over hers and caressing her arm.

Stacy's eyes dropped to his hand, knowing what he was thinking. Getting up, she led him over to an area where the cameras didn't reach. There was a table in the corner; she sat him down there, and sat down next to him. She unzipped his trousers and reached her hand in, taking his limp member out. She stroked it until it came alive. She could hear his ragged breathing, and the next thing she knew he came all over the underside of the table. She smiled, satisfied that he'd help her now.

Fred left a few minutes later, a very satisfied grin on his face. Stacy went back to her cell and thought about what other lies she could tell in court to keep Kevin from taking Emily.

"She what?" Kevin asked, looking at the wormy-looking lawyer.

"Ms. Mallory stated that you have struck her and Emily," Fred repeated.

Kevin stared back at the little lawyer, then glanced at Erin. She shook her head. Kevin had warned her that this wasn't going to be easy. That Stacy didn't just give up—she fought back.

"Where are the police reports on these supposed incidents?" Kevin asked.

"She states that she never reported it because of your status as a peace officer."

"That would have been the perfect thing to do, report me," Kevin said. "If I'd really done what she said, I would have gotten fired."

"Perhaps she was worried about the welfare of your daughter if you lost your job," Fred said, smiling triumphantly.

"If she was more worried about Emily's safety than she was about Kevin's income, she would have reported it, if it had really happened," Erin said evenly.

"If there were no reports of this alleged abuse," said Jacob Berringer, Kevin and Erin's lawyer, "then she'll have to prove it, or come up with some kind of corroboration."

Fred nodded, making a note to himself. Then he looked at Erin, thinking what a very pretty woman she was. She had a quality of total sweetness about her. She looked like a nun compared to Stacy—that did not help much.

"Ms. Shandley, what is your experience as a mother?" he asked.

"I've been one for over eight years now," Erin replied calmly.

"You have?" Fred asked, surprised. Why hadn't Stacy told him that?

"Erin has an eight-year-old son," Kevin said. "Steven lives with us full time."

"If you already have one child in the home, where does Emily sleep?" Fred asked, thinking this might be a point of contention.

"She has her own room," Kevin replied. "Our house has three bedrooms."

"Do you own or rent?" Fred asked, trying another angle.

"Own," Kevin replied, his smile wintery. He knew what the lawyer was trying to do, and he wasn't going to let him win.

Fred once again nodded, unhappy that he wasn't finding more issues with Kevin and Erin. His client looked much worse than these two did. They were married, both working, owned a house.

"You're an alcoholic, aren't you, Mr. Elmasian?" Fred asked, his tone condescending.

"Yes," Kevin replied, his look direct.

"How long have you been sober?"

"Over four years."

It was the truth. He hadn't actually managed to get a good drunk on the entire time he'd been on his recent tangent. The closest he'd come was on the yacht, and even that wasn't drunk so much as reeling from the fact that he'd had a drink again. The lawyer hadn't asked when the last time he'd had a drink was—that was a whole other question.

Fred nodded. "And what about your Attention Deficit Disorder—is that considered under control?"

"Yes," Kevin replied, nodding.

"According to who?"

"My doctor."

Fred looked disappointed, scribbling notes on his pad.

"Will you authorize me to speak with both children?" he asked.

Kevin looked at Erin. She nodded slowly.

"I want our lawyer present," Kevin said, his tone no-nonsense.

Fred agreed, knowing he had no choice. "I'd also like to schedule a home visit with a social worker."

Kevin narrowed his eyes, but nodded all the same.

Twenty minutes later they were out of the offices and Kevin was smoking like a train.

Erin sat by, knowing that he needed to calm down before they could talk.

"I can't believe that bitch had the nerve to lie about me hitting her or Emily," Kevin said, shaking his head. "I went to extreme measures to keep from beating the shit out of her when she pushed me beyond my limits."

18

"She has no proof that what she claims happened, Kevin," Erin pointed out calmly. "She's desperate and she's making up anything she can to try to beat us. It won't happen."

Kevin took a deep breath and blew it out, shaking his head. "I hope not. Emily's quality of life was crap before—it will be worse if Stacy gets her back."

"That's not going to happen, Kevin," Erin said stridently.

The more Emily came out of her shell, the more she opened up about how Stacy really treated her. Often there was no food in the house, other than stale bread and milk that was either near or past the expiration date. "It tastes funny," Emily said, making a face, when she described the milk. Stacy never made dinner or breakfast. Emily said she loved "lunch" at school, because she got dessert and everything.

It broke Erin's heart that the child was thrilled beyond belief that Erin made dinner every night, and made sure that Emily not only had breakfast before she left the house but packed her a lunch for school every day. It wasn't right. Emily deserved a normal childhood.

Emily was like a sponge for attention. At first when Erin would sit on the couch to read a book, Emily would come into the room and stand staring at her. One evening Erin glanced up to see her there as she had a few times before.

"Would you like to get a book to read and come sit with me?" Erin asked.

Emily's eyes had grown wide, as if she couldn't believe Erin was serious. She'd run back to her room, grabbed a book, and run back to the living room. It was obvious from the look on her face that she fully expected Erin to have changed her mind about the offer. Erin had patted the couch next to her.

"Come sit right here," she'd said.

Emily had settled next to Erin on the couch and opened her book, trying to hold it like Erin did, with one hand. She dropped the book a couple of times, before Erin grinned and told her she'd probably have more success if she used both hands. Emily had nodded, and proceeded to try to read. Glancing over a few minutes later, Erin noticed that Emily hadn't turned the first page yet.

"Are you having trouble?" she asked.

Emily nodded, looking scared.

Erin put her book down on the coffee table, uncurling her legs and patting her lap.

"Why don't you sit here, and we'll read your book together," she said. "I haven't read *Cat in the Hat* in a long time."

Emily's smile could have lit up the entire state of California. They'd spent two hours that night reading *The Cat in the Hat* over and over again. Kevin had walked in at one point, and stood watching Erin and his daughter. It was a picture he mentally carried with him often. He wanted more than anything for Erin to be Emily's legal mother. He thought his daughter deserved the best, and Erin was it. He'd fight Stacy tooth and nail to keep Emily now.

CHAPTER 2

Dave and Cat were on a stakeout, watching a dealer to see if he'd lead them to his stash. Cat's phone rang. She hit the hands-free.

"Roché."

"Cat?" came Elizabeth's English-accented voice.

Cat glanced quickly at Dave and reached over, picking up the phone. He could only hear her half of the conversation.

"Hey," Cat said. "You did? When? Holy shit, where? Does it have the proper zoning? When can you see it? Oh, you did? Then what's the decision? Oh… okay, well, when do you want me to see it?" she asked, leaning her head against the driver's window of her Blazer. "I can't right now," she said, grinning and shaking her head. "'Cause I'm working." She nodded. "Well, after work, I could… Yeah, okay, well then meet me at the apartment at five thirty, okay? Great, perfect, see you then."

Cat hung up the phone a few moments later.

Dave said nothing for a moment, then looked over at Cat.

"That was Elizabeth, wasn't it?" he asked, his tone friendly.

"Yes," Cat said, nodding as she reached for a cigarette. Dave's eyes tracked the movement.

"I didn't know you knew her," he said, his tone still conversational.

Cat nodded, lighting her cigarette and taking a long draw.

Dave nodded too, then looked over at her pointedly. "Your association with her wouldn't have anything to do with drugs, would it?"

To her credit, Cat's eyes didn't even flicker. "Why would you say that?"

Dave's lips quirked in a wry grin. "Because for one thing, I know you overheard my conversation with my wife, who happens to be Elizabeth's sister, about her taking Nick down."

"You're assuming I knew who Nick was," Cat countered mildly. "And if I recall the correct conversation, you never mentioned Elizabeth's name. Again, you're assuming I knew who your wife's sister is."

Dave pursed his lips. "And there was the department-wide scuttlebutt going around about Nick Masterson, Assistant Chief Masterson's son, dating the chief's wild niece," he said, holding up his hand to forestall her comment. "Before you say it, yes, I'm assuming you know who the chief's niece is, and not my wife. What I need to know," he went on, narrowing his sky-blue eyes, "is how bad her drug problem is."

Cat looked back at him for a moment, meeting his eyes. "She doesn't have a drug problem," she said calmly.

"Do I hear the word 'anymore' in there?"

Cat didn't answer for a long, pointed moment. "I didn't say that."

"No," he said, shaking his head, his eyes still narrowed. "You didn't. Look," he continued, reaching over and touching her hand, "I just need to know that she's okay. She's my sister-in-law—I care about her, Cat."

Cat nodded slowly. "She's fine, Dave, I promise you that."

Dave nodded. "And I'm betting I have you to thank for that."

"Not necessary," Cat said. "I like her—she's a trip to hang out with."

Dave grinned. "I can only imagine. So can I ask what that call was about? Or is that top secret too?"

Cat grinned. "She's looking into starting a restaurant and club."

"Wow," he said, shaking his head. "That's kind of a shock."

Cat shrugged. "She needed a hobby," she said simply.

Dave laughed at that, nodding.

Cat was surprised when she got a call from Midnight Chevalier a day later.

"Cat, this is Midnight," the chief said casually.

"Uh," Cat stammered, glancing around her nervously. "Hi, Chief," she said, trying not to sound nervous.

"Do you happen to be free for lunch?"

"I, uh, yeah, sure."

"Great, how about meeting me at Anthony's, on the bay, at noon?"

"Yes, ma'am," Cat replied automatically. Midnight could have said "Meet me on the moon at noon" and Cat would have agreed. This was the Chief of Police talking—who was she to argue?

At noon, when she was shown to a table out on the terrace of the restaurant, she was shocked to see both Chief Chevalier and Lieutenant Debenshire sitting there.

"Thanks for meeting us," Midnight said, gesturing to a chair.

Cat sat down, nodding, looking speculatively between the two of them.

Midnight's eyes narrowed slightly as she easily detected Cat's nervousness. Midnight never realized that she made people nervous without meaning to. When she wanted to intimidate people, no problem, but she wasn't trying to intimidate Catalina Roché at all.

23

"Cat," she began, glancing at Rick, then back to Cat. "I want you to understand that this is a strictly personal meeting, not business at all, okay?"

Cat blew her breath out slowly and nodded. Then it was about Elizabeth. She knew she should have kept her mouth shut.

Midnight sat back in her chair. "I understand that we owe you a fairly huge debt of gratitude."

"Why's that?" Cat asked, the narc in her kicking in. Her eyes didn't even flicker.

Midnight's lips curled into a grin. All Dave's people were getting as good as he was.

"We understand you helped Elizabeth out recently," Rick said, his blue eyes narrowed.

"Sworn to protect and serve," Cat said, inclining her head.

"This was above and beyond."

"I don't think so," Cat countered.

"We do," Rick said evenly.

Cat looked at Rick. He was a very handsome man—it was easy to see what kept the Debenshire marriage alive and well. He had beautiful sapphire-blue eyes, much like Elizabeth's, with a finely boned face that spoke of sophistication. His long brown curly hair ruined that effect, however. He had a taste of wild to him, and Cat imagined it was something that attracted women to him in droves. But this was the man that had been devastated beyond belief when his wife had been thought dead years before. It had been all over his face during her funeral. He was staring at her at that moment with the direct look of a man who was used to getting his way.

"Alright," Cat acquiesced.

"Are you convinced that she's clean?" Midnight asked, concerned.

24

"She's clean."

"But will she stay that way?" Rick asked.

"I think she will," Cat said. "She's got motivation now."

"What would that be?" Rick asked, his look wry.

"Not getting nailed by her Chief of Police aunt, or lieutenant uncle, for one thing," Cat said, her look dry. "Also, she's taken an interest in starting her own restaurant and night club. I think that'll keep her busy."

Midnight nodded. "Do you know how long she'd been using?"

"About a year and a half."

Midnight glanced at Rick. He blew his breath out and sat back. It was obvious they were blown away by this information.

"We've spent so much time getting her out of trouble..." Rick began, by way of explaining why they'd missed it.

"Too much time," Cat countered before she could stop herself.

"Meaning?" Rick asked.

Cat hesitated, glancing at Midnight, who wore a curious grin.

"Well, the problem is, everyone's gotten her out of trouble every time she's gotten into it, and no one's really asked her why she found it necessary to get into trouble in the first place."

Rick looked surprised by this, then his expression turned cynical.

"Is that the bullshit she sold you?" he asked.

"No," Cat said, shaking her head. "I'm a narc, Lieutenant. I don't get sold anything I don't want to buy. The fact of the matter is, it's been a bid for attention all along. It's pretty classic, actually."

Midnight lifted her chin, grimacing.

"Cat's right, Rick. It's a classic. When a child feels like they're not getting enough attention, they behave badly, if only to get negative attention. I can't believe I never saw that..." she said, her voice trailing off as she shook her head.

"She hid it pretty well, I think," Cat said, giving them an out.

"We weren't paying attention."

Cat said nothing, not sure what to say. She had no way of knowing what all they'd done. Elizabeth wasn't their child, so where was her mother?

"Either way," Midnight said, "thank you for all that you've done to help her."

Cat shrugged. "No need to thank me—she's my friend, that's what friends do."

"Were you friends before you helped her?" Rick asked.

"Well, no," Cat said, grinning.

"Uh-huh," Rick said, laughing.

"Then let us appreciate you, okay?" Midnight said.

"Fine," Cat said, making a face.

Midnight laughed then. This girl definitely hadn't helped Elizabeth to garner herself attention. Dave had told Midnight about Cat helping Elizabeth, and Kana had confirmed it. Midnight had felt obliged to thank Cat.

"We wanted to thank you personally," Midnight explained, glancing at Rick. He nodded in confirmation. "And to tell you that if there's ever anything you need…" Her voice trailed off as she held her hands out.

"Not necessary, ma'am," Cat said, smiling.

"Understood," Midnight said.

Cat left the lunch feeling a sense of unreality. She had never thought that helping Elizabeth would get her anything, least of all a personal thank you from the chief. She'd actually believed that she'd get into trouble if Midnight ever found out. Interesting people she worked with, that was for sure.

***

Randy walked off the plane, holding Kat and JT by the hand. She smiled warmly when she saw Joe standing at the end of the gangway. The kids saw him a moment later, squealing in delight as they let go of her hand and ran to him. Joe knelt down, scooping up both kids in his arms and hugging them tight. People turned their heads to look, smiling at how excited the children obviously were to see their father.

Joe stood as Randy walked up. He held his arms out to her, and she stepped into them, hugging him as he hugged her.

"How are you?"

"I'm okay," she said, smiling up at him before glancing over at Jordan, who had stood off to the side during the reunion. "Hi, Jordan," she said, smiling at the other woman.

"Hi, Randy," Jordan said, laughing as the kids noticed her for the first time, pulling away from Joe to run to her and hug her too.

"How was the flight?" Joe asked as he turned, his arm around Randy, and reached out to take Jordan's hand. Kat held on to Jordan's hand, and JT put his hand in Randy's free one. They walked toward baggage claim to get the kids' bags.

"Pretty long," Randy said, sighing. "But they were good," she added, winking down at JT.

Randy had insisted on accompanying the kids to Florida. "Just for the flight," she'd told Joe. She'd been too worried about letting them fly alone to spend two weeks with Joe and Jordan while they took a break. Joe had agreed fully with his ex-wife's accompanying the kids to Florida, since he had plans of his own once Randy got there.

They got down to the baggage claim and waited. The adults talked while JT and Kat watched all the bags going around on the carousel.

Joe noticed that Randy looked extremely tired. He knew she was burning herself out big time, trying to run the center and keep up with the kids as well. She'd just completed her PhD in child psychology, and he was very proud of her. She frequently told him that it was because of him that she'd managed to accomplish what she had. He was never willing to take credit for any of it.

Once they got the kids' bags, they went out to the Cadillac Escalade Joe had rented to pick them up. Randy got into the back with the kids.

"This is so silly," Randy commented as they drove.

"What is?" Joe asked, glancing back at her.

"It's so far to the hotel, and you're just going to have to drive me back here tomorrow morning."

Joe had insisted she stay the night at the hotel before flying back the next day. He'd told her that he and Jordan wanted to take her to dinner for her birthday, which was three days away. Randy had agreed to stay.

"Well…" Joe said, his voice trailing off as he grinned.

Randy narrowed her teal eyes at her ex-husband. "What?" she asked suspiciously.

Joe glanced over at Jordan, who was also grinning.

"We kinda changed plans," Joe said, glancing back at Randy again.

"Excuse me?" Randy said, sitting forward, even as she noticed that both of her children had guilty looks on their faces as well. "Joseph Michael Sinclair, what have you done?"

Joe laughed at that—she sounded like a mother.

"You're not going back to San Diego tomorrow," he said, reaching into his inner pocket.

"I'm not?" Randy asked, starting to look panicked.

"Nope," Joe said, shaking his head as he handed her an envelope.

"Joe…" Randy began, her voice trailing off as she opened the envelope. Inside was a ticket. It said, *Disney Cruise Lines*. "Oh my God, Joe…" she said, shaking her head. She read the dates on the ticket. "A week?" she asked, sounding almost hysterical.

Joe laughed again, nodding. "We're going on a cruise, babe. All of us."

"But, Joe, I can't…" Randy said, shaking her head again. "I have appointments, kids I have to look after, meetings—"

"Derrick is taking care of all that."

"But—"

"But nothing, Randy," Joe said, his tone no-nonsense. "You need a break, and you're taking one, you got it?"

"I don't have any clothes," Randy said futilely.

"Handled," Joe said, nodding at Jordan.

"We're going shopping today," Jordan told Randy, winking at her.

"Oh, no," Randy said, shaking her head. "I can't let you two do this, it's too much."

"We're doing it, and you're going to like it," Joe said, his tone serious but his grin spoiling the effect.

"It's from both of us, Randy," Jordan said, turning to face her. "And the kids too."

Randy laughed softly, glancing down at the kids, seeing that they were smiling too.

"We're going on a big ship, Mommy!" JT said excitedly. "With Goofy, Mickey, and Captain Hook!"

"That's what it sounds like," Randy said, smiling. It was hard to resist her son's engaging smile.

She leaned forward, putting her hands on Jordan's and Joe's.

"This is so much," she said softly. "But thank you, it's very sweet." She leaned her head against Joe's shoulder. "You're not supposed to be this nice to your ex-wife, you know."

He turned his head, kissing her forehead. "You're not my ex-wife—you're one of my very best friends, love."

Randy smiled, feeling the tears sting the backs of her eyes. She glanced at Jordan, who looked back at her with a warm smile. Randy sat back, thinking about how lucky she was. She had divorced her husband of fifteen years, wanting to set him free to find what he needed for himself. He'd found himself a superstar. And the super-star turned out to be a really nice woman, who seemed to understand Randy's relationship with Joe. It was amazing.

At the hotel, there was one more shock to be received. When Joe escorted her to her room for the night, inside waited John Tearney, the officer she'd been dating for the last year.

John was the captain in charge of the juvenile division. They'd met years before Randy had ever been divorced. John had liked her right away. She had a sweet quality about her, but was very deter-mined to help children. Randy was a peace officer married to Joe Sin-clair at the time.

There had been a lot of controversy within the department in-volving Randy and Joe. At one point Randy had been accused and put on trial for the attempted murder of not only Joe but Midnight as well. She'd been acquitted of the crime, and Joe and Randy had stayed married, and obviously in love for many years after that.

John and Randy had started working together when she opened her shelter years before. John was a nice, quiet, unassuming man, with a dignified strength about him. At the age of forty he'd never been married. He was a gentleman to the maximum—it was some-thing Randy liked very much.

When the divorce had become known to the members of the department, John had waited a respectful amount of time and then asked Randy out. Randy had talked to Joe first, worried that it would embarrass him for her to date someone in the same department. Years before, she'd been foolish enough to have an affair on Joe, and it had been with a man that worked for the department. It had been a critical mistake, and Randy didn't intend to make that same mistake again. Joe had encouraged her to date John, telling her that he just wanted her to be happy.

Their first date had gone well; they'd had endless things to talk about. They discussed the center, law enforcement, life, love, everything. It had been great. She'd felt very connected with him, and it had felt good. At the end of their first date, he'd walked her to her door, kissing her softly on the cheek. It had been months before they'd ever progressed farther than a kiss at the door. John had been interested in getting to know her. He never asked her about Joe unless she brought him up.

Eventually, they'd talked about the divorce, and why it had happened. She'd told John that she felt that Joe and she had just grown apart, that their needs had changed, but they were now the very best of friends. It was true. Randy felt like she could tell Joe anything, and he could do the same. One of the things Randy liked most about John was that there had never been any kind of jealousy over her and Joe's marriage and subsequent friendship.

John honestly seemed to respect Joe. He often said that Joe Sinclair was one of the best cops he'd ever met. Randy knew she could never be with a man that didn't like Joe. She also knew she couldn't be with anyone that talked badly about him. Randy was fully aware that if it hadn't been for Joe, she'd never be where she was in life.

During the divorce, Randy had asked for nothing, except shared custody of their children. Joe had been the one to counter by giving her a million-dollar cash settlement, the house they'd lived in together, Sinclair House—the house he'd bought for her to run the center out of—as well as not only child support but alimony too. Joe was a wonderful, loving, fantastic man, and Randy refused to date anyone that didn't believe that. She knew it was asking a lot, but she also knew that she had a right to want what she wanted.

John Tearney met all the criteria she had for a man. For that reason, she felt herself falling for him little by little every day. It wasn't the blind puppy love she'd felt for Joe the first time she'd met him. But it was a deep feeling of a connection with a man that she knew she could be with.

When they'd made love for the first time, Randy found that John was a very good lover. He wasn't crude or rough; he was sweet, gentle, and very attentive to her needs. He told her over and over again what a beautiful, special woman she was. It had been a very special union. That had been three months ago. They'd taken their time taking that last step. Randy was glad that they'd waited—she felt very sentimental about Joe, and hadn't wanted to rush into another sexual relationship. John had understood, and given her all the time she needed.

Now she stood staring at him as he got up and walked over to her. She smiled brightly.

"Were you in on this too?"

John glanced at Joe, grinning as he shook his head. "Joe called me and asked if I'd like to come."

Randy turned around and reached up to hug Joe tight, then pulled back to look up at him. "You are crazy, you know that, right?"

"Yep," Joe said, grinning as he nodded. "Jordan will be over here in about an hour to take you shopping. John, I'm going to take the kids down to the pool, if you want to join us."

"Sounds good," John said, nodding.

"See you then," Joe said, inclining his head to Randy with a grin, then walked away.

Joe had called John Tearney to ask him about joining them for the cruise. He knew that Randy was dating him, and he also knew that Randy really liked the man. She may even love him. Joe wasn't sure how he felt about her falling in love again, but he knew it was the right thing for her. He had fallen in love with Jordan, right? It was only fair that Randy find love again. Knowing it was right and fair didn't make it easy to handle. But Joe was finding his respect for John Tearney growing day by day.

When Joe had contacted John, he'd offered to pay for John's ticket. John had politely refused to let Joe pay for either his ticket for the cruise or the flight from San Diego. Joe liked that; it meant the man wasn't really interested in money. It also built some respect for the man, and Joe knew he needed to respect whoever Randy ended up with. After all, he would have a hand in raising their children. Joe liked John Tearney. Even Jordan had said that she thought he was a very nice man. Joe figured they'd find out during this cruise.

Randy discovered quickly how much more relaxed Joe was since taking over as Jordan's security. She commented on it the second day of the cruise.

"You don't seem near as stressed, Joe."

They were sitting by the pool. The kids were at a "lunch with the stars" show. John had gone back to the cabin to take some aspirin for a headache, and Jordan had just walked over to the bar to get them drinks.

Joe grinned. "I guess I'm more relaxed right now."

"Are you seriously considering leaving the department?" Randy asked, leaning back and tilting her face up to the sun.

"I don't know yet," Joe said, then shrugged. "If Midnight gets AG, I may not want to stay anyway."

Randy glanced over at him. "Who do you think will take over if she leaves?"

"Probably Kyle for the time being. But no matter who they promote, or put in that spot, it won't be Night."

Randy nodded, knowing that Joe felt very strongly about Midnight being the best chief the department had ever had. It was true—Midnight had made a great deal of strides in a lot of areas. She was forward-thinking, with enough understanding of law enforcement to be able to take chances on new ideals. That was going to be a hard act for anyone to follow. Randy didn't envy anyone that tried to fill Midnight's shoes if she left.

"How's the election going?" Randy asked, knowing that Joe would probably have talked to Midnight quite often, regardless of whether he was in town or not.

"You know Night," Joe said. "She never imagines she's doing as well as she is. The polls are putting her at about sixty-nine percent of the vote. Women love her, men love her, Republicans love her, Democrats hate her but can't argue her stats, so…" His voice trailed off as he shrugged.

"So she'll probably win," Randy said, smiling.

"Probably," Joe said, rolling his eyes. "God help the state government then."

Randy laughed, nodding. Midnight would take them all by storm.

"So what about you?" Joe asked. "How's the center going?"

"Good," she said. "It's going really good. I've got six full-time doctors now, and three assistants. I need another assistant, and a receptionist, but at least I've got the kids covered."

Joe nodded. Randy's center was one of the forerunners in the social services field. Randy's concept of giving the children a warm, loving environment was making huge waves. She had written her doctorate on the benefits of a home-style environment versus a clinical environment on children displaced during law-enforcement upheavals. She'd found in her studies that children responded better, and were far less traumatized by law-enforcement actions where one or both parents were taken into custody, when they felt comforted rather than shunted from one barren, cold place to another.

Randy worked closely with foster homes, as well as toward permanent adoption to place children who were eventually removed from their parents' custody. It was a rewarding job, and the fact that she'd come up with the concept herself was extremely commendable.

Jordan walked back over to them, carrying a bottle of beer for Joe and margaritas for herself and Randy. She looked incredible in a black bikini, her tanned and toned body on show. Randy felt a stab of jealousy—the woman was just too beautiful. With her long dark hair shot through with rich auburn highlights and her liquid-gold eyes hidden by Serengeti shades, Jordan Tate was perfect, and Joe's light blue eyes definitely did a once-over as she walked up.

Jordan sat down on the chaise lounge next to Joe. She handed Randy her margarita, and then gave Joe the bottle of beer, which had been clasped against her side.

"Thanks, babe," Joe said, smiling as he took a drink.

"They didn't have Tequiza, so you have to settle for Corona," Jordan said, grinning.

"That's it, we're outta here," Joe replied, laughing.

Randy grinned. "Planning on swimming back, Joe?"

Joe pursed his lips. "Guess it would be a bit of a swim."

"A bit," Jordan confirmed.

"Guess I'll drink Corona and be silent in my protest."

"Good plan," Jordan said, winking at him.

The three of them sat together, drinking their drinks and relaxing on the chaise lounges. They talked about inconsequential things, enjoying their time in the sun.

"I think I'll go make sure John's okay," Randy said, standing up.

"He's not getting seasick, is he?" Jordan asked.

"No," Randy said. "He said he had a headache."

"Isn't that supposed to be your excuse?" Joe asked, raising an eyebrow with a grin.

"Haha, very funny," Randy said, walking past him and smacking him on the arm.

"So, we'll see you two for dinner? Or will you be dining in?" Joe asked, his tone lecherous on the last.

"Oh Lord," Jordan said, rolling her eyes and shaking her head.

"I'll get back to you," Randy said with a wink and a lecherous grin of her own.

"Ohhh…" Joe said, grinning, his eyes following his ex-wife as she sauntered away.

Randy looked good—she always did, with long golden curls and teal-blue eyes. Her body was naturally shapely. She wasn't all toned muscle like Jordan, but she was beautiful and sexy in a soft, sweet way. She wore a white one-piece bathing suit that showed off her body without being too revealing.

"Careful…" Jordan purred in his ear.

Joe grinned, knowing he'd been caught ogling his ex-wife. He turned his head, catching her lips with his, kissing her deeply. She moved to the chaise lounge he was sitting on, their lips never parting. Her hands slid up his bare chest, and he moaned against her lips. His arms around her waist gathered her closer as he deepened the kiss. It took a few minutes before he realized they were sitting at a very public pool with half the ship watching them kiss. He broke into a grin, and Jordan began to laugh.

"I think we need to go back to our cabin," Jordan said, smiling.

Joe glanced at his watch. The kids were scheduled to be back at their cabin in two hours. He stood up, pulling her up with him.

"Let's go," he said, his light blue eyes sparkling mischievously.

Joe and Jordan had arranged for three cabins that were all connected by doors. The children were in the cabin in the middle. The adults took turns leaving their door open for the kids if they needed anything in the middle of the night. It was working out perfectly. The kids were thoroughly enjoying having both parents available to them. Kat, as usual, also loved spending time with Jordan, since they had a love of art in common. JT liked John too, so things worked out well.

Randy walked into the cabin she and John were sharing. John was lying on the bed, his arm over one eye. She looked at him for a long moment. He was tall, not as tall as Joe but still tall at six foot. He was lean and handsome. His hair was dark brown, and he had hazel eyes. He also had the sweetest disposition she'd ever known. In a family full of intense, passionate men, it was nice to finally find one that was affable and easygoing.

Moving to the bed, Randy lay down next to him. John moved his arm to look down at her.

"You didn't have to leave the pool for me."

"I wanted to check on you," she said, moving to her side and touching his cheek.

John moved to his side too, looking down into her eyes. He was still constantly amazed that he was actually with her. She had always been the unattainable, yet here she was.

Leaning down, he kissed her softly, his fingers brushing her cheek gently.

"Can I ask you something?" he asked quietly.

"Sure," she replied, smiling up at him.

"Does seeing Joe with Jordan bother you?"

Randy hesitated before answering, then shook her head. "I thought it might. I mean, I've seen them together before, but not on a constant basis. But it really doesn't. Joe still means a lot to me, but I think Jordan is so good for him now. He needs someone to make him feel young again. I think I just made him feel old and tired."

"I don't think you made him feel that way, Randy," John said, staring into her eyes. "I think he was feeling that way, and he maybe needed a change to bring him back."

Randy considered that, and then nodded. "Maybe you're right. I wasn't saying that I was the only cause, I just think everything in our lives contributed to the divorce. It was just time."

John nodded.

"Now," Randy said hesitantly, "can I ask you a question?"

"Of course," he said, smiling gently.

"Does seeing me with Joe bother you?"

It was John's turn to hesitate, his look contemplative. Then he nodded slowly. "I'd be lying if I said it didn't a little bit, but mostly because I know that he knows you so well. It's easy to see how comfortable the two of you are around each other." He reached out, touching her cheek. "I just hope I get there with you someday."

Randy stared back at him for a long moment. It pleased her no end that he had been honest about being jealous of Joe. It had also made her happy to note it had nothing to do with Joe's money. The only other man she'd ever been with had been extremely jealous of Joe, and it had nothing to do with her—it had everything to do with Joe's money and position in the department. He had been a ruthless, angry man, and a dirty cop to boot, who'd attempted to frame Randy for trying to have Joe murdered. It had made her quite leery of any man she dated. She couldn't handle anyone that was jealous of Joe's money or standing in the department. That had been part of the reason she'd hesitated to date anyone within the department.

Instead of answering him, Randy moved forward, pressing closer to him and kissing his lips. John's hands slid around her, pulling her closer. They kissed for a long time, then he began removing her bathing suit, kissing her skin. She unbuttoned his shirt, touching him and caressing him. They made love slowly, enjoying each other.

Afterward they lay together, Randy in his arms, the back of her head against the hollow of his shoulder, both of them staring at the ceiling.

"I have a confession to make," John said, his thumb stroking her arm.

"What's that?" she asked, her voice still dreamy.

John smiled, knowing he was being a silly fool for telling her this.

"I have had a thing for you for the longest time," he said wistfully.

Randy turned over, propping herself up on her elbow, looking down at him with a quizzical grin on her lips. "Oh really?"

"Yep," John said, grinning boyishly. "When you started coming to see me about your idea to start a mentoring program, all I could think about was how beautiful you were." He sighed, shaking his head, a whimsical grin on his lips. "But you were the very married, very much in love with her husband, big beautiful ring on her finger Randy Sinclair. And who was I? Some schmuck lieutenant in the juvenile division."

"You weren't a schmuck," Randy said, narrowing her eyes. "You were a very nice man who never made one single pass at me."

"I wouldn't ever do that," he said, shaking his head. "Not to a married woman, especially one that couldn't stop smiling when she mentioned her husband."

Randy bit her lip, her teal-blue eyes shining.

"I began to think of you as…" He paused, rolling his eyes. "As corny as this is going to sound… you were like this beautiful butterfly—you'd float into my office, hover long enough to talk to me about what you needed, what you wanted to accomplish, and then you'd float right back out again. I couldn't touch you, because I might damage your wings, and I couldn't think of a damned thing to say to make you stay."

Randy felt tears sting the back of her eyes. What he was saying was so sweet. It made her feel so special—no one had made her feel that way since Joe.

"Then you didn't show up for a long time, and eventually I heard about the divorce," he continued. "I knew you'd started the center, and I knew that was keeping you busy. I'd get calls from you, but you didn't come into the office. Then you finally appeared a month after word about the divorce got out. I was dying to ask you out, but I didn't think I should."

"But you finally did," Randy said, smiling softly.

"Oh yeah, major stud that I am," John said, rolling his eyes. "I meekly asked you out for coffee."

"And the big chicken I was, I was afraid to even accept that," Randy said, making a face.

40

"What made you change your mind?

"Joe," Randy said simply, then saw she needed to explain. "I was afraid to date anyone at the department, after all that with Dickerson so many years ago…" Her voice trailed off as John nodded, his look grave.

The entire department remembered the trial, where Dick Dickerson had tried to accuse Randy of planning the murders of Joe and Midnight. It had been a nightmare in Randy's life, and she had never wanted to make that mistake again.

"Plus," Randy continued, "I didn't want anyone thinking that I had divorced Joe to be with anyone else. I guess I just didn't want to cause any more heartache than necessary. Anyway, I talked to Joe about it, and he said he didn't care about what the department thought, that he wanted me to be happy. So I decided that I did want to go have coffee with you, and get to know you better." She smiled shyly. "You'd always been so nice to me, a perfect gentleman, and I had to admit you were good-looking…" She said the last touching his lips with her fingertip.

John smiled. "Well, I was jazzed as hell when you told me you wanted to have coffee with me."

"I was terrified!" she said, laughing. "I had no idea how to go out on a date—I'd never done it before. You have no idea how relieved I was when you didn't seem to mind when I mentioned Joe's name. I was afraid I'd ruin everything, or make you feel bad."

"Why would I mind if you mentioned Joe?"

Randy shrugged. "I don't know, I guess I was remembering Dick, how he hated Joe's guts. He was always putting him down and making nasty comments about him."

"That's not really my kind of thing," John said, shaking his head. "I don't have to put people down to make myself feel better. Besides,

Joe Sinclair is a good guy. I can't think of anything I don't like about him." He grinned mischievously then. "I especially like him for letting you go so I could finally get you in my clutches." With that he pulled her to him playfully and kissed her lips.

Randy laughed, and wriggled as he tickled her. John was definitely a good man, and Randy knew that it was right being with him. He was good to her and good to the kids too.

That night they met Joe and Jordan for dinner. They had the kids with them. It was a nice evening. Afterward, Joe and Jordan took the kids with them, so John and Randy had a chance to spend the evening drifting along the deck, talking about whatever came to mind. They even danced when they wandered by a dance floor with slow jazz music playing. It was a very nice evening.

They got back to their cabin about midnight. Randy walked into the cabin next door, checking on the children. Kat was asleep with her favorite stuffed elephant in her arms, and JT was asleep on his stomach with his arm draped over a large toy PT Cruiser Joe must have bought for him. Leaning down, she kissed each of them on the cheek, smiling to herself. They were definitely beautiful children, and both very sweet. She'd gotten lucky with them.

Walking back into her room, she saw John looking out the window, watching the moonlight play on the water all around them. She went over to him, feeling a rush of joy. Here she was on a beautiful ship, her children sleeping happily in the room next door, her extremely thoughtful, sweet ex-husband probably doing God knew what to Jordan Tate the next cabin over, and here she was with a man who made her feel special again. What could be better? Putting her arms around his waist, she rested her cheek against his back. His hands came up to cover hers. It felt good.

After a long while, he turned around, looking down at her. He glanced at the clock; it was 12:22 a.m.

"Happy birthday," he said, smiling and leaning down to kiss her softly on the lips.

Randy smiled. "I guess it is my birthday, isn't it?"

"Yes," he said as he reached over into his suitcase sitting on a stand near the closet. He pulled out a small square box with a ribbon wrapped around it. Handing it to her, he winked.

"John…" she whispered. "You didn't have to."

"I wanted to, Randy. It's your birthday," he said, smiling indulgently.

She smiled, tugging at the ribbon. When she had the box open, she just stared at the bracelet nestled inside. It was gold links with blue topaz stones set in the center of each. It was beautiful.

"John…" she said, her voice trailing off in awe. "It's gorgeous. Thank you."

She said the last reaching up to hug him, kissing his cheek.

John hugged her to him, closing his eyes as he whispered, "I love you, Randy."

Randy's breath caught in her throat. Somehow she'd convinced herself that no man would ever say those words to her again. But hearing them now, she knew, she knew…

Pulling back, she looked up at him, her teal-blue eyes, the exact shade of the topazes in the bracelet, shining with tears.

"I love you too," she said softly, having just realized it was true. It wasn't the white-hot love she'd shared with Joe, but it was definitely love. A deep, wonderful feeling of being connected to someone.

John's surprise was evident. He had been half afraid to tell her, for fear she'd think he was crazy. The last thing he'd expected was that she'd say it back to him. But she had—she just had. Was the world about to end? The brightest smile crossed his face then, and he gathered her up in a hug, kissing her deeply. He wasn't able to wipe the smile off his face that whole night, even as they made love again. She had just made him happier than he'd ever thought possible.

Jordan smiled in her sleep. She was wearing all white and walking down the aisle toward Joe. Everyone was there. She glanced around, seeing BJ, Mackie, Cassie, Midnight, Rick… and there was Joe. He looked so handsome, and he was smiling. When she took his arm, he reached down and touched her stomach. *Oh my God!* Her stomach was huge! Suddenly she remembered that she was pregnant—how could she have forgotten? Her heart soared as they turned to the priest… but why a priest? Maybe it was Joe, maybe—and suddenly she woke up. Looking around, she realized she was in the cabin on the ship. It was around dawn, because it was just starting to get light. Joe was lying on his front, his arm over her stomach. She turned on her side and snuggled against him. His arms automatically tightened around her.

She rested her head against his chest and thought about the dream. She'd been pregnant and marrying Joe. What a dream! Examining it closer, she felt a stab of disappointment that it wasn't real. That awful feeling when you realize your dream wasn't real. She couldn't go back to sleep, as much as she wanted to, hoping the dream would come back.

She lay against Joe, thinking about things between them. How did she feel? Did she want to marry Joe? That was an easy answer—yes, she did. Did she want to have a baby with him? That wasn't as easy an answer. She'd never thought about having children before. Never really wanted them, but with Joe, she wanted a lot of things she hadn't wanted before.

Jordan shifted, moving to her back again and staring up at the ceiling. Joe stirred, then opened his eyes and looked down at her.

"Can't sleep?" he asked, his English accent thicker because he was tired.

She shrugged. "I had a really cool dream, and naturally because I wanted to go back to sleep to get back into it, I couldn't."

"Hate when that happens," Joe said, grinning.

"Me too," she replied, grinning as well.

They were both quiet for a while. Joe closed his eyes, nuzzling his lips against her temple. Jordan reveled in being with him. It was so nice to wake up next to him every morning. She knew that was the attraction to marrying Joe, so she'd know it would be him she'd wake up to every morning for the rest of her life. She'd never wanted a man like she wanted him. At times it scared her. What if he left her? What if he found someone else? What if Randy pulled him back? Jordan was fairly sure that if Randy ever tried, she could get Joe back. She just hadn't tried yet.

"Joe?" she queried after a long while.

"Hmm?" he murmured sleepily.

"Have you thought about...I mean..." Jordan stammered hesitantly. "Will you ever get married again?"

Joe opened one light blue eye, looking down at her. "Why?"

"What do you mean, why?"

"I mean, why are you asking this at..." He glanced at his watch. "Six in the morning?"

"Is it that hard of a question to answer?"

Joe gazed back at her for a long moment, his look perplexed. Finally he blew his breath out, shaking his head.

"I can't honestly say I've thought much about getting married again, Jordan."

"Is that because you don't want to?" she asked, knowing she was pushing it.

"It's because I don't see anything wrong with the way things are with us right now, babe," he said, touching her cheek.

"So you're saying getting married would ruin that?" she asked defensively.

"I didn't say that," Joe said, narrowing his eyes slightly. "I'm just saying I don't see that being married would change anything. It's a piece of paper and a ring on your finger."

"It's an important piece of paper, and it's a ring that makes things more permanent," she countered irritably.

Again Joe stared down at her, his lips quirking in a sardonic grin. "I was married for fifteen years, had that piece of paper and important jewelry, and neither meant shit when she wanted out."

Jordan stared back at him, knowing she wasn't getting anywhere.

"Okay, so you don't care if we're married or not," she said, nodding.

Joe looked back at her openmouthed, his light blue eyes reflecting bafflement. "Jordan, what the hell are you talking about? Why are we on this topic? Since when did you want to get married?"

"I want to be with you, Joe," she said simply.

"You are with me."

"But I want to mean more to you than just your girlfriend," she said petulantly.

"I love you, Jordan. How much more can you mean to me than that?"

She didn't answer, lowering her eyes from him and absently tracing a pattern on his chest with her finger. She was silent for a while, not sure if she should tell him what else she wanted from him. Would he laugh in her face? Or would he treat her like she was nuts? She had to ask. She had to.

Raising her eyes, she noted that he was still watching her.

"Would you, I mean…" Again she trailed off uncertainly as she gritted her teeth. She hated the feeling of nervousness in her stomach. "Shit!" she snapped.

"Would I what, Jordan?" he asked, sounding very English.

Again she hesitated, then looked him straight in the eye. "Would you ever want to have a baby?"

His look didn't even flicker. "I have two children, Jordan."

"I know that, Joe," Jordan snapped. "I meant with me."

"I know what you meant," he replied calmly. "I'm not in a place in my life where I want to start a whole new family."

"I know how old you are, Joe. I was at your birthday party, re-member?" she said, irritated and not knowing why.

His look told her that she was starting to irritate him. He had an infuriating way of being even more calm when he was annoyed.

"Yes, I remember you being there," he said.

"So you're saying that you wouldn't want a child with me?"

He looked back at her for a long moment. Then his expression changed slightly as his light blue eyes narrowed.

"Jordan, are you trying to tell me something?" he asked evenly.

"No," she said, shaking her head. "But believe me, if I were, you can damned sure bet I wouldn't now."

His look was quelling. She was being unfair to him, and she knew it. She had brought up the subject, and was getting mad at him just because she wasn't getting the answers she'd hoped for. Joe had never said he wanted to get married; he'd never said he wanted more kids. None of that. Jordan knew it just bothered her that Randy was forever the mother of his children and the woman he had once been married to, no matter what happened between him and Jordan.

They were both silent for a while. Joe moved to lie on his back; Jordan stayed where she was, on her side facing him. There was so much tension in the room it was tangible. Jordan was mad at herself for starting this. Why did she have to start these kinds of conversations? Now he was mad, and she'd probably ruined the day. Or... *Oh, shit!* She glanced down at him, seeing the contemplative look on his face. And she knew, somehow she knew.

As if reading her mind, Joe moved to sit up, turning to face her. Jordan sat up too, dreading what he was about to say. She knew it before he said it.

"Jordan," he began, his tone serious. "If this is something you really want—I mean, having a baby and all—I think it would be better if—"

"No!" she screamed, knowing exactly what he was about to say. She put her hand to his mouth, shaking her head vehemently. "Don't even say it, Joe, don't! I'm not letting you go, I'm not going to go find someone else. No, don't say it," she repeated, seeing the look in his eyes.

Reaching up, he took her hand, holding it as he looked into her eyes.

"Jordan..." he said, his tone reasoning.

"Damn it!" she exclaimed. "I said no, Joe, okay? This isn't some goddamned turning point, okay? It's not! It was a stupid dream that I had, okay? It got me thinking. But that doesn't meant that I want any of that over being with you—I don't. Okay? I don't."

Joe stared back at her for a moment, the look in his eyes somber.

"You say that now..." he began.

"Bullshit," Jordan said. "I'm saying it for good. I don't want anyone else, Joe, no one. I only want you. And I'll take you any way I can get you, period."

"So you'll settle for not having kids or being married," Joe clarified.

"No," Jordan said, her gold eyes narrowing. "I'll settle for living my life with the man I love, if that's okay with you."

Joe said nothing, slowly shaking his head as he got out of bed. Without a word he pulled on his jeans, picked up his cigarettes and lighter, and walked out onto the small veranda outside the cabin. He stood there smoking.

Jordan sat on the bed watching him, cussing at herself for starting this crap. She knew that when she started what he considered her "drama" it pushed him farther away. She was always afraid it would be too far to get him back. Lying back down on the bed, she couldn't help but cry. She felt so stupid for doing this. Why? Why did she have to ask him about all of this? Did it really matter to her that much? No, it didn't really—she had just been in the mood to ask. Now she had him worrying that she was feeling like she was missing out on something. No, she wasn't. She'd never been in love like this before. She just wanted everything with him. All those stupid little things she'd never wanted before. She wanted the 2.5 kids, the little house with the white picket fence, the stupid Cocker Spaniel, and even the stupid minivan. But if she couldn't have any of that, she'd just be with him, because that's what she wanted more than anything. Him. Joe.

Getting off the bed, she wiped at her tears. Walking out to the veranda, she reached her arms around him from behind, putting her head against his back. She felt him take a particularly deep drag on his cigarette and heard him blow it out in frustration. He flicked his cigarette away into the ocean, turning around in her embrace and pulling her to him.

"I'm sorry," she whispered desperately. "I love you. That's all I need. You're all I need."

Joe nodded, leaning down and kissing her. Lifting her off her feet, he carried her back to bed, kissing her the entire time. She clung to him, worried that nothing she could say now would convince him that she didn't need a baby or a wedding ring. He made love to her, and she took refuge in the feelings and sensations he created with his body. It was always good with him, always explosive and exciting.

"I love you, I love you, I love you," she repeated over and over again as her body exploded into tiny particles around him.

Afterward, he was quiet. Jordan said nothing, afraid to ask him what he was thinking. They spent the rest of the day celebrating Randy's birthday, drinking, gambling, and having fun. Joe was reserved; Jordan sensed it all day, but he said nothing else about the discussion that morning. Somewhere in her heart of hearts she knew he was mulling it over in his head. Joe never forgot anything; he never let anything go until he was ready to, and he wasn't letting this go just because he wasn't talking about it. She'd opened a can of worms, and now she couldn't control what happened. It scared her to death.

CHAPTER 3

Kevin was in his Durango, heading into the office from the field, when his cell phone rang.

"Mace," he answered.

"Kevin? Hi, it's Stacy. I'm at the airport, can you pick me up?"

"You're in San Diego?" Kevin asked, stunned.

"Yeah," Stacy said, laughing. "You didn't think they'd keep me in that stupid place forever, did you?"

"No, but ninety days would have been nice," Kevin muttered, more to himself than to her.

"Can you pick me up?" she asked again, undaunted by his cold reception. "We need to talk."

Kevin shook his head. The woman didn't have a clue about people working for a living. It was two o'clock in the afternoon—did she imagine he sat around twiddling his thumbs, waiting for something to do? Gritting his teeth, he forced himself to calm down. Maybe she'd come to her senses about fighting for custody of Emily.

"What terminal are you in?" he asked calmly.

"Uhhhh..." Stacy stammered. "I dunno. I came in on Southwestern Airlines—does that help?"

Kevin rolled his eyes, shaking his head. "Yeah, I'll be there in about half an hour."

"Half an hour?" Stacy queried. "That long?"

"Stacy, I have a job, you know. I can't just disappear."

"Oh," she replied dumbly. "Okay, see you soon then," she said, all smiles on her end.

Kevin hung up, thinking how unreal this was. He got into the office and went in to let Dave know that he needed the rest of the afternoon off and give him an update on his case. Dave grinned when Kevin told him about Stacy's "surprise attack" and then wished him luck.

Kevin also put a call in to Jacob Berringer, asking him if he had to release Emily into Stacy's custody if she was here to try and take her.

"She said you had ninety days with her, correct?" Jacob said.

"That's how long she was supposed to be in jail for, yes."

"Then no, she can't take Emily out of your custody right now," Jacob assured him.

"Good, thanks," Kevin said.

A half hour later he drove up to the terminal, and cussed a blue streak because she wasn't outside. He parked the Durango at the curb, showing the airport security officer his badge, then walked inside. He found her at the bar, talking to some guy and playing up the "poor me" angle.

"Ready?" he queried from behind her.

"Kevin!" she exclaimed, hopping off the barstool and throwing her arms around him like they were long-lost lovers.

Kevin disengaged himself, setting her back from him and giving her a fairly stern look.

"Let's go," he said, nodding toward the doors.

"Okay," she said, looking undaunted.

Once they were in his Durango, he lit up a cigar, opening the window and blowing a stream of smoke out. He glanced over at her. She was looking around at the interior of the SUV. The term "sizing it up" came to mind. She didn't say anything. Finally Kevin lost his patience.

"So why are you here, Stacy?" he asked evenly.

"Like I said, Kevin," she said, her look innocent, "we need to talk."

Without warning, he pulled off the street, parking in a lot that faced the bay. He put the Durango in park and turned off the engine.

"So talk," he said simply.

Stacy looked at him. He wasn't exactly acting happy to see her. She knew he was always very cool, but she thought he'd at least be a little excited to see her. She'd flown down here to him; she'd wanted to surprise him. He didn't seem fazed. But damn he looked good! She could never really get over what a sexy-looking guy he was. He was all cool ice, with this tough edge that excited her no end. There had been so many times when the sex with him had been rough, because they'd been fighting and he was usually drunk. He had a temper, and when she pushed him just the right way, he responded viciously, but if she excited him in the process it meant for some seriously explosive sex. She missed that. No one did it like he did.

He was wearing blue jeans and a black shirt with black boots. He had a small silver hoop in each ear, and a black onyx stud in his left ear. The top of his shoulder-length brown hair was pulled back into a tail. He looked rakish and sexy, with his dark sunglasses on. Sunglasses that hid bright moss-green eyes. She could get excited just thinking about the way he used to look at her when he was horny. And now she wanted him back.

She realized with a start that he was looking at her, his cigar clenched between his teeth.

"When did you start smoking those?" she asked, pointing to the cigarette-sized cigar.

"When I quit drinking."

"Oh," she said, not wanting to talk about that. "Why those instead of cigarettes?"

"What do you want, Stacy?" he asked, ignoring her question.

"God," she said, giving him an annoyed look. "I'm trying to make civilized conversation, is that okay?"

He looked at her, saying nothing, his eyes hidden by the shades, giving him an even more sinister look.

Finally she sighed. "Fine, okay," she said, sounding petulant, which didn't faze him in the slightest. "Look, I know you don't want to risk losing Emily…" she began, her voice trailing off as she sensed, rather than saw, his eyes narrow. "I mean, I know you want her full time," she hurried on.

"That's my plan, yeah," Kevin said evenly.

"Well, what if you could have her full time?" she asked slyly.

"I intend to."

"If you win in court," she retorted.

"Once again, I intend to," he said confidently.

"We both know that no court is going to give you custody," she said haughtily.

Kevin didn't reply. He had no intention of getting into a pissing match with her.

Stacy took that as agreement, and reached out to put her hand on his thigh. Kevin looked down at her hand, then back at her, his face a calm, unaffected mask.

"Kevin, you haven't ever been around for Emily," she said, her tone reasoning.

"That would be because you left me and took her with you, Stacy," he replied calmly.

"Well, what if I came back now, and brought her with me?" Stacy asked, sure that he was hoping for just that.

Again Kevin said nothing, his look so unreadable, especially in those damned sunglasses.

"Will you take those fucking things off?" she snapped, gesturing at them.

His lips curled sardonically as he reached up, taking the glasses off and setting them on the dashboard. He looked back at her calmly. She still couldn't read any emotion in those moss-green eyes.

"Don't use your narc shit on me, Kevin," she growled, irritated that he hadn't responded to her question at all.

"Is that what I'm doing?" he asked, his look unchanged.

"You know it is!" she yelled, clenching her fists, wanting to hit him, he was making her so mad.

Kevin's eyes flicked to her hands, clenched in her lap. Again the sardonic grin appeared on his lips as his eyes connected with hers.

"You didn't answer me," she said finally, when it was obvious he wasn't going to say anything else.

"What was the question?"

She narrowed her eyes at him. She knew he was trying to piss her off, and it was working like a charm, but she wasn't ready to give up yet.

"Do you want me and Emily with you again?"

He looked back at her for a long moment, then turned his head to look out the front windshield.

"Did you miss the part about me being married to Erin?" he asked simply.

"No," Stacy said, disgusted, "but you and I both know you only did that so you could have a chance in hell of getting Emily away from me."

Kevin pursed his lips. "Actually," he said, not looking at her, "that didn't even occur to me when I asked Erin to marry me. She brought the idea up later."

"Why does that bitch want my daughter?" Stacy snapped.

Kevin's hands tightened on the steering wheel. "Watch how you talk about Erin, Stacy," he warned her, his tone tightly reined-in steel.

Stacy sat back, sensing the violence in him instantly. No matter what she'd claimed, he had never struck her, but she had always felt that if he did he'd probably be capable of killing her. It scared her and excited her at the same time.

She glanced at his hands on the steering wheel. She remembered his hands well—they had grabbed her, touched her, excited her quite often when they'd been together. As she stared, she realized he wasn't wearing a wedding band.

"If you're married, why aren't you wearing a ring?" she asked cynically.

"I'm married, Stacy, trust me on that," Kevin replied mildly.

"If it wasn't a bullshit attempt to get Emily, why wouldn't you have a ring on? Or don't you want anyone to know you're married? Will that cut down on your sex life?" she asked sarcastically, remembering how sexual he was.

"Well, you got part of it right," Kevin said, his tone irritatingly calm.

"Which part? You don't really love her, do you?" Stacy said knowingly.

"Oh, I love her," Kevin said, nodding.

"Then why aren't you wearing a ring, declaring yourself off the market?"

"I'm a narc," he said simply. "You think I want those scumbags knowing I have a wife?"

"Good excuse," Stacy said, unconvinced. "You just don't want anything saying you have a shorty."

"I didn't say that," he said, his eyes dancing with vengeance.

Stacy looked at him, her face a mask of cynicism. "So what are you saying? You have a ring you wear sometimes? When you choose to?"

"No, it's permanent," he said calmly.

"What is?" she asked, bewildered.

Without a word, he unbuttoned his shirt, turning to face her. Pulling the tails of his shirt out, he opened it, baring his chest. At first Stacy thought he was getting naked for her—the idea thrilled her. He had an incredibly nice chest, well defined without being too much... That's when her eyes touched on the tattoo. She remembered well when he got the heart surrounded by the chains and golden lock. Narrowing her eyes, she noticed something new. Moving toward him, she looked more closely.

There was a key now, a gold key, outlined in black, with the name *Erin* in blue script.

She looked at him, her eyes burning with anger.

"She has the key to your heart?"

He nodded, his eyes widening slightly in amusement at her reaction.

Stacy sat back, her look disgusted. "Isn't that just too cute."

Kevin shrugged, not replying.

"And what was that key, Kevin?" Stacy asked, her voice dripping venom.

"A heart of her own," Kevin replied simply.

"You bastard," Stacy growled, not liking the direction this was going. "She can't have my daughter, and neither can you."

"I think that's up to the court to decide," Kevin said mildly.

"What makes you think they'll take Emily away from her natural mother?"

"The fact that natural or not, you suck as a mother."

"You fucking bastard!" Stacy screamed, launching herself at him, her nails flailing, catching him in the face and chest before he could restrain her.

Stacy struggled against his hold.

"Let go of me!" she screamed. "Or I'll scream rape!"

"Go ahead and scream, Stacy," Kevin said. "And when the cops come, they'll see the blood on my chest, neck and face, and not a mark on you—who do you think will go to jail?"

Stacy stopped struggling immediately, knowing he was right. She moved back to the passenger seat, still looking like she wanted to kill him.

"Now," Kevin said, reaching up and touching the blood on his chest, rubbing it between his fingers thoughtfully. "I'm going to take you back to the airport," he continued. "And I'm going to drop you off. You're going to get your ass on a plane and get the hell out of my town. Do you understand?" His eyes narrowed slightly at the last.

Stacy nodded, looking subdued. Kevin did precisely that, driving back to the airport and stopping at the curb. Stacy got out, and Kevin drove away without looking back.

Kevin went straight to the house, arriving before Erin got home for the day. He took a shower, washing off the already drying blood. Erin walked in while he was still in the shower, trying to soak away the tension he was already feeling in his neck and back. His back was to her when she walked in.

"Kevin?" she queried worriedly. She'd heard from Dave that Stacy had called Kevin from the airport. Kevin hadn't called her, not wanting to worry her unnecessarily.

He turned around, and that's when she saw the claw marks.

She gasped, putting her hand to her mouth, even as her eyes narrowed. "That bitch, I'll kill her!" she snapped.

Kevin shut off the shower, stepping out and grabbing a towel to wrap around his waist. Erin was there immediately, gently touching the scratches, her eyes showing her concern.

"It's okay, babe," he said gently.

"It's not okay, Kevin," she said, worried. "She gets violent with you every time she sees you—it's getting worse."

"No one ever said Stacy didn't have a temper," Kevin said, shaking his head ruefully.

"And if she has one with you, what does she have with an eight-year-old that gets on her nerves?" Erin asked, her tone disgusted. Then she suddenly realized what she'd just said, her eyes widening as she looked at Kevin.

He went very still. Erin was right. Stacy's temper was vicious, always had been. Had she ever let her temper loose on Emily? Emily was certainly timid enough.

"Jesus fucking Christ…" he muttered, his stomach tightening in a knot at the thought of Stacy hitting his daughter.

"Okay, okay," Erin said soothingly. "We need to find out," she continued reasonably. "We need someone to talk to Emily that knows how to ask her. We can't do it ourselves—if we do, Stacy's lawyer will only say that we made her say it, that we put the idea in her head. We need a professional."

To that end, Kevin talked to Dave, who called Donovan into his office.

"What's up?" Donovan asked, glancing at Kevin and then at Dave.

"Mace needs some help."

"You got it," Donovan said, nodding at Kevin. "What do you need?"

Kevin looked over at Dave, his look showing confusion.

"He needs your sister's expertise. Didn't I hear that Randy just got her PhD in child psychology?"

Kevin's eyes widened as he looked from Dave to Donovan hopefully.

"Yeah," Donovan nodded, turning to Kevin. "She's on a cruise for her birthday, but she's supposed to be back tomorrow. Is this about the court case to get Emily?"

"Yeah," Kevin said. "Think your sister could see her?"

"No problem," Donovan said. "I'm sure Randy'd be happy to talk to Emily. Want to clue me in on what she's looking for?"

"Nope," Kevin said. "I just want her to talk to Emily and form her own opinion. Think she'll do that?"

"I know she can," Donovan said, certain.

"That would be great, Pony," Kevin said, wondering if these people were ever going to cease to amaze him with their generosity.

That shock didn't lessen later that day when he was on a surveillance with Christian. They got to talking about Stacy, and her visit, and what she'd wanted.

"She doesn't seriously think she's gonna win, does she?" Christian asked.

Kevin shrugged. "I don't know that she won't."

"Not gonna happen, man," Christian said confidently.

"What if they find out about this last incident?" Kevin asked, his biggest concern coming to bear.

"They won't," Christian said. "There were no official reports."

"Yeah, but you guys can't lie for me…" Kevin said, shaking his head.

"So far we haven't had to," Christian said. "They keep asking if we've seen you take a drink or seen you drunk. We haven't, so that's not a lie."

"Okay, so what if they change the way they ask the question?"

"Then we lie," Christian said, grinning.

"And you'd do that for me?" Kevin asked, his tone disbelieving. "Commit perjury?"

Christian looked considering for a moment, then shrugged. "We figure it's the lesser of two evils."

"Meaning?"

"Meaning either we lie a little bit, to get you custody of your daughter, or we go up to Seattle and help you beat the shit out of the woman for not taking care of your daughter," he said, his grin sly.

Kevin laughed at that, shaking his head. It was unreal, the loyalty these people showed. He couldn't believe it. He told Erin about it later that night.

"They know this is the right thing for Emily," she said, turning over to rest her head against his chest as he smoked.

"Yeah, but… they're going to lie in court for me?" Kevin said, unable to believe that part.

"They bend rules when there's a principle involved."

Kevin nodded. "I'll owe them, big time."

"They're your friends, your teammates," Erin said. "They'll always be there for you, Kevin, just like I will."

Kevin nodded, still not sure how to handle that knowledge but feeling very comforted by it.

"I love you," he said, touching her cheek with his free hand.

Erin smiled, looking up at him. "I love you too, honey."

His eyes connected with hers, his thumb stroking her cheek, his look very serious.

"I want you to know, you are the best thing that's ever happened to me."

Erin smiled. "Well, besides Emily," she qualified.

"I think you're neck and neck," he said, smiling.

Erin was surprised by that. She knew that Emily was the one person Kevin had always loved. For him to say that she was as important to him as his daughter made a definite statement.

Reaching up, she touched the tattoo on his chest, the key with her name on it making her smile. He hadn't told her about getting it done, he'd just come home one night after work with a bandage on his chest. Erin had been worried that he'd gotten hurt. He'd been mysterious about it, saying it was a minor injury. Two days later, he'd taken the bandage off, showing her what he'd had added to his tattoo. She'd been shocked and thrilled beyond belief. It was a testament to his commitment to her. It was a permanent statement that said he belonged to her, and she to him. She loved it, and him.

***

Christian stood listening to the message from Stevie's doctor. His eyes narrowed as the doctor mentioned Halcion, a narcotic used for problems with sleeping. The doctor was saying that if she needed a refill on the prescription he'd given her, she'd need to come in and see him first. Christian wasn't aware she'd been taking the drug to sleep. It bothered him.

Stevie hadn't talked about the attack she'd sustained at Sergei's hands. Christian had given her space, knowing that if he pushed her she could push back. He'd been on her bad side one too many times, and didn't intend to go there again if he could avoid it. Now he didn't know if he could avoid it.

His lips twitched in agitation as he rewound the message and left it on the answering machine for Stevie to get. He'd come home in the middle of the afternoon to change his clothes. He and Kevin had run down a suspect that morning. Christian had been the one to catch up to the guy and tackle him to the ground, getting extremely dirty in the process. So he'd come home to change, and Stevie was out with Cat on another case.

He proceeded back to work, smoking all the way. His smoking continued as he went on a surveillance with Dave. Dave noted the chain-smoking, and recognized that Christian was agitated.

"So what's going on?" Dave asked mildly as Christian lit up his sixth cigarette in a row inside of an hour.

"What?" Christian asked, then saw that Dave was looking pointedly at the cigarette in his hand. "Oh," he said, grimacing. "Shit with Steve…"

Dave nodded. "Is she having a rough time with all that?"

Christian blew his breath out, shaking his head. "I have no idea, Dave. She won't talk to me."

"Not good."

"Yeah," Christian said. "And I find out today, by accident, that she's been taking Halcion…"

"She's that bad?" Dave asked, looking surprised.

Stevie had been acting perfectly normal around everyone. She was one hell of an actress.

"Obviously," Christian said, curling his lips in self-disgust. "And I'm such a great fucking husband I noticed, right?"

"Blue, if she's been hiding it, she didn't want you to notice."

"I'm her husband. I should have known."

Dave shook his head. "Blue, man, that girl could be an Academy Award–winning actress if she wanted to. If she didn't want you to know something, there's no way you'd know."

Christian blew his breath out, shaking his head. "Okay, but why is she hiding it from me?"

"She's hiding it from all of us," Dave pointed out. "I had no idea she was still reeling."

Christian nodded. "Okay, but why do you think?"

Dave shrugged. "Maybe she just doesn't want to face it herself. She reacted quite violently last time she was attacked—maybe she's afraid of how she'll react if she really looks at what happened."

Christian nodded, looking grim. He remembered hearing about the last man that had tried to attack Stevie, a couple of years before. She'd been working for a drug dealer named Marco Tiempo, as his bodyguard. She'd done it to get close to Tiempo, wanting to make him pay for the death of her brother-in-law, a cop.

When one of Tiempo's associates had decided that Stevie was a fringe benefit for him, he'd attacked her, even bringing a knife into play when she refused to give in to him. Stevie had shot him, repeatedly, because he wouldn't stop advancing on her. She'd finally killed him with a shot to the heart. The medical report had showed that the man had been on PCP, and that had been the reason he'd survived being shot so many times. He'd been determined to get to Stevie, and she'd been determined to stop him from raping her. It had been a lethal combination.

"Well, if she's taking narcotics to keep from dealing with this, Dave, I need to do something."

"I agree," Dave said, nodding.

Christian looked pensive. "But how do I manage to push her to talk to me without ending up in Siberia again?"

Stevie wasn't one to be pushed on anything. When Christian pushed, Stevie would push back, usually harder. She was no wilting flower when it came to battles. She took every battle head on, and the consequences be damned. It was one of the things that had attracted him to her in the first place. She wasn't the kind of woman he could walk all over. If he pushed her away, she walked away—it was as simple as that. She wasn't one to beg, plead, or pander. She did as she pleased, refusing to cater to his ego. He loved that about her. He also hated it, since it meant that he had to be careful which battles he picked with her.

This battle was worth the fight. She needed to work through her emotions about the attack, otherwise it would hurt her in the end. Christian couldn't risk that.

"Well," Dave said, "my suggestion is that you talk to her about it, don't confront her—you know Stevie, if you back her in a corner, she'll come out fighting. Just ask her about the Halcion, ask her if she wants to talk. Even suggest a professional. I think she's got a lot of things going on in that head of hers. She needs to work them out, and I don't know that any of us have the ability to get to what's really going on. You know?"

Christian nodded, blowing his breath out. "I don't know if she'll like the idea of a shrink, though."

"Probably not," Dave said. "But it would be what's best for her, if she'll do it."

Christian nodded, looking frustrated. "I just don't want to end up on the wrong side of her again, ya know?"

"It's not a nice place to be," Dave said, his grin sardonic. "But it's worth the risk if she's really knotted up."

"True," Christian said. "She's been a bit distant since then, you know? I mean, not cold or anything, but we definitely don't have the connection we usually do."

Dave nodded. "Talk to her, man, see what happens. Don't push at this point, just let her know you're worried. Marriage is about communication, and she's going to need to learn to do it, just like you need to. This might be the time to start."

Christian nodded, and was silent for a while.

"So how are things with Susan?" he asked then. "How's the pregnancy going?"

"She's finally over the morning sickness, thank God," Dave said, grimacing.

Christian laughed, shaking his head. "If I know Zan, she's probably willing to put up with anything to have a baby."

"Oh, she is," Dave said. "I just can't handle it."

Christian grinned. Country's best narc couldn't handle his pregnant wife's morning sickness.

"Disgusting what love'll do to ya, isn't it?" he said, grinning.

"Yeah," Dave said, smiling too. "Tell me about it."

"I'm glad she found you, though," Christian said sincerely. "She deserved someone like you."

Dave grinned, raising an eyebrow at Christian. "I don't know if that's a compliment to my wife or an insult."

Christian laughed, shaking his head. "Nah, it's a compliment to both of you. She needed someone who would love her like you do."

"And you found what you needed too," Dave pointed out. "Things work out the way they're meant to, Blue. And this thing with Stevie will too. Trust yourself to know what's right."

Christian nodded. Dave was too damned logical for his own good sometimes, but he was usually right too.

That night, Christian got home around ten o'clock. He'd wanted to get home sooner, before Stevie went to sleep, but he'd gotten held up working on the paperwork from the collar that day. When he walked into their bedroom, he fully expected her to be asleep, like she had been just about every night since the attack. To his surprise, he noticed that while she was in bed with the light off, she was not asleep. Instead she was tossing and turning.

"Everything okay?" he asked as he walked in.

"Yeah," she said. "Just can't get to sleep tonight for some reason."

Christian nodded, knowing why she couldn't get to sleep. She didn't have any more Halcion.

"I'm going to take a shower. I'll be in soon."

"Okay," she said, turning over.

Christian took his shower, taking his time. He was fairly sure she'd still be awake. He had done a little checking into Halcion, and the side effects from being on it too long were restlessness, sleeplessness, and overall agitation. He knew he needed to avoid irritating her any more, but he was hoping she'd wear herself out a bit by tossing and turning.

He was right. When he climbed into bed next to her an hour later, she was still awake. She was lying with her back to him, her foot moving in agitation. Sliding his hand around her waist, he pulled her back gently to him. Leaning down, he kissed her temple softly.

"I love you," he said, his voice sincere.

He felt her relax against him. After a few minutes, she turned over, putting her face into the curve of his neck and sighing contentedly. Christian held her, stroking her hair and back, his lips nuzzling her temple. After about an hour he felt her breathing become even.

She'd fallen asleep without the Halcion. Good. He allowed himself to fall asleep then.

Christian woke with a start as he heard Stevie cry out, her nails, clenched at his chest, cutting into his skin.

"Stevie!" he exclaimed, seeing that she was awake now and breathing heavily. "Baby, it's okay, I'm here, it's okay," he said soothingly, holding her to him.

She was nodding, making an effort to get her breathing under control.

"It's okay, Steve, I'm here, I'm here," he said over and over.

Stevie swallowed a few times, as if physically swallowing her fear.

"I'm okay," she said quietly.

"No, babe, you're not," Christian said gently, tilting her face up to his, his light blue eyes searching hers. "Baby, I love you, and I don't want you to hurt any more than necessary," he said, his tone still soft. "But we've got to deal with what happened. You can't keep running from it, because it won't go away—it's inside you, and it's only going to hurt you in there."

Stevie looked back at him. He could see a myriad of emotions in her eyes. He didn't know if it was because she was still half asleep and not consciously hiding her feelings or if he was actually getting through, but either way, he plunged ahead, hoping for the best.

"We need to work through this, baby..." he said.

"I'm not running away," she said. Her tone was petulant but not defensive, which he took as a good sign.

"Honey, you are," he said gently. "You're avoiding it, and sleeping when you can't."

"Sleeping," she repeated, without much of a question in her voice.

"Yes," Christian said. "I know about the Halcion."

Stevie's eyes widened slightly, searching his eyes. She was looking for signs that he was mad at her for hiding it from him. He knew that if she detected even the slightest hint of anger in him, she'd go on the defensive. He didn't look away; he let her search. He wasn't mad, he was worried.

"I just wanted to sleep without dreaming," she said, dejected.

"I know, babe," he said. He hadn't known that part of it, but it made sense. "But you can't do that forever. The dreams will go away once you deal with the emotions causing them."

Stevie's lips tightened in a grimace. "You're talking about a shrink, aren't you?"

Again he only looked back at her, allowing her to see that he was worried, not aggressive or angry.

"I think it might help, babe, yes," he said gently.

Stevie looked rebellious for a few moments, her emotions obviously warring with each other.

"I really don't want some guy running around in my head," she said, her voice indicating distaste for the idea more than rejection of it.

"So we'll get a woman shrink," Christian said, grinning engagingly.

Stevie narrowed her eyes at him, but his grin was contagious, and she couldn't get mad at him. She closed her eyes for a moment, then pressed her face against his neck again.

"Will you go with me?" she asked softly.

"Of course I will. Whatever you want, babe, whatever you need," he said, hugging her, feeling relieved and extremely grateful for Dave's advice that day. Dave had been right—he hadn't confronted Stevie, so she hadn't felt the need to fight back.

"I need you," she said softly. "I need your strength."

"Then you've got it, babydoll, and you've always had me and always will."

Stevie sighed, snuggling against him. Inside she felt herself let go. She didn't know if she could ever describe to him how much he fulfilled her. In Christian she'd found the one man she could be weak with. In him she'd found the one person she would let her guard down for. The overwhelming feeling of security he gave her, knowing that no matter what happened, no matter what came, he'd be there with her. He was what people called her soul mate. Christian gave her the freedom to be herself, and the love that kept her wanting to be with him. It was a perfect balance.

Rhiannon was sure she'd heard wrong.

"You're what?" she asked, looking across her desk at Stevie.

"Going to a shrink," Stevie repeated, grinning.

"Okay, who are you, and what have you done with my sister?" Rhiannon asked, narrowing her emerald-green eyes at Stevie.

Stevie laughed. "I know it's a total one-eighty for me, but…" She shrugged as her voice trailed off.

"I think it's a great thing," Rhiannon said, nodding.

"Yeah, yeah," Stevie said, waving her hand. "We'll see."

"Couldn't hurt."

"The hell you say," Stevie said, wrinkling her nose up. "Some idiot traipsing through closely guarded memories and feelings. It could hurt a lot."

"So what made you decide to go?" Rhiannon asked, still shocked that her ever-cynical, stubborn sister was willing to get professional help with her problems.

"Not what," Stevie corrected. "Who. And that who is my husband."

Rhiannon's face reflected the fact that she was impressed. "I'll have to kiss that brother-in-law of mine next time I see him."

"Yeah, well…" Stevie muttered.

Rhiannon laughed. "It's not that bad, Stevie, really. They don't even make you lay on a couch anymore."

"No?" Stevie asked. She grinned. "Damn, I was hoping for a nap…"

"Stevie Marie O'Neil-Collins!" Rhiannon exclaimed, laughing all the while.

"I better get going," Stevie said, glancing at her watch. "Christian is meeting me there. I don't want to be late and have him think I'm chickening out."

"Can't have that," Rhiannon murmured.

"Shaddup," Stevie said, leaning down to kiss her sister on the cheek.

Twenty minutes later she was walking up to the offices of Myra Robinson. Christian waited outside, smiling when he saw her. Stevie could never get over how handsome the man was. He just beat out every man she'd ever seen. Walking up to him, she put her arms around his neck, kissing him on the lips.

"Mmmm…" he said. "What was that for?"

"You're just too gorgeous not to kiss," she said, smiling up at him.

"Well, you're feeling awfully good this afternoon," he said, his light blue eyes shining.

"Is that a bad thing?"

"Nope," he said, taking her hand and leading her inside.

Stevie was pleasantly surprised by the therapist's office. It wasn't really like an office at all. It resembled a very cozy house, with an overstuffed couch, lots of throw pillows, and two comfortable-looking chairs around a low coffee table.

Myra Robinson was an older woman, with graying dark hair and kind brown eyes. She smiled at both of them as they walked in.

"I'm Myra," she said, smiling and extending her hand to Stevie.

"Stevie," Stevie replied, shaking hands with the woman.

"And you are?" Myra asked, turning her eyes to Christian.

"Christian."

"Let's sit down, okay?" Myra said, gesturing to the couch and chairs.

Stevie and Christian sat down on the couch, both obviously tense.

Myra noticed, smiling as she sat. "Relax. I promise, I don't bite at all."

Stevie and Christian both grinned.

"Now," Myra said. "I need to ask you a few questions so I can understand the two of you a little better. Do you mind?"

"No," Stevie said. Christian shook his head.

"You two are married?"

They both nodded.

"How long?"

"A year and a half," Stevie replied.

Myra nodded. "Now, can you both tell me how you feel things are with the marriage?"

Stevie and Christian looked at each other and smiled.

"That pretty much tells me," Myra said, laughing softly. "So you're definitely not here for marriage counseling," she continued, winking at the two of them. "Do you want to tell me what it's about? Or would you rather just talk and let me pick that up for myself?"

Stevie was silent, looking pensive. Christian sat back, fighting the urge to speak up for her. This was her call, not his. After a long pause, Stevie started talking.

"I was attacked, a month ago. The guy was someone I was working for a case."

"Working?" Myra asked.

"He was a suspect in a case, a drug dealer," Stevie explained.

Myra nodded. "Go on."

"My partner got there in time before the guy actually managed to succeed in raping me, but I haven't really been able to sleep since then, and... well, I keep having these dreams. I mean, I know it's totally normal and stuff, but..." Her voice trailed off as she shrugged.

"But you felt it was important enough to talk to someone about?" Myra asked.

"Yeah, I guess so."

Myra nodded. "How would you describe yourself, Stevie?"

"In terms of what?"

"In terms of personality—are you a submissive personality?"

Christian couldn't hold back the sarcastic snort at that.

Stevie gave him a quelling look, but grinned all the same.

"No," she said. "I've a pretty strong personality."

Myra looked at Christian. "How would you classify your wife's personality?"

"She's the strongest woman I know," he said, his light blue eyes on Stevie.

"Strong?" Myra repeated.

"Emotionally," Christian said. "She's been through hell and back, but she gets through it all."

Myra looked back at Stevie. "Hell and back? Tell me about that, Stevie."

Stevie took a deep breath and launched into the story of her life. Losing her father at eleven years old, losing Jason years later. Quitting the force to go after the man responsible for Jason's death. Getting attacked by one of Tiempo's contacts and having to kill the man before he raped her. Then making the case and almost getting killed by Tiempo's men before the trial by AK47 fire.

Myra listened to all of it with interest, jotting down notes as Stevie talked. Christian looked on as his wife told Myra the story of her life. At one point he reached out to take her hand when she became particularly emotional. She grasped his hand with both of hers and continued to talk, undaunted. Myra's eyes took in the gesture, and she glanced at Christian, then back to Stevie.

When Stevie finally ended the story with marrying Christian and getting to this point, Myra again nodded. Stevie breathed a sigh, leaning back against Christian, who put his arm around her, hugging her to him.

"So, your father was killed in the line of duty?" Myra asked.

"Yes," Stevie said.

"And your brother-in-law also died in the line of duty," Myra continued. Stevie nodded.

"You killed this man trying to attack you, and that brought about the uncovering of your duplicity with this drug dealer."

"That got Dave sicked on me, yes."

Myra nodded. "And you were almost killed before you could testify against the man that was responsible."

"Right."

"There's been a lot of violence in your life," Myra said. "Violence that has changed your life drastically each time. It's no wonder that your mind doesn't want to accept that this latest occurrence of violence doesn't mean a big change for you."

Stevie looked back at Myra for a long moment, thinking about what she'd just said. She glanced up at Christian, who looked back at her thoughtfully.

"Even your attempt to check out meant a huge change," Stevie said softly.

Christian nodded.

"Check out?" Myra asked, her look questioning.

Stevie said nothing, her chin coming up a notch, indicating that she had no intention of answering that question. As far as Stevie was concerned, that was between her and Christian; this woman didn't need to know that part. She was protecting Christian. So Stevie was surprised when he answered Myra.

"I tried to overdose when I lost Stevie to another man almost two years ago," he said evenly.

Myra looked surprised by the admission, but only nodded. "And what change resulted from that?" she asked, looking at Stevie.

Stevie grinned and held up her left hand, wiggling her ring finger.

"Ohhh…" Myra said, grinning. "A good change, for a change."

"You could say that," Stevie said, laughing softly.

"You better say that," Christian intoned.

Stevie smiled.

"So, do you think that's accurate?" Myra asked. "That violence has caused the majority of the upheavals in your life?"

Stevie nodded. "And you're saying that my mind won't believe that nothing's got to change now, right?"

"I think your mind is waiting for the other shoe to drop, yes."

"So how does she get around that?" Christian asked.

"Well," Myra said, "she needs to talk through it. Stevie, you need to ask yourself, what are you afraid to lose?"

Stevie nodded.

Myra glanced at her watch, then at the two of them. "I think that's enough hot-coal walking for today," she said with a grin. "I'd like to see you both again the day after tomorrow, if you can make it."

"Sure," Christian said, glancing at Stevie, who nodded.

The three of them stood up.

"Same time, okay?" Myra asked, walking them to the door.

"Same time, same place," Stevie said, grinning.

At the door, Myra turned to them both, taking their hands in hers.

"I think the two of you have everything you need to get through this," she said confidently, looking back and forth between them. "You have a very strong bond, and it's obvious you love each other very much. Use that to your advantage, lean on each other, and trust that there's a reason you were brought together."

Stevie and Christian looked at each other, then back at Myra, nodding.

As they left the office, Christian got a page from Dave.

"I need to call Dave."

"I'm going to take some time to think for a bit," Stevie said, leaning up to kiss him.

He nodded. "Are you okay, though? I mean…"

"Yeah, babe, I'm okay," she said, smiling. "I just need to sort some stuff out in my head, that's all."

"Okay," he said. "I'll see you at home tonight then?"

"Yeah," she said, and hugged him.

He watched her get in her Trans Am and drive away, not sure if he liked the idea of her running off to "think," but he knew he had no choice. Sighing, he picked up his cell phone and called Dave back.

That night, Christian was home, waiting for Stevie. He was edgy because he had no idea how she was feeling about the session. He sat on their bed, wearing black sweats, bare-chested, with the radio on. He was smoking, tapping his fingers on the headboard. He was mentally pacing, as he'd been physically doing most of the evening. He'd been home for two hours. He'd avoided calling her on her cell phone, knowing that she would feel suffocated. So he waited.

An hour later, the long nights and the day's events were catching up with him. Leaning his head back against the wall, he closed his eyes.

He was awakened by the feel of lips on his chest, moving upward, slowly kissing every inch of exposed skin.

"Mmm…" he murmured, opening his eyes and putting his hand to her head.

Stevie moved to his lips, kissing him deeply. He pulled her closer, deepening the kiss. Her hands touched his chest, moving to his shoulders, grasping at him, pulling him to her. It was her way of telling him that she needed him, and they could talk later. She'd already dropped her clothes. Christian pushed her back on the bed, kissing her deeply as he slid his body inside hers. She cried out at the contact, grasping at him and moaning over and over again.

They made love with all the heat and passion they always had, communicating desires and wants without words, using only actions and the touch of their hands to guide each other. Afterward, Christian moved to lie on his back, pulling her down with him, her body lying over his. They were both panting as they tried to catch their breath. His hands caressed her skin, reaching up to touch her cheek as she moved to look down at him.

"God, I missed this," he said, his voice still husky.

She grinned.

"Not the sex," he said, then rolled his eyes. "Well, yeah, the sex too, but that's not what I meant."

"What did you mean?" she asked softly.

"I meant our connection, the way we communicate without words," he said, leaning up to kiss her lips.

She pulled back, her eyes wide, her mouth open in shock.

"That's it," she said, her tone awed.

"What's it?" he asked, perplexed.

She shook her head. "I spent hours sitting at the beach, trying to do what Myra told me to. Trying to figure out what I was afraid to lose. And that's it, Christian. I'm afraid to lose what we have, lose our connection."

"We'll never lose that, babe," Christian said sincerely.

"You don't think so?" she asked, her tone worried.

"No," he said, his tone assured. He touched her cheek, smoothing his thumb over her skin. "I love you more than I've ever loved anyone or anything in my life. I'm willing to do anything it takes to make this work. I'll change anything I have to to be with you."

"I don't want you to change, Christian. I love you as you are. I love everything about you."

Christian grinned. "And that's why we belong together, Steve."

She looked back at him, her eyes searching his. "I was so afraid to lose our connection, we lost it a little bit, didn't we?"

"It dimmed a bit. But we didn't lose it. I could feel you pulling away, and I wanted to pull you back, but I knew that you needed to deal with what happened first."

"You do realize," she said, putting her finger to his lips, "that no one has ever gotten me to go to a shrink."

"No?" he asked, surprised.

"Nope, not even my mother could make me go when Dad was killed. I refused. I even ran away a few times to prove my point. I didn't want anyone messing with my head."

"So what made the difference?"

"You. I knew you were worried, and I knew that things weren't right with us. I was scared, but I didn't know why. Now I do."

"Because you felt like we were losing us."

"Right," she said, nodding.

"Then I'm glad I made this time different," he said, his eyes shining.

"Me too."

They were both silent for a while.

"I think we should keep going," she said, her face pressed against his skin.

"We?"

"Yeah, we," she said, grinning against his neck. "I need you there with me, babe. Or I'll say whatever I think she wants me to."

Christian grinned. "My wife, the actress."

"I'm a narc," she said, shrugging. "It's habit now."

"Uh-huh," he said cynically.

She bit his neck, making him jump. "Be nice."

"I was," he replied. "I didn't say 'bullshit.'"

She laughed, snuggling closer to him. "I love you," she said softly.

"And I you, Stevie Marie O'Neil."

"You got that bad habit from my sister," she said, narrowing her eyes.

"And?"

She growled at him, then started kissing his neck. Within minutes they were making love again. This time, as they reached their peak, she sucked hard at his skin in her passion. When they finished, he felt her lick his neck. He glanced down at her.

"Did you draw blood?" he asked mildly.

"Oops," she said, grinning.

"Oops my ass," he said, giving her a narrowed look.

"Paybacks are a bitch, and so am I," she said, smiling brightly.

Christian laughed. "It's gonna be dark…" he said, his voice trailing off.

"So? You're mine. I can make sure everyone knows it if I want to."

"I'm always yours, love," he said, kissing her again. "But you can mark me as you feel it necessary. Just remember," he added, moving his lips to her neck as his hand came up to hold her chin so she couldn't move, "I always reciprocate."

"You brat!" she exclaimed, trying to wiggle away from him. He laughed, sucking on her neck undaunted.

They spent most of that night playing, making love, and talking. It felt good.

***

Palani couldn't believe she was actually seeing Kana. *She never comes here!* came the thought screaming through her head. Kana always went to Bourbon Street, but here she was at The Flame. Suddenly Palani knew she was in the wrong place with the wrong people. She was there with Jerry, Jane Anne, and the woman she was somewhat dating at the moment.

"Isn't that Kana?" Palani heard Jerry say.

Palani could only nod mutely. She didn't trust her voice at that moment.

"Oh, the famous Kana?" Nancy stated flatly. "Let's go take a peek, shall we?" she said as she began to lead the way across the bar, making a beeline for Kana.

Palani knew that Kana had seen her, because she was staring straight at them. Glancing at the woman she was with, a very butch-looking dominatrix named Nancy, Palani suddenly felt incredibly out of place. Regardless, she followed as Nancy led her directly toward Kana. As they neared the table, Palani saw Kana's chin come up. She could see the ice in her eyes; she didn't want to look. She wanted to run away at that moment, but Nancy's hand was holding hers firmly.

"You're Kana," Nancy practically spat.

Kana didn't reply, merely looked back at the woman, who, although she was tall, was still a head shorter than Kana. Palani could see that Kana was doing what she liked to do to throw people off—she was remaining silent. Nancy's tension only grew.

"I'm Nancy, and I just want you to know that Palani's with me now."

Kana's eyes reflected no emotion whatsoever. The only indication she gave that she'd heard the woman was the slight smirk on her lips. Palani remembered that smirk well. She was doing her best to stay away from Kana as much as possible; regardless, she felt Kana's gaze on her. "I see your taste in women has changed," Kana said mildly, her eyes flicking back to Nancy appraisingly. "Drastically."

Nancy noted the disparaging look in Kana's casual once-over, and apparently took offense to it. She took a step forward, her manner threatening. Kana gave the woman a wintery grin, showing very white teeth.

"Oh, you just throw down, honey, make my night," Kana said, her tone supremely confident, Palani trembled, knowing that Kana would wipe the floor with Nancy.

Nancy had the temerity to look nervous then.

"Kana?" a woman queried from the side of the group. "Everything okay here?" Palani could read passiveness and a bit of a challenge in her stance. She was blond, blue-eyed and beautiful. Palani felt herself starting to seethe.

Finally she looked over at the woman and then up at Kana, and with as much malice as she could muster said, "And I see your taste for blondes hasn't changed at all."

Kana didn't reply for a moment, allowing a slow grin to spread across her features, showing that she'd noted Palani's obvious jealousy.

"The last brunette I had gave me heartburn," Kana said, her tone wry and cutting.

Palani's eyes flared as she felt a stab of both anger and pain go straight through her heart. Dropping Nancy's hand, she turned on her heel and walked away As she did, she heard Kana say to Nancy, "Looks like you have a sub to retrieve." That had Palani striding faster.

After the scene, Cat proceeded to buy Kana drinks for the next hour and a half until last call. When the bar closed, she drove the Navigator back to Kana's house. She opened the front door with Kana's keys and led her inside. Kana was swaying on her feet by that time. She'd had way too much to drink and knew it. Cat led Kana to her bedroom, sitting her down on her bed and kneeling to pull off her boots. Then she undid Kana's belt and pants, carefully removing her holstered gun from the back of her belt and setting it on the dresser, and pulled off her pants. She took off Kana's cover shirt, leaving her in only underwear and a black tank top.

Cat proceeded to push Kana back on the bed, pulling the covers over her. Leaning down, she kissed her cheek. Kana's eyes were already drooping slightly. Cat took the clothes, draping them over Kana's wardrobe next to her dresser. Then she turned off the light and walked out of the bedroom, heading down the hall.

Kana lay in her bed, her mind going in a thousand different directions.

Palani was with someone else! Palani was still seeing women! What happened to the baby? Was it already born? Yes, yeah, it was—it had been almost a year now since they'd broken up. Where did Cat go? Was she coming back to the bedroom? Why was Palani at the bar? It was calculated! Was it? Where was Cat? She was coming back, right? Of course she was, Cat always stood by her. *Why do you treat her like shit then?* Why was Palani still seeing women? The room was starting to spin, and Kana knew it wasn't a good sign. She didn't know how long she'd lain there, but she knew she felt really sick all of a sudden.

Getting up, she went into the bathroom and threw up. Now she felt worse. Sitting down on the floor of the bathroom, she closed her eyes again.

Why was Palani at the club? Did Matt know about her being gay now? Was this all some kind of game? Where was Cat? Did she leave? Why? Shit, shit, shit! Getting up off the floor, Kana made her way down the hall, feeling a bit unbalanced from the alcohol still in her veins. The lights in the house were all off. Getting to the kitchen, she turned on the light. On the counter was a quickly scribbled note.

"It's been fun. Take care." It was signed simply "Cat."

Kana stood at the counter for a long time, staring at the note. Finally she shook her head. What the fuck was she doing? Cat was the one that had brought her out of her emotional coma. The one she'd been put in by Palani's deceit. Seeing Palani had thrown her; she hadn't expected it, but did she want to lose Cat over that? No, she didn't.

Striding back down the hall, still feeling a bit unsteady, Kana went into her room. She grabbed a pair of jeans and threw them on, then sat down on the bed to pull on her boots. She left the house five minutes later.

Cat had taken a cab back to her apartment. She'd methodically undressed, washed off her makeup, and brushed out her long hair. There was a message on her answering machine; she wondered if it would be Kana. It was Elizabeth, just asking how she was doing and telling her to call whenever she got back in. Climbing into bed, she lay on her side, staring off into space. She was forcing herself not to feel anything. She knew she'd done what she had to do in leaving Kana. She couldn't go on feeling like this.

The phone rang. She didn't answer it; the machine picked up. Elizabeth's voice chimed in.

"It's just me. Guess you're staying with—"

Cat picked up the phone.

"I'm here," she said dully.

"Oh, you are," Elizabeth said. "I didn't wake you, did I?"

Cat glanced at the clock; it was 3 a.m., and Elizabeth was honestly asking that question?

"I wasn't asleep."

"Cat, what's wrong?" Elizabeth asked, hearing the dead tone in her friend's voice.

"Shitty night."

"What happened?"

"Nothing good," Cat replied, her tone non-committal.

"Did you and Kana have a fight?"

"No," Cat said. "We just broke up."

"What!" Elizabeth exclaimed. "Why? When? What happened?"

"We went to the club, ran into her ex, she drank herself into a stupor, I took her home and put her to bed, and left," Cat said, rattling it off like it was a laundry list.

"Left the house."

"Left her."

"Oh…" Elizabeth said, her voice trailing off as she grimaced. "Are you okay?"

Cat was silent for a long moment, then sighed. "No," she said honestly. "But I will be. I can't go on playing the rebound girl forever, you know?"

"I know," Elizabeth said softly.

"I'm gonna try to get some sleep."

"Okay," Elizabeth said. "Call me if you want to talk, okay?"

"Ten-four."

"Goodnight."

"Night," Cat replied, and hung up.

Cat woke up, sensing someone in her room. She moved her hand toward the gun on her nightstand. The hand moved away just as quickly when she realized it was Kana that stood there.

"Jesus, K," she said, worried instantly. "Tell me you didn't drive here."

Kana ignored the question, moving to sit down on the bed. She reached out her hand, touching Cat's cheek. Cat's chin came up warily.

"I'm sorry, babe," Kana said. "I didn't mean to get so drunk, I just… I'm sorry."

"Kana, tell me you didn't fucking drive here," Cat said, her tone sharpening. She could tell Kana was still very drunk.

"I needed to talk to you," Kana said. "You left, I needed to talk to you."

"You're going to get yourself killed, Kana, damn it!" Cat exclaimed. "Or is that what you're going for now?"

"No," Kana said, shaking her head. "Cat…" she began, then it was like something clicked. Without another word, Kana stood up, her eyes reflecting the pain of realization. The alcohol in her veins was making things seem more intense.

"I need to go," she said, starting to turn toward the door.

"Bullshit!" Cat said, grabbing Kana's hand and dragging her back down on the bed with all the strength she had.

Kana looked at her, her dark eyes pained. "I can't do this to you, it's not fair."

"Kana, stay here tonight, okay?" Cat said, worried. "We'll talk in the morning. It'll be better then, okay?"

"No," Kana said, moving to stand again. "I need to leave you alone. I'm sorry," she said, shaking her head.

Cat lunged for Kana's hand, pulling her back, and moved to straddle her lap. "You're not driving like this, Kana," she said sternly. "I won't let you do it."

"Cat…"

"Please, K, just stay tonight," Cat reasoned, well past worrying about her hurt feelings and worried instead about Kana's safety.

"I can't. It's not fair to you, I can't," Kana said, shaking her head.

"Damnit, getting yourself killed because of Palani and her bullshit isn't fair to me either, okay?" Cat growled, angry suddenly

Kana blinked as if she'd just been slapped. She looked back at Cat for a long moment, her lips quivering as she swallowed convulsively.

"Stay here, K," Cat said softly, leaning in to kiss her softly on the lips.

Kana's hands slid around her back then, pulling her closer. Cat slept in the nude, so she wasn't wearing a stitch of clothing. Cat pulled back to look at Kana. Kana's lips reclaimed hers hungrily. Cat moaned against her lips, sliding her hands into Kana's hair. The kiss turned extremely passionate then, and Cat gave in to it, allowing it to happen.

As they kissed, Kana caressed her, making her writhe.

"I'm sorry," Kana murmured against her skin as she continued to excite Cat. "I'll make it up to you, little one, I promise you... I'm sorry."

Cat's hands slid through Kana's hair, guiding her. Before long she was crying out in her release. Kana continued to kiss her skin, moving slowly, taking her time. Cat moved over her then, taking charge of the situation. In the end, she had Kana begging for release. As she brought her close to it, Cat moved to Kana's ear.

"No more games, K. You're either with me or without me—you need to choose, once and for all," she whispered harshly.

She brought Kana to release then, and Kana grasped at her, pulling her closer.

Afterward, Kana moved Cat to lie on her side, pulling her into her embrace and cuddling her close. Leaning down, she kissed her temple.

"With you," Kana said simply.

Cat nodded, snuggling closer to her. She knew in her heart she'd never have Kana's heart like Palani did, but she also knew that at this point Kana needed her. What was she to do? She was addicted to Kana, and she loved her. She didn't kid herself that she was *in* love with her. She loved her for all that she was, but she honestly didn't think you could be in love with someone that wasn't in love with you.

It didn't work that way. Only time would tell what would happen with them. Cat fell asleep that night thinking exactly that.

CHAPTER 4

Preparations had been made for Midnight to do a city tour, giving speeches. She was dreading it, since it would mean being away from home and away from her department for a month and a half. She paced her office most afternoons, talking endlessly to Kyle, briefing him on everything. Kyle sat back, jotting down notes and grinning.

"What's so funny?" she asked at one point, turning to him with her hands on her hips.

Kyle broke into a laugh, shaking his head. "I'm just thinking that you're leaving the country and not telling anyone."

"You wish!" she said, laughing.

"Hell no!" he said, glowering at her. "I never said I wanted to play chief, Midnight. Assistant Chief works for me. You being gone will be stress enough. If you get elected, I'm quitting."

Midnight's face became serious then. "You can't, Kyle."

"Who says?" Kyle replied flippantly.

Midnight chewed at her lip as she moved to lean against her desk in front of where he sat. "Is that what everyone's planning to do if I get elected?" she asked, worried.

Kyle looked back at her. As a young man, he'd dated the young, fiery, copper-blond Sergeant Midnight Chevalier. They'd met at a conference in Sacramento. There'd been an instant connection between them. Midnight was an upfront, beautiful, and intelligent woman, and she unknowingly oozed sex appeal out of every pore.

He'd been unable to resist her, not that he'd tried. She'd been interested in him too.

He lived in New York, she lived in San Diego. They'd seen each other off and on for over a year. He'd quickly found that she wasn't the clingy type of female. When he was in town they were together; when he left, she didn't call or bother him at all. He'd found it quite a draw.

Many years later, Midnight was the Chief of Police for one of the biggest and most successful departments in the country. She'd put out a bulletin for an opening for an Assistant Chief. By that time, he'd worked his way up at NYPD to Assistant Chief. Having recently lost his wife to breast cancer, Kyle had been ready to make a change. Midnight's bulletin couldn't have arrived at a better time.

He'd applied, and Midnight had scheduled him for an interview not knowing who he was. She'd known him by his nickname of Masters; she hadn't known Kyle Masterson was that same man. It had been meant to be—he'd gotten the job and met the woman he was married to now. The woman who had brought him back to life.

Kyle knew better than anything that everything happened for a reason. Looking at Midnight now, he saw her concern. She'd worked hard to build her department into what it was today. She was afraid that in moving on to bigger things, she'd be leaving it behind to fall to ruin.

"I don't know what everyone's planning, Midnight," he said gently. "But you can't spend your time worrying about that."

"Kyle, if they leave…" she said, shaking her head as her voice trailed off.

"Why don't you ask them?" he said, his tone still gentle. He knew this was hard for her.

"I'm asking you," she said, her gold-green eyes staring straight into his. "Will you stay if I get elected?"

Kyle didn't respond for a moment, his eyes searching hers. He could see she was very serious, and that his answer was important to her. Finally, he blew his breath out slowly and nodded. Midnight nodded too, moving to take his hands in hers.

"If I get elected, I'm going to recommend that you take over as chief."

"Were you going to tell me that?"

"I just did," she replied, grinning.

"Yes, but…" he began, then saw the sparkle in her eyes. "Never mind," he said, shaking his head. He knew her well enough not to get into a debate with her over intentions versus happenstance. She'd win—she always did.

Midnight called a meeting of the Gang later that morning. They all made it in, making various excuses to dealers, Deputy District Attorneys, etc. Even the non-law enforcement members of the Gang were invited to this one, including Susan, Erin, and Tammy. The only absence was Joe, and everyone was already guessing that he'd never be back. It dragged at some of them; it was worse still that Midnight might be gone soon too.

Rogue Squadron grouped together in one corner. Kana and Tiny walked in, and Kana moved to lean on the table next to Cat. Tiny went to his wife, Jess, who was sitting at the small conference table. Susan arrived, glancing around and spotting Dave with Rogue Squadron. He held his hand out to her, and she walked over to him, taking it. Christian leaned across and kissed her cheek, reaching down to touch her tummy, which was just beginning to show the slight bulge of the baby.

Spider walked in, looking harried. Tammy, his wife, who was also sitting at the conference table, grabbed his hand and pulled him down. Spider leaned down to kiss her lips softly, then moved to kneel on the floor in front of her, his back to her. She immediately started massaging the muscles in his neck and back. It was obviously a routine for them when he was stressed.

Rhiannon and Erin arrived together, still discussing some property issue. Erin walked over to Kevin. He took her by the waist, turning her around and pulling her back against him. Leaning down, he kissed her neck, making her smile. Everyone noticed. Kevin was becoming much more comfortable with the group now. Rhiannon walked over to Kyle, who was standing by the windows, his back to her.

"Don't jump," she whispered, sliding her hands around his waist.

Kyle grinned, putting his hands over hers and drawing her closer. She rested her cheek against his back.

Rick and Midnight walked in to complete the group. Cassandra, Midnight's secretary, came in last, closing the door behind her.

Midnight moved to perch on the front of her desk, looking at all of them.

"I needed to talk to all of you," she said, her eyes touching on each of them. "I need to know what your intentions are."

"In terms of what?" Kana asked, her look serious.

"In terms of my department."

Kana nodded, glancing at Tiny. Tiny glanced at Spider, Spider at Dave. They were her core members; they'd always been with her, their entire careers. The four of them looked back at Midnight. She waited patiently, knowing they were going through their usual almost telepathic way of communicating.

"That depends," Spider said evenly.

"On what?" Midnight asked, canting her head to the side.

"On whether or not there are any great job offers forthcoming from the state level for gang members."

"I don't see any gang members here," Midnight said.

"Reformed gang members," Dave qualified.

"Ah," Midnight said, nodding, looking serious. "Well, I can't see myself raiding my own department…"

"But?" Kana asked, hearing what everyone had heard.

"But," Midnight said, holding her hands out plaintively, "if it's lose all of you or raid, I'll raid."

The four looked satisfied with that answer.

"I will tell you," Midnight went on, "that Kyle has agreed to stay if I'm elected, and I'm going to recommend that he be made chief."

There were a few sighs, and Rhiannon glanced up at her husband. His lips twitched, telling her that he was still unsure of the decision. Rhiannon looked at the rest of the group as Midnight continued to talk.

"I want to know who of you intends to stay on."

Again there was silence.

"Is this standard procedure?" Cat asked curiously, her look innocent.

Kana glanced down at her, even as Midnight turned her head to look at the girl.

"What?" Midnight asked.

Cat shrugged, guileless. "Is it standard procedure to ask what your employees' intentions are in terms of their future with the department."

"When there are key people in important positions," Midnight replied, her eyes narrowing.

"But we're not all key," Cat countered.

"What do you care?" Rick snapped.

"Easy…" Kana said.

Cat glanced up and saw that Kana was looking at Rick, not at her. She didn't know if Kana knew what she was doing, but she was definitely defending her.

"I just think it's important that we understand the situation," Cat said, pinning Rick with a look. "This isn't standard, these people aren't standard, and neither is the person asking the question. If we all understand *why* they're being asked, it might make a difference in *how* they answer." She canted her head to the side, giving Rick a sidelong look. "Don't you think so?"

Rick's sapphire-blue eyes narrowed further, this time in an assessing way. This girl was smart. She was making sure that everyone here knew that Midnight's own future was hinging on their answer. If they were all leaving, she wasn't going to continue to run. Midnight wasn't willing to risk decimating the department she'd worked so hard to build for the sake of an election.

Midnight understood it too; she knew what Cat was doing. Her gold-green eyes were turned on Cat, pinning her.

"You're being asked too, Sergeant," Midnight said, her way of telling Cat she was indeed included in what Midnight considered to be her family.

"I'm staying," Cat replied without hesitation, glancing up at Kana, who was grinning down at her with a gleam in her eyes.

"So am I," Kana said then, glancing at Tiny.

"I'm in," Tiny said, turning to Spider.

"Count me in too," Spider said, his eyes on Dave.

Dave looked back at Spider, grinning. "Eh, what the hell? I'll stick around and see if the train can handle it."

"Dave!" Midnight, Rick, and Kyle all exclaimed at the same time, even as everyone that understood the term started laughing.

After that, Midnight pinned the members of Rogue Squadron with a look.

"What?" Christian said when she started with him. "You think I'm leavin' now? I just started making what I made as the computer consultant here," he said, winking at her.

"Geek," Donovan put in.

"Hacker," Christian and Stevie countered.

Midnight's eyes were on Stevie then. She shrugged. "It's the family business," she said, smiling.

Midnight smiled too, then looked at Donovan.

"I'm staying, unless you want me to change over to BNE," he said, grinning, naming the Attorney General's version of a narcotics division.

"Do they have a boy scout division?" Christian mused.

"If they do, you won't qualify," Jeanie said, laughing, then looked at Midnight. "My husband stays, I stay."

Donovan grinned. "She swore she'd never leave me again."

"Smart move," Erin said, winking at Jeanie.

Erin noticed then that Midnight's gaze was on her. She hadn't figured she was part of this official survey; she wasn't a cop or anything. That pointed look told her she was wrong.

Midnight noted Erin's hesitation. "You're integral here, Erin," she said. "You keep the property records straight—it's key."

Erin looked surprised, but then nodded.

"My husband works here," she said, glancing back at Kevin.

"Yes, he does," Kevin said, glancing at Midnight too.

Midnight looked at Jess then. Jess grinned, glancing around her.

"Everyone else is staying. Who am I to break with tradition?"

Midnight nodded, relieved.

"You all do realize," she said, grinning, "that all bets are off if I get in there and everyone there sucks, right?"

The group burst into laughter.

"Good way to cause a fight…" Kana said to Cat later when they were headed out of Midnight's office.

Cat shrugged. "Wanted to level the playing field."

"Uh-huh," Kana said, giving her a narrowed look.

"Did you even know why I was saying that?" Cat asked, moving to lean against the wall outside the office, glancing at people as they walked by, then back up at Kana.

"I wasn't sure," Kana said. "No."

"But you were defending me to Debenshire?"

Kana stared down at her, her look measured. "You're my girl—that's my job."

"Not against your family, K," Cat said, shaking her head.

"Against anyone, Cat."

Things had been really good between them since that night at the bar. Kana seemed to be dedicating herself to the relationship now. Cat was enjoying it thoroughly, but she knew it wasn't forever. She didn't tell Kana that, but she just knew. Kana's reaction to seeing Palani with someone else had said it all.

Kana had finally told her the whole story about Palani. Cat had been surprised. She'd been shocked to hear that Kana had dated a woman that was not only bi-curious but also married. Kana's comment had been that she just couldn't resist the extremely beautiful, intriguingly innocent model. With prompting, Kana had even shown Cat the pictures Palani had taken in Hawaii, the pictures that had made her doubly famous in the swimsuit edition of *Sports Illustrated*. She was beautiful, smiling with the sun setting behind her.

Kana also showed Cat the private picture Palani had reserved for Kana alone. It was a stunner to say the least. She looked incredible in a black metallic bikini, her hair loose, her makeup perfect. But the look on her face was what made the picture incredible. She was looking straight at the camera, her eyes alight with love, and she was biting her lip. It was a very sexy picture, and even Cat couldn't help but be affected by it. Palani was beautiful, there was no question about that.

***

Dave walked Susan out to her car, smiling as she ran her hand over it reverently. He'd bought her the Mercedes for her birthday the previous year. It had been a testament to how much he loved her. He'd wanted her to have the best, because he felt that was what she was. Now he was further pleased that he'd bought her the car, because it was considered very safe. Since she was now carrying his baby, he wanted to assure himself that she was safe at all times. It had been part of the reason he'd signed up to take the lieutenant's test. The test and interviews had taken place the week before. Dave was waiting for the results.

"What time's your appointment today?" Dave asked, putting a gentle hand on her belly as she leaned against the car, looking up at him.

"Four thirty."

"And it's okay for me to be there?"

"Yes, David, I want you there," she said, smiling up at him.

"Did you decide if you want to find out what the baby is?"

97

"I'd like to, but you never said what you thought of the idea."

Dave grinned. "I like to be prepared."

Susan laughed softly, nodding. "That's a yes then."

"Basically," he said, grinning.

"Will you meet me there?"

"I'll come home and pick you up," he said, leaning down to kiss her lips softly.

That afternoon, Dave found out he was going to be the father of a baby boy. He was ecstatic; Susan was very happy. That night they lay in bed talking.

"I just don't know if I should paint the nursery blue or not…" she said, shaking her head.

Dave grinned.

"What?" she asked, catching his grin.

"I was just marveling at the difference in my conversations between here and work. Earlier I was talking about taking down a drug dealer that's moving up to hits on the competition, and now I'm discussing colors for the nursery."

Susan smiled, moving to sit up and look down at him. "Isn't that a good thing though?" she asked softly.

"Yes," he said, moving to sit up too, touching her cheek. "It's a very good thing. I need you in my life to give me a haven to come home to."

Susan smiled, staring up into his eyes. "I never dreamed that someday I'd be considered someone's haven."

"Well, you're mine."

They lay back down, going to sleep a little while later. In the middle of the night Susan woke, feeling strange cramping. Getting out of bed, she went into the bathroom, silently praying to herself. She was relieved when she didn't see any blood, but the cramping didn't stop. Dave was up a moment after she was out of bed.

"What is it?" he asked, concerned.

"I don't know," she said, her breathing labored.

A half hour later Dave carried his wife into the emergency room. He insisted on them checking her out. He was no-nonsense with the nurses on duty.

"She's five months pregnant, and she's having cramping. Do something, now."

"Her doctor is coming in now," the nurse said, nodding.

An hour later the doctor arrived to a waiting room full of people. As always, the Gang turned out in force when one of their own was in trouble.

"Mrs. Dibbins is just fine," the doctor said. "She was having pre-term labor, but we've given her medication to stop it. She's resting comfortably now. Her husband is with her."

"And the baby is okay?" Christian asked.

"Yes, the baby is fine."

Everyone nodded, many of them sighing in relief. The doctor couldn't believe this many people had turned out at midnight over something this minor. He even recognized the Chief of Police, who was currently running for Attorney General.

Someone had notified the press, because later that night, when Midnight and Rick went to leave the hospital, they were there waiting.

"Chief Chevalier, is everything okay? Who was shot?" asked one overzealous reporter.

"Shot?" Midnight asked, looking dumbfounded. She shook her head. "A member of my family was having an emergency," she said, not relaying too much information.

"Why was half of San Diego PD here?" another reporter asked suspiciously.

"These people are basically my family," Midnight explained. "When I have an emergency, so do they."

The reporters jumped at that, eager to film the people leaving the building now. The members of Rogue Squadron had already gone out the back exit, always careful not to be identified. The reporters attempted to talk to Tiny, Kana, and even Kyle when he and Rhiannon left the hospital; none of them had any comment to make. All the same, the press printed Midnight's comments about these people being her family. It was all over the papers the next morning.

"You're famous," Dave said, grinning at his wife.

"I'm what?" Susan asked, getting dressed so she could leave the hospital.

Dave showed her the paper: *Chief's niece in hospital. "Family" turns out for support.*

"Good Lord," Susan said, scanning the story. "Why are they bothering with me now?"

"You're the niece of the next Attorney General, a woman everyone wants to know right now."

Susan shook her head. "Those people really need something to do with their time," she said blithely.

Dave laughed, nodding. He's been terrified the night before that she was losing the baby. The doctor had assured him that the baby was fine, even letting Dave and Susan hear the heartbeat of their son for reassurance. Susan was told she'd need to take it easy, however, since they felt that the labor was caused by overworking herself. She was taking care of the Sinclair children during the day and endeavoring to pamper Dave at night. He'd allowed her to because he knew she took a great deal of pleasure in taking care of him, but things were going to change now.

The week that followed, Dave was home at five every night and insisted on helping with everything in the house. He refused to allow her to clean, even threatening to hire a maid if she wouldn't stop insisting that everything had to be spotless constantly. He did everything he could to look after her and keep her from overworking herself.

***

Midnight left on her city tour the following week as well. The night before she was to fly to Los Angeles, she started packing. She was surprised when Rick did as well.

"What are you doing?"

"Packing," he said with a grin.

"Why?" she asked, a hopeful gleam in her eyes.

He turned to her, looking down into her eyes. "You didn't think I was letting you go alone, did you?"

"Rick…" she began, relieved. She hugged him.

"I figured you might need some moral support," he said as he hugged her back.

"You know it," she said, smiling happily. "What about the kids?"

"Marie is here with Roberto. And I've arranged for us to fly back on Friday nights to spend the weekends with them."

"I love you," she said sincerely.

"I know," Rick said, grinning.

So she left the next morning holding her husband's hand. Of course, that evening when they showed up to the rally together, it was everywhere that Rick Debenshire was accompanying his wife.

"Your 'good husband' stock is going up everywhere," Midnight said that evening at dinner.

"All I care about is that my wife thinks so," he said, reaching over to touch her under the chin, looking into her eyes.

That picture was on the front page the next day. Once again the press ran reports and pictures of Midnight's "funeral" years before. Reels of Rick at the funeral, sinking to his knees during the playing of *Taps*, aired on all the news stations. They also ran the story about Rick stepping in front of a bullet a couple of years before to protect his wife. The media seemed to love Midnight Chevalier-Debenshire and her gallant, handsome husband.

***

Randy sat looking at the girl, watching the way she played, observing and making notes. Emily was playing with two dolls, one that looked like a child and an adult doll. She was talking for them, saying that they were going shopping to buy some things.

"Emily?" she queried.

The little girl turned her eyes to her.

"What are they going to buy?"

Emily shrugged. "Stuff at the store," she said, still intent on her game.

Randy nodded. "Is it a grocery store? Where they have food and things?"

Emily nodded.

"So what kinds of things are they going to get there?"

Emily was silent for a minute, then said, "Ice cream, Pop-Tarts, candy, and beer."

"Beer?"

Emily nodded.

"Do you know what beer is?"

Emily nodded, wrinkling up her nose. "It tastes yucky."

"You've tasted beer?"

Emily nodded again. "Sometimes after the parties, I find all the sodas no one finished. I thought one can was a soda, but it wasn't. It was yucky."

Randy nodded. "Did you find a lot of soda?"

Emily shook her head. "It was mostly beer."

"How often do you get soda that way?"

"Mostly after the check comes."

"The check?"

"From Daddy."

Randy nodded, as if understanding. "How do you know when the check comes?"

"Because Mommy always buys me candy," Emily said, smiling.

"Does she buy you other stuff too?"

"No, mostly candy," Emily said, playing with the dolls again. "One time, she bought me ice cream from the ice cream truck."

Randy nodded, smiling. "That was fun, huh?"

"Yeah," Emily said, smiling fondly.

"So when you get home from school, what do you do?" Randy asked, getting comfortable on the floor next to where Emily sat playing.

"I watch cartoons and draw."

"You like to draw?"

Emily nodded.

"My daughter loves to draw too," Randy said. "In fact, she's just a year older than you."

"You have a daughter?"

"Yes, and a son."

"It's neat, having a brother," Emily said.

"You like having Steven for your brother?"

"He likes cars and stuff," Emily said, wrinkling up her nose. "But he sticks up for me at school."

"How are you doing in school?"

Emily shrugged, becoming more intent on her playing.

"Is it hard for you?"

Emily nodded, looking worried.

"It's hard for a lot of children," Randy said. "Sometimes it's because they don't understand what they're being taught, other times they're like your daddy and just can't concentrate on what's being taught."

"My daddy is like that?" Emily asked, looking surprised.

"Yes," Randy said. "Your daddy has something called Attention Deficit Disorder. Have you ever heard of that?"

Emily shook her head.

"Well, it just means that your daddy has a hard time concentrating on one thing at a time. When things get really noisy around him he gets very tense. Have you ever noticed that?"

Emily looked thoughtful for a moment. "Sometimes when Steven is playing PlayStation, Erin tells him to turn it down because my daddy can't take the noise."

"Right," Randy said, nodding. "It's makes it hard for him to concentrate on whatever he's trying to do."

Emily nodded. "Maybe I should be quieter around Mommy."

"Why's that?" Randy asked, watching the girl closely.

"She gets tense too," Emily said. "Do you think she has Attention Deafs Disease too?"

"Attention Deficit Disorder," Randy corrected with a gentle grin. "I don't know if she does," she said noncommittally. "Does she get really tense?"

Emily nodded vehemently. "She yells at me to go to my room when I'm being too noisy."

"Do you go to your room?"

Again Emily nodded. "I try not to cry."

"Why's that?"

"Because that makes Mommy mad."

"Mad?"

Emily nodded. "She says that I shouldn't be a cry baby and that if I want to cry she'll give me something to cry about."

Randy took a deep breath, blowing it out slowly. "What happens if you can't stop from crying?"

"She hits me," Emily said, her tone normal.

"You mean she spanks you on the bottom?"

Emily shook her head.

"Where does she hit you, Emily?" Randy asked, her teal-blue eyes searching the little girl's face.

"She what?" Kevin exclaimed, getting up from the table and starting to pace.

"Hits her in the face," Randy repeated, glancing at Erin, who was shaking her head unhappily. "And in the back, and the head, wherever she manages to get to in her fury, apparently. Emily says she gets all red in the face and 'scary' when she does it."

"God…" Kevin said, feeling sick. "I'll fucking kill the bitch."

"No," Erin said, standing up and moving to him. "We'll get Emily away from her for good."

Kevin looked at Erin, his obvious fury warring with his wife's desire to calm him. He glanced over at Randy.

"Will you write the report?"

"I'll write the report, and I'll testify in court for you," Randy said. "That child deserves you two for parents, not that woman that gave birth to her."

***

Kana and Cat had spent the weekend going out and cutting loose. Kana regretted it Sunday morning at 4 a.m., when she got a call from Tiny.

"We have a hit on one of our guys."

"Who?" Kana said tiredly, glancing at the clock.

"AJ," Tiny said with a grin.

"Shit… no way," Kana said, shaking her head.

They'd been after AJ Perone for months. He'd shot two people in cold blood, reportedly because he felt like it. There was no motive, just a love of killing. Kana wanted this guy off the street as soon as possible.

"Where's he at?" she asked, moving to sit up and rubbing at her eyes. She and Cat had gone to bed not an hour before.

"Holed up in a house down in Chula."

"You got a warrant?"

"Would I have woke you if I hadn't?"

"No," Kana replied simply. "What time to do you want to hit it?"

"Six," Tiny said. "I'd like to catch the little bastard still asleep."

"True," Kana said. "Okay, call for some air support in case he runs."

"You got it, boss," Tiny said, grinning.

"Fuck you, Tiny," Kana said, grinning too.

"Not your type, K, remember?" Tiny said, laughing.

"I remember," she said, her eyes on Cat, who was awake now too.

"Meet me at the corner of Broadway and D at five thirty. I'll have the plan there."

"See you there."

They hung up a moment later. Kana lay back down, sighing deeply.

"That wasn't a raid I heard you agreeing to, was it?" Cat asked.

"Uh, yeah, it was, actually," Kana said, grinning.

"Uh, no," Cat said. "Call him back and tell him you can't go."

"Cat…"

"Bullshit, K," Cat said, looking worried. "You just went to sleep like an hour ago!" she exclaimed, shaking her head. "You're not up for this."

"Well, I will be," Kana said. "This is Perone, Cat. I need to get him."

"Let Tiny get him," Cat said, grabbing Kana's arm.

"I'm still his backup."

"You're his lieutenant, K."

Kana didn't reply, simply shook her head.

"Please, K, I'm serious," Cat said. "You're not up for this."

"Stop," Kana said, moving to sit up, putting her hand on Cat's lips to stop her from talking. "I've done raids on even less sleep than this, okay? I'll be fine, babe, trust me."

"K…" Cat said, her face a mask of concern.

"Shhh…" Kana said, leaning forward and kissing her lips softly. "I'll be back by noon, and we can sleep the rest of the day, okay?"

In the end, Cat got up and made her coffee, strong Kona coffee. Kana drank it gratefully, leaning down to kiss her deeply.

"Go back to bed," she said as she picked up her gear bag. "I'll join you as soon as I can."

Cat smiled, reaching up to touch her cheek.

Kana left for the raid, and Cat went back to bed, feeling uneasy.

At the corner, Tiny laid out his plan for hitting the house. Kana agreed to it, completely. She and Tiny would be on the entry team. They drove over, stopping two doors down. Kana had just gotten out of her vehicle when she heard the helicopter. She glanced at her watch; it was 6:10.

"Fuck!" she yelled, knowing that helicopter was going to give them away. Sure enough, she saw a blind being lifted in the house. "Damn it, Tiny! We've been made!"

Grabbing her gun, Kana ran toward the house.

"Kana!" Tiny yelled, still strapping on his body armor.

Kana made her way to the door. Without pause she took one step back and kicked hard with her right foot. The door gave immediately. She moved through the living room, checking it quickly, her gun in front of her, finger on the trigger. She got to the bedroom and saw that the door was closed. "Fuck," she muttered to herself. Once again she went to kick the door, but no sooner had she stepped back than it was thrown open and there was a blast.

Kana saw a muzzle flash and felt a searing heat in her chest. She fell and was out cold before she hit the ground.

"Kana!" Tiny yelled, shoving one of his team aside and moving past him. That's when he saw a sight that would haunt him for months to come. Kana was lying in a pool of her own blood.

"Sonofabitch! Call the paramedics, officer down!" Tiny shouted. Turning, he made his way through the house, his fury making him faster than he'd ever been.

Perone was headed out a window at the back, the Remington shotgun still in his hand.

"Freeze, Perone!" Tiny yelled.

Perone turned to look at him, bringing the shotgun up. Tiny shot him five times, dead center.

Three hours later, Dave stood at Cat's front door. He knocked, feeling sick at what he needed to do.

Cat answered, took one look at him, and strode into her kitchen, leaving the front door open. Dave walked in just in time to see her take an extremely long swig of tequila. She set the bottle down.

"What happened?" she asked, feeling her insides quivering in fear already. If Dave was there, it meant something had happened to Kana. It could be big, it could be small, but...

"We need to go," Dave said, taking her arm.

"Shit, what happened?" Cat repeated, walking with him all the same.

"She got hit with a shotgun blast," Dave said, grimacing.

Cat stopped dead in her tracks, her face going pale. This couldn't be happening. Her mind stalled. It couldn't be happening. She felt a numbness shroud her brain. It couldn't be... it couldn't be... Kana couldn't be... but she had to ask.

"Dave, is she dead?"

"No," Dave said, shaking his head. "But..." His voice trailed off as a lump rose in his throat.

Cat nodded, tears in her eyes instantly. It was too much, but she had to go. She knew she had to go.

They arrived at the hospital just as most of Rogue Squadron did. Tiny was there with Jess. Spider and Tammy were already there, as was Randy. Kyle and Rhiannon arrived just after that, so everyone heard what Tiny told Kyle.

"We got to the scene, and air support was too early, or we were too late, I don't know," Tiny said, shaking his head. It was obvious he was distraught. "Either way, Kana yelled at me that we were made, and then she just grabbed her gun and took off toward the house."

"She wasn't wearing body armor?" Kyle asked.

"No," Tiny said. "She always gears up at the scene, but then that happened."

"When she gets better, Joe'll kick her ass for that one," Christian put in, his tone somber, even if his words were hopeful.

Kyle grinned slightly, nodding, appreciating that Christian was trying to give them all some semblance of hope.

"What happened next?" Kyle asked Tiny.

"I was running toward the house when I heard the shotgun blast," Tiny said, looking sick. "I got there as fast as I could…" He shook his head. "But when I got there it was too late. She was down," he said, looking like he was going to be sick. "I yelled for the team to call for paramedics and went after Perone. I caught him trying to go through a back window—he still had the fucking shotgun in his hands. I yelled for him to freeze—he started to bring up the shotgun. I fired."

"Perone dead?" Kyle asked.

"More than—I fired five times," Tiny answered, his eyes fiery.

"Good."

"IA didn't just hear that," Jess said evenly.

Tiny looked at his wife, considering. He didn't care what happened; he was glad Perone was dead too. If Kana didn't make it, he was doubly glad.

"Good thing IA isn't here, right?" Jessica said then, winking at her husband. It was her way of saying she was his wife right now, not Internal Affairs, the people that would look into the shooting of AJ Perone and determine if Tiny was justified in using lethal force.

"Anyone get ahold of Midnight or Joe yet?" Tiny asked.

"Cassandra's working on it," Kyle said. "Dig in, everyone. It could be a long day."

Everyone moved to sit, stand, or lean on something in the waiting room. Rogue Squadron grouped around Cat, who hadn't spoken since they'd gotten to the hospital. She was holding it together; she hadn't even cried yet. Her team intended to be there when she broke down.

An hour later, Elizabeth arrived with Susan. Susan made her way to Dave, and Elizabeth walked over to Cat.

"Cat?" she said, worried.

"Hey, Bet," Cat said, her tone listless.

"Come on," Elizabeth said, reaching down to take Cat's hand. "You need to smoke."

Cat nodded, getting up. Elizabeth led Cat down the hall toward the open quad where smoking was permitted. Christian, Stevie, Donovan, Jeanie, Dave, and Susan all watched them walk away, glancing at each other and shrugging.

Out in the quad Cat lit up with shaking hands, the one physical manifestation of her worry. Taking a long drag, she looked over at Elizabeth.

"Are you alright?" Elizabeth asked.

Cat didn't answer for a long moment, taking another drag on her cigarette. "Alright isn't exactly how I am, no," she said, her voice tightly controlled.

111

Elizabeth nodded, watching Cat. She could tell that Cat was holding on to her control with every ounce of her strength; the dam would have to burst at some point.

They stayed in the quad for a half hour, neither of them speaking. Just smoking and doing their best to forget why they were there.

Midnight and Rick walked into the hospital two hours later. Everyone came to attention with her in the room, crowding around her as she got the report from Kyle.

"Damn it, she knows better than that," Midnight said, shaking her head. "Have we gotten word yet on her status?"

Kyle shook his head. "She's been in surgery for going on nine hours."

Midnight shook her head, glancing around her. She saw Tiny's grim expression and went over to him.

"There's nothing you could have done," Midnight said, giving him a hug. "Except maybe get shot yourself. Perone was determined to take someone out."

Tiny shook his head miserably.

Midnight glanced around, not seeing Cat. Finally she located her sitting in a chair at the other end of the room. She walked over, kneeling in front of the girl.

Cat saw Midnight walk in, watched her talk to Kyle, then Tiny. She then saw Midnight heading in her direction. She wasn't sure what she could say; this was just a slow-moving nightmare at this point.

"How are you holding up?" Midnight asked, concern etched in her features.

Cat looked at Midnight for a long moment, then nodded slowly. "I'm okay."

Midnight nodded, searching the younger woman's face. Cat just looked back at her, not sure what the woman was looking for but bound and determined not to become someone else Midnight had to deal with. She wasn't going to scream and cry and carry on; the last thing anyone needed was a scene. Inside Cat was screaming; inside she wanted to find Perone in whatever body bag he was in and kick the crap out of his corpse. She was holding on to her self-control with everything she had.

Joe waited for Jordan to get off stage at the end of her show, pacing back and forth. Jordan came running off stage, grabbing a towel from an assistant.

"I gotta go," Joe said unceremoniously.

"Where?" she asked, surprised.

"Home," Joe said. "Kana's been shot."

"Oh my God," Jordan said, wide-eyed.

Joe took her hand, leading her back toward her dressing room.

"I don't know how long I'll be gone. I called Mackie—he can be with you in twenty-four hours."

Jordan stopped, looking at him strangely.

"What?" he asked, impatient to get out of there and back to where he was needed right now.

"Joe, I'm going with you," Jordan said. "A member of your family's been shot. I'm not staying here and pretending everything's okay."

"Jordan, you've got shows…"

"I don't care," Jordan said. "You're going to need moral support, and I'm going to be there."

Joe looked at her for a long moment, then nodded, walking over to hug her close.

"Thank you."

She snuggled into him. Things had been strained since the cruise, and she reveled in his embrace again.

Four hours later they were walking into the hospital. They arrived three hours after Midnight and Rick. Joe walked straight over to Midnight, taking her into his arms and hugging her. He knew what she'd be going through at that point. He shook hands with Rick.

"Have we heard anything yet?" Joe asked, knowing they hadn't heard anything when Kyle called him five hours before.

"Nothing," Midnight said, shaking her head. "Joe, she's been under for twelve hours…" They both knew the longer someone was on the table for surgery, the worse it was.

Joe grimaced, shaking his head. Blowing his breath out, he glanced around him.

"Kana's stronger than any of us," he told them. "If anyone can make it through this, she can."

He turned to Cat. "Cat, how are you doing?" he asked solicitously.

She looked back at him for a long moment, blinking a couple of times. She felt like she was in a haze at this point. The pain in her heart was making the rest of her body numb. She felt like she couldn't focus on what Joe was saying to her. She felt Joe take her hands in his. Why were his hands so hot?

"Cat?" Joe queried again, giving her hands a gentle squeeze. "You hear me?"

Something clicked in Cat's head then, and she finally nodded, still looking dazed.

Joe nodded too, giving her hand another squeeze. "Hang in there, we'll get through this," he said, then stood up and walked back over to Midnight.

"She's going into shock," Joe told Midnight. "Her hands are ice cold."

Midnight glanced over at Cat, concerned. "She hasn't shed one tear yet that anyone's seen." She looked at Joe then. "What do you think we should do?"

Joe glanced back, seeing that Rogue Squadron were stationed around Cat in varying degrees of attention. Christian was leaning against the wall, behind the chair where Cat sat. Stevie was leaning against the back of the chair next to Cat's. Donovan was sitting to Cat's right; Jeanie sat on the floor, next to Donovan's leg closest to Cat. Dave and Susan were across from her, Susan on the couch, Dave on the floor in front of her, watching Cat closely from behind his sunglasses.

"Rogue Squadron's got her," Joe said. "Might just want to let Dave know about the possible shock. I'll go talk to the hospital maintenance about getting the heat turned up in that area." Joe grinned. "Warn them it's about to become summer again," he said with a wink.

It was another hour before the doctor finally walked out to talk to them.

"For Kana Sorbinno?" he queried.

Midnight stepped forward, Rick at her back. Everyone else ranged out behind her.

"I'm Chief Chevalier—she's one of my people," Midnight said. "How is she?"

The doctor looked at her for a long moment, then sighed. "There was a great deal of damage. We worked on her for twelve and a half hours." He shook his head, rubbing at his eyes tiredly. "She lost a lot of blood, and we weren't able to repair everything we wanted to. It was too risky keeping her on the table that long. Either way, I don't think it would have made a difference."

Midnight closed her eyes. *Oh God, he's about to tell me she's dead.*

"I wish I had better news," the doctor said, sounding like he truly did. "But I don't think she'll make it through the night. I'm very sorry. When she's brought down to recovery, we'll make sure you can get in to see her... to say goodbye."

Midnight was sure her heart had stopped beating. She reached blindly for Rick, her tears overwhelming her. Rick was there instantly, holding her and doing his best to keep his composure.

"This isn't happening," Midnight said, shaking her head, the tears that flowed down her cheeks mirrored in her voice. "This isn't happening."

Palani came up on the scene. She saw all the familiar faces of Kana's extended family. She searched for Kana even as she called to Midnight. She'd been watching TV an hour before and there'd been a special report saying that a member of San Diego PD, a lieutenant, had been shot and was in critical condition. Something had told Palani she needed to get to the hospital. So she'd gotten in her car and driven down to the hospital the news had indicated Kana had been taken to. Now, seeing Midnight upset, her fear doubled. She didn't see Kana...

"Midnight?" she called quietly.

Palani's eyes finished their scan, and before she'd even said it, she knew. "Oh my God. It is Kana, isn't it?" she said, tears already starting. "She was the officer shot..." Palani begged Midnight with her eyes to tell her she was wrong.

Midnight closed her eyes for a moment, then opened them, nodding.

116

Palani felt her heart pumping blood so hard, it hurt to breathe. Was she breathing? She couldn't tell—it felt like the whole world had just tilted slightly.

"She's going to be okay, though, right?" Palani asked, wanting Midnight to say, "Of course!"

Instead, Midnight winced, glancing at Rick, then back at Palani, shaking her head slowly. "They don't think she's going to make it through the night," she said, as gently as humanly possible.

"No!" It was a primal cry that was ripped from Palani's throat. Suddenly everything was going dark.

Palani woke slowly, thinking she'd just had the worst nightmare ever. Maybe this was a sign; maybe she should try to work it out with Kana. But then she came fully awake and realized where she was. She was at the hospital. And then it came flooding back—Kana was dying. It was all she could do to hold it together. She glanced around her and noticed the woman that had been with Kana at the club that night a month ago. She noticed that the woman was watching her for a long moment, and that she looked as dazed as Palani herself felt. The blonde stood up and strode out of the room. She was gone for a while, and when she came back Palani could smell the cigarette smoke clinging to her as she walked by. The woman took up the same chair she'd been in and continued to wait with everyone else.

When they were finally told they could see Kana, but that there wasn't much hope for her to recover, Palani watched as her friends filed into the room one or two at a time to say their goodbyes. Palani wanted so badly to see her, but felt that she didn't really have the right. When Dave yelled down to Midnight that Kana was waking up, Palani couldn't stop herself from heading for the room, like many others did. She was part of the crowd watching as Dave tried to talk

117

to Kana, to tell her to fight for her life. Palani watched in tears as Kana clenched her hands in fists as she writhed in agony. There was nothing she could do—she couldn't move, she couldn't leave...

As she stepped aside to let the nurse into the room with the IV in her hand, she heard Dave continuing to try and calm Kana. She thought that Dave would get her to stay for all of them. But then she heard Kana tell him that she wouldn't fight, that she was tired and couldn't do it anymore. She heard Dave tell Midnight that they were losing her, and Palani couldn't stop the involuntary scream that left her throat. Without caring what her rightful place was in the group anymore, she moved forward, and with tears flowing down her cheeks told Kana she had to stay, she had to fight for her life. She had no idea what all she said—all she knew was that she couldn't let Kana go. Suddenly she was being told to keep talking to Kana, and she did as they told her.

"Kana? Kana, listen to me. I need you to stay here. I need you to fight. You need to stay with us, with me... please? Please, honey, please..."

Finally the machines monitoring Kana's vital signs were registering normal. The crisis had passed. Palani had never felt so relieved in her entire life as she did at that very moment.

Cat breathed a sigh of relief with everyone else, but her heart took on a new ache. Palani was there, and Kana had responded to her... Blinded by the tears in her eyes, Cat picked up her cigarettes and walked out to the quad, then made the snap decision to go home. She couldn't do this anymore. It was out of her hands. She went out to hail a cab. Inside she gave the guy her address and sat back. All the way to her apartment, all she could think was that Kana had Palani now, and she had no one again. She hadn't been lying when she'd told

Kana that she loved her; she did, even knowing that Kana would never love her back. It was stupid, and she'd known it, but she'd been unable to resist the pull. Now, who knew, it was still really likely that Kana would die, and that broke Cat's heart—she just couldn't stay to see it. She'd said her goodbyes, and now she just wanted to go home and forget everything for a while. That's what she intended to do.

Once home, Cat turned on her stereo, selecting the very darkest music she had to blast. Grabbing a bottle of tequila, she went to sit on her balcony and smoke and drink. She sincerely hoped she could do so until she passed out so she could forget all about this day.

Evanescence's dark-toned debut album, *Fallen*, came on, and "Tourniquet" was playing when Elizabeth found her. The song really portrayed how Cat was feeling at that point. The line about trying to kill the pain, but how it only brought more, was what screamed through every part of Cat's being.

As a shadow fell over her, Cat wasn't completely surprised to glance up and see Elizabeth standing there, looking down at her.

"What are you doin' here, Bet?" she asked, her voice slightly slurred.

"I thought you might need some company," Elizabeth said, moving to squat down in front of Cat's chair.

Cat looked back at her for a long moment, thinking about it. She didn't see why she needed company—she was fine, and she had Jose Cuervo to keep her company. Finally she shrugged dismissively and lifted the tequila to her lips again.

"Cat," Elizabeth said cautiously. She reached out, touching Cat's arm.

Cat snatched her arm away as if Elizabeth had burned her. "Why are you here?" she asked again. Now she was annoyed. If Liz was there to kill her buzz, thanks but no.

"Because you need me."

"No," Cat said, shaking her head.

"Yes," Elizabeth countered, looking at her searchingly.

Cat looked away, grimacing. She didn't want to need anyone—look what good that had done her...

"Please let me help you," Elizabeth went on doggedly, her voice gentle. "You've done so much for me. Please let me help you now."

It was all Cat could take—the kindness in Liz's voice, the worry she saw in the other woman's eyes, it was too much. She'd been holding on by a thread all day, and now it snapped. She folded against Elizabeth, her tears flowing, her sobs loud and soulful. Elizabeth was shocked by the sudden change, but held on to Cat, hugging her, stroking her hair, even rocking her back and forth in an effort to soothe her.

Cat let everything pour out of her, all the anguish, all the pain, everything. She cried for what seemed like hours, and then she just felt drained. She felt Elizabeth stand up and pull her to feet, and let her lead her to her room. Elizabeth sat down on the bed and drew Cat down with her, getting her to lie down and then covering her up. Cat finally let go and fell into an exhausted sleep.

"Where's Cat?" Dave asked when he came out of Kana's room.

Everyone started looking around.

"She was just here..." Spider said.

"I saw her near the room."

"Shit, where is she?" Dave exclaimed. "Rogue Squadron, come with me," he said, and started walking down the hall.

Once outside, he sent them off in different directions. He charged Stevie and Christian with checking Kana's house, while Donovan and

Jeanie were to check The Flame and Bourbon Street. Dave was headed to Cat's apartment.

On the drive over, his cell phone rang. It was Midnight.

"Let me know if you find her," she said. "If I need to, I'll put out an APB for her."

"Thanks, Midnight," Dave said. "I'm headed to her place right now."

"Okay, keep us posted."

Dave hung up, knowing that Midnight was so used to crisis management that she covered all the bases. Cat was a part of the family, with Kana or not. She'd been welcomed in as a member of Rogue Squadron and had proven herself long before she'd gotten together with Kana. Her relationship with Kana had been a bonus, as far as the rest of the group was concerned. Cat had helped heal what was hurt in Kana; that counted for a lot with them too.

Driving up to the apartment, Dave noted Elizabeth's black Porsche parked at an odd angle. An angle that lent itself to the idea that the driver had been in a hurry. He also noted Cat's Blazer parked in her spot. Feeling the beginnings of relief, he dialed Midnight's number as he walked toward the apartment.

"Midnight, it's me. She's at her place, and Elizabeth apparently beat us all to the punch—she's here too."

"Elizabeth is there?" Midnight asked, surprised.

"Yeah," Dave said. "I'll brief you once I've got confirmation on it, but her Porsche is here."

"Okay, great, thanks," Midnight said, sounding relieved.

"Can you call the rest of my team and let them know I've found Cat?"

"You got it."

They hung up then.

Dave knocked on the door, but he could hear music coming from the apartment and figured they probably couldn't hear him. Trying the door, he found it unlocked. He walked inside, glancing around. He checked the balcony and noted the mostly empty bottle of tequila, one that had been almost full earlier that morning. Walking back inside, he headed down the hallway to the bedroom. He was greeted with the sight of his sister-in-law pointing a gun at him. She lowered it instantly upon recognizing him.

"You even know how to shoot that?" he asked in a whisper, his eyebrow raised.

Elizabeth shrugged, grinning. "I'd learn quickly if I needed to."

Dave's eyes fell on Cat, who was lying next to where Elizabeth was sitting up. Elizabeth's arm was up over Cat's head in a proprietary fashion. Dave wondered at that, but said nothing.

"Is she okay?" he asked, still whispering.

"She cried for a long time," Elizabeth said. "But I think she'll be okay."

Dave nodded, hoping she was right.

"How's Kana?" Elizabeth asked.

"Her vitals are stable, but they're still not upgrading her condition—she's still listed in critical."

"Is Palani still with her?"

"Yeah, she seems to be the one thing Kana's responding to right now."

Elizabeth nodded. "See, that's the problem…"

"Problem?"

"For Cat," Elizabeth said. "I know she wants Kana to be okay, but you've got to imagine how hard it is for her to stand by and watch someone else be the one Kana responds to." She shrugged. "I mean,

122

imagine if something happened to Susan and the only person she responded to in her comatose state was Christian, and not you…"

Dave nodded, closing his eyes for a moment. He'd already thought about that, in terms of Kana and Cat, but having it put in a such a graphic illustration pertaining to his own life made it even clearer.

"Would you stay with her here?" he asked.

"I had every intention of doing just that," Elizabeth said, a look of conviction in her eyes.

Dave grinned. "I can't think of any way to say this without sounding condescending, but I'm really proud of you, Liz. You've grown up a lot lately."

"Cat's the reason for that, Dave," Elizabeth said, glancing down at the woman sleeping beside her. "I owe her."

Dave nodded. "Well, if you need anything from any of us, give me a call, okay?"

"I'll do that," Elizabeth said. "And please, let me know how Kana is doing."

"I will."

He left the apartment feeling both relieved and surprised. His sister-in-law was the last person he'd ever count on, and yet she'd been the one to be there when Cat had crumbled. Wonders never would cease.

CHAPTER 5

Midnight's plans were on hold. The press, of course, reported faithfully that Midnight Chevalier was at the bedside of a dear friend and employee of the department. They'd cornered Joe and Jordan on their way out of the hospital one evening shortly after the incident.

"Captain Sinclair, how's the officer doing?" one press person asked.

"She's still in critical condition," Joe stated.

"Is it true that this is a family member?" another reporter asked.

"Kana is like family to Midnight—she's been with Midnight for over twenty years," Joe replied.

He and Jordan walked away then.

Two days later it came out in the press that Lieutenant Kana Sorbinno was gay. Midnight was sure it had been Longelo's camp that ferreted that information out. Of course, Longelo, a Democrat, started bashing Midnight for not truly being a Republican, as the average Republican platform was conservative, especially pertaining to alternate lifestyles.

Longelo started commenting on whether Midnight herself was hiding being gay. A speech he gave at a rally in Sacramento directly accused Midnight of such. "Perhaps there is more in Chief Chevalier's closet than we realized. Perhaps that's why Lieutenant Sorbinno warrants the attention of many key officers in the San Diego Police

Department. Captain Sinclair did indicate that the lieutenant is 'family' to Midnight. That is the gay community's term for someone who is gay. I believe the public has been duped by Chief Chevalier. As Attorney General, I will look into any misconduct on Chief Chevalier's part in terms of this election. The citizens of California deserve better than lies from its officials."

Midnight received a copy of the paper from Rick that morning while having coffee at home.

"He's attacking Kana?" she asked disbelievingly as she looked up at Rick. She started shaking her head as she reached for the phone.

"What are you doing?" he asked evenly.

"He's not going to attack my people," Midnight said. "Me, okay, but never my people."

"Some people might construe this as fighting back for your lover," Rick pointed out, with a twinkle of mischief in his eyes.

"I don't fucking care how they construe it," Midnight said, narrowing her eyes, as she dialed. "I don't care if they believe Kana and I have been lovers for the last twenty years. Either way, it's none of their fucking business," she growled as she waited for the line to connect.

"Not gonna say it quite that way in the press conference, are ya?" Rick asked, openly grinning now.

"Shut up!" Midnight said, grinning too.

She scheduled a press conference for two that afternoon.

When the Gang got wind of that speech, they came out fighting.

Tiny was quoted as saying, "Longelo wouldn't know the truth if it bit him in the ass."

Spider went on record saying that Kana Sorbinno was a close friend of his, and he couldn't care less what her sexual preference was.

125

Dave made the statement that Longelo needed to make things up to win the election, since he couldn't come close to Midnight's record of accomplishments.

Fortunately, all threats to string Longelo up were kept to themselves and shared only with Midnight in the privacy of her office. They all ended up in her office at one point or another. They were all damned if Kana's name was going to get slandered while she wasn't even conscious to defend herself. They all knew she'd be mortified when she found out that the entire state and probably country knew she was gay now. It wasn't something she hid anymore, but she didn't feel it necessary to proclaim her sexual preference from the rooftops either.

At two that afternoon, Midnight walked into the press conference she'd called. She looked sedate in dark blue slacks and a jacket nipped in at the waist. She wore a cream silk camisole and navy blue heels. Her hair was pulled back from her face in a long braid. Her badge was prominently displayed on her belt next to her gun at her hip; as always, Midnight was a cop first—everyone knew that.

"I called this press conference to clarify a few points," Midnight said, her cat-like green eyes surveying the press. "Art Longelo has been making accusations about a lot of things in the last couple of days. Accusations about my misusing my officers' time, my lying to the public about being a Republican, and about my sexuality. Let me address the first two first—I'll get to that last one in a minute.

"First of all, Lieutenant Kana Sorbinno has been with the San Diego Police Department since she was eighteen years old. For over twenty years, she's dedicated her life to fighting the crime in this city. For someone like Art Longelo to simply dismiss her as unimportant because she's gay is beyond outrageous. But I digress—I'll deal with that issue at the end of this speech. Lieutenant Sorbinno has a number of good friends in this department. Her immediate family live in Hawaii, so her surrogate family—myself, Rick, and all the rest of her friends—are supporting her through this horrific incident.

"Lieutenant Sorbinno was shot doing her job, attempting to arrest a man that murdered two people. If I didn't support her as a friend, I'd damned sure support her as her chief. Her friends, who also happen to be officers in this department, are also supporting her. I haven't ordered anyone to spend time at the hospital with Lieutenant Sorbinno. I defy Longelo to find someone that will state otherwise.

"As for my being a 'real' Republican. My beliefs are, for the most part, conservative. But I will tell you now, besides being a Republican, I'm also a woman that's had to stick up for herself over the years. Has that changed some of my beliefs? Yes, it has. Life is about experience and learning new things. So, I guess I'm what would be considered a modern Republican. I believe that the government should stay out of people's lives. I believe in the death penalty. I believe in gun control, in as much that there is a fifteen-day waiting period, not to the point that people shouldn't have the right to bear arms. I just don't think people need an AK47 in their sock drawer for home protection.

"I don't think anyone should just believe in one platform wholly. I think that everyone should look at all the options and make choices from there. As I've stated repeatedly, my record stands for itself. I'll be handing out a copy of the statistics for this department in the time that I've been chief. I'll also personally hand out my own personnel file. Publish it—I don't frankly care.

"And finally, my sexuality..." Midnight trailed off as she glanced over at Rick. He grinned at her, his eyes sparkling with subdued humor. Midnight smiled at him, her eyes shining. She glanced down at

127

her wedding rings, then back at the press. "I think anyone that believes that I'm not very much in love with my very male husband is either blind, deaf, or dumb, but that's neither here nor there. I don't feel the actual need to defend my sexuality to anyone. What I do feel the need to say is that yes, one of my best friends in the world is gay, and so are a few other members of my extended family. Have I felt the need to mention that before? No, I haven't—why should it matter? Have I felt the need to hide it? I never have—why would I start now? Do I feel that this will cost me votes for Attorney General?"

Midnight looked out over the group of reporters, right into one of the news cameras.

"To be honest, I don't think that anyone who doesn't believe that love knows no gender will be truly represented by my beliefs. Therefore, I'm perhaps not the Attorney General for them. I refuse to compromise what I believe in, the people I love, or the job that I do, for anything, including an election or a vote."

With that, Midnight walked offstage and out of the room. The press, of course, erupted into a commotion. Rick walked out after Midnight and found her waiting down the hall for him. He took her in his arms.

"Good speech," he said, kissing her temple.

"Probably an election killer. But I really don't care at this point. I won't pretend that I'm not irritated that Longelo is willing to drag anyone through the mud to get to me. I am, and I think the people should be too."

"You're right," Rick said, nodding.

"I know," she said, sighing. "It pisses me off so much that he went after Kana, the bastard."

It was Rick's turn to sigh. "Politics is nasty business, Night... We knew that going in."

"Yeah, and I was willing to take the hit on *my* personal life, but not Kana's, or any of my members' for that matter."

Rick nodded. "But I think you're not giving them enough credit, babe. Hell, Kana would probably be the first one to tell the press that if they had a problem with her being gay that would be *their* problem, not hers."

"True," Midnight said, nodding as Rick started to lead her out to the private garage. "I just don't like this guy's tactics. He's trying to pick a fight, and he so doesn't really want that with me." She said the last with narrowed eyes.

"I know I'd love to see you wipe the floor with him," Rick said, grinning.

"Shhh!" Midnight said, giggling at the visual.

They left the building, leaving in their wake a press that was, as usual, impressed with the tiny powerhouse that was Midnight Chevalier.

As it turned out, rather than killing her election chances, Midnight was shocked to find her ratings on the rise. The gay community appreciated her candor on her feelings about alternative lifestyles. They also liked her comment about love not knowing gender. Midnight also found that people thoroughly liked a candidate that not only spoke her mind but flat out refused votes from people that she didn't feel she could fairly represent. In Midnight's statements, they read a sincere desire to represent the citizens of the state of California. They saw an honest woman, not a slick politician, and they liked it.

***

Kana hadn't regained full consciousness in the week after she'd been shot. She'd stirred a few times, moving around, but never opened her eyes more than a slit, and then was unconscious again. Palani stayed by her side the entire time.

Palani was used to the whole group visiting. It reminded her of how much Kana's extended family cared about her. They came routinely to see how Kana was, asking if there were any changes, celebrating even the slightest good news. They talked to her, often joking that this was a hell of a way to get a vacation or take a rest.

Cat had even returned after a few days. She'd walk into the room, her eyes searching Kana's face, then sit down. Palani would excuse herself and leave the room, wanting to give Cat some time alone, since it was obvious that she wouldn't talk to Kana if she was there. She was right; on Cat's third visit she'd walked back to the door, having forgotten her purse, and heard Cat talking to Kana. Cat's comments weren't joking. They also weren't angry or accusatory.

Palani had heard statements like "You have to get better, K" and "Everyone's here for you." Cat was being supportive. Palani had knocked politely before walking back into the room. She'd glanced at Cat, noting that there were no tears, almost no emotion at all. Palani hadn't been sure what that meant.

It was another two days before Palani noticed Kana shifting around again. She'd grimace, twitch her hands, and move her head around. Palani stood up, looking down into Kana's face.

"Kana?" she said softly. "Kana? I know you can hear me. Come on, babe, open your eyes."

Kana's head turned in her direction and her eyes opened slightly. Palani bit her lip, trying not to get too excited by this.

"Come on, Kana. You can do it, open your eyes," she entreated softly.

Kana's eyes opened wider, and she looked around her, then back at Palani. She started to sit up; Palani put her hands out to stop her.

"Don't, Kana. Don't move too much," she said, slightly alarmed.

Kana eased back against the pillows again, looking around.

"Why?" she asked, her voice a hoarse whisper.

"Why?" Palani repeated, puzzled.

"Why… am… I here?" Kana stammered

"Oh," Palani said hesitantly. "You were shot."

Kana's eyes took on a faraway look as she tried to remember. The thought came to her.

"Perone."

Palani nodded.

Kana nodded too, and closed her eyes again. She was asleep again then. Palani sat back down, happy that Kana had finally awakened and was speaking and obviously remembering things. That was a very good sign.

Cat went back to work four days after Kana was shot. Everyone was very careful around her. It didn't take long for it to annoy her.

"Why is everyone treating me with kid gloves?" she asked Christian after that first week. "It's not like I was the one that was shot, remember?"

"True," Christian said, nodding, his face unreadable.

"So?" Cat asked after a long few moments when he said nothing else.

"So," Christian said, his lips twitching in a grin, "we want to make sure you're okay. Is that a bad thing?"

"No, but I'm fine, so you can all just relax, okay?" she said pointedly.

Christian looked back at her, his features schooled in a sarcastically obedient expression, his light blue eyes sparkling.

"Fine, huh?"

"Fine," Cat repeated.

Christian nodded, looking unconvinced.

"She says she's fine?" Donovan asked, standing at his cutting board, chopping vegetables.

"That's what she says, man."

"You believe her?" Jeanie asked, reaching over and plucking a carrot off the board and popping it in her mouth.

"No," Christian said. "But I tend to think if we push her too hard, she'll come back fighting."

"And that's the last thing we want," Stevie put in, gesturing with her shot glass.

"Is she coming today?" Dave asked, leaning against the dining room table.

"I don't know," Donovan said, shaking his head. "She knows everyone is coming over here today… She never said if she was coming or not."

"Hopefully she will come," Susan said, moving to sit in one of the chairs.

Dave went to help her. She'd been having backaches a lot lately. The doctor said it was totally normal, that the baby was putting some strain on her back. She was told to take it easy and not pick up the children in her charge at all.

Dave also caught the twinkle in his wife's eyes as she sat down.

"What did you do?" he asked, his eyes narrowed.

132

Susan smiled, shrugging. "I just sent in… I believe you call them a wringer."

Cat was outside on her balcony smoking when Elizabeth walked out.

"What are you doing here?" Cat asked, grinning all the same.

"I could ask you the same question," Elizabeth replied, sitting down in the chair next to Cat's.

"Meaning?" Cat asked mildly, taking a long drag on her cigarette.

"Isn't it your boss's birthday today?"

"Isn't it your brother-in-law's birthday today?" Cat echoed, raising an eyebrow.

"Quite right," Elizabeth said, sounding very English. With that she stood up, taking Cat's hand and pulling her up out of the chair.

"What are you doing?" Cat asked.

"Going to my brother-in-law's birthday party," Elizabeth replied, leading the way out of the apartment.

Fortunately, Cat was dressed and had makeup on and her hair brushed; otherwise she probably would have argued. Instead she followed Elizabeth out to her Porsche with an indulgent grin on her lips. Elizabeth had turned out to be quite a good friend when she'd needed it. They'd become closer since Kana was shot.

Liz had a way of making her laugh when she needed to, and also a way of pushing her without being pushy. Like the birthday party for Dave. Cat had known about the party; she had decided against going, even though she'd gotten dressed thinking she would. Everyone was driving her insane with their "concern," and she knew if she dealt with it too much more, she'd scream.

Now here she was, sitting in Liz's black Porsche. She sighed, reaching for another cigarette.

At the party, Cat realized that someone must have warned everyone not to be too solicitous of how she was feeling because they all avoided the topic. Midnight arrived and gave everyone the good news that Kana had finally awakened and was talking.

"She's not totally out of the woods yet, but she's getting there," Midnight said, smiling with obvious relief.

Cat poured herself a double shot of tequila, and found that Christian, Stevie, Donovan, Jeanie, and Mace had joined her.

It was an interesting day. Joe and Jordan Tate showed up. One by one everyone from the Gang but Kana arrived to celebrate Dave's birthday. He was ribbed a great deal about it being his fortieth. He took it all good-naturedly, making comments about being one of the youngest members of the original Gang. That went over with a number of boos and hisses.

Donovan cooked for everyone. There was music, plenty of food, and lots of alcohol. At one point Matchbox Twenty's *More Than You Think You Are* was on.

The song "So Sad So Lonely" was playing, an upbeat, insolent song, and Rogue Squadron knew all the words. The six of them sang with gusto. It was obvious they were enjoying themselves thoroughly. The singer lamented about not wanting anyone and no one wanting him. One part of the song talked about how when things went wrong he sincerely hoped they got what they deserved—that line was shouted at the top of their lungs. It was clear steam was being blown off that night.

Elizabeth looked on with everyone else, relieved that Cat seemed to be having a good time. She also seemed to be drinking a lot. Elizabeth joined her, almost managing to keep up with her friend.

By the end of the night, both Cat and Elizabeth were trashed, as were most of the members of Rogue Squadron and a few others as well. At one point they played a drunk game of football, but the ball eventually ended up down the hill from Donovan and Jeanie's house. Dave volunteered to go and get it; his wife strongly suggested that he stay where he was. The hill was quite steep and littered with sharp rocks. Dave was at least three sheets to the wind by that time, and there was no way he was being allowed to retrieve the ball. Susan had told Tiny to handcuff her husband if he attempted it again. Tiny agreed, grinning.

It was a fun day and evening.

***

Back at Joe's townhouse that night, Jordan got a phone call. She walked out onto Joe's balcony to take it, but there was no hiding what the call was about. Her tour manager was giving her hell for taking off, warning her that promoters were threatening to sue her if she didn't get back to doing her shows. It had been well publicized that Jordan Tate was in San Diego with her boyfriend because a friend of his had been shot. It wasn't like they were married, and it wasn't like it was his family or anything. People didn't understand. Her tour manager didn't understand.

"I know, Tom, I know!" Jordan said, raising her voice not for the first time. "But Joe needs to be here, and I need to be where he is, okay?"

In the house, Joe grimaced at the way she put it. There were a lot of things these days that were dragging at him. And he knew they needed to talk. He'd been putting it off since before Kana had been shot. Things hadn't been right with them since the cruise. Too many things had been said, and they were things that Jordan couldn't take back no matter how much she wanted to.

Later that night, they lay in Joe's bed. Jordan had been irritable after the conversation with her tour manager, so Joe had gone in to take a shower. He knew when she was irritable they'd inevitably fight about something, and he wanted to avoid that. He knew if his temper was ignited at this point he'd say things he didn't want to say in the heat of anger. It wasn't the way he wanted to approach things with her. Jordan was such a volatile personality that pushing her could make her go off the deep end one way or the other. He didn't want that.

When he was done with his shower, he put on a bathrobe and walked out to see what she was doing. She was on the phone again, apparently trying to assuage someone. Taking his cigarettes, Joe walked out onto the balcony. Lighting up, he sat down on the chair by the door. His hair wasn't dry, and he knew he was playing a dangerous game sitting in the chilly night air, but he was on edge and he needed the relief smoking gave him.

He stayed outside for a half hour, smoking three cigarettes, his mind wandering over everything and coming back to the same problems over and over again. When he walked into the house, Jordan was still on the phone. She looked at him, shaking her head and rolling her eyes. Joe grinned, nodding. He went over to her, leaning down to kiss her lips softly.

"I'm going to bed," he mouthed.

She nodded, covering the mouthpiece of the phone with her hand. "I'll be there soon."

Jordan finally made it to bed an hour and a half later. Joe was still awake, lying bare-chested with one arm behind his head.

"Still awake?" Jordan asked, her gold eyes showing the wariness she was already feeling.

When Joe stayed up waiting for her to come to bed, it usually meant he wanted to talk. Jordan knew that it wasn't going to be a conversation she was going to like. Taking off the bathrobe she'd put on when they'd gotten back to the townhouse, she climbed into bed next to him. As usual, his arm went out to hold her, and he leaned down to kiss her lips gently.

Jordan turned to him, sliding her arms around his neck and kissing him back, hoping to put off the conversation a bit longer. It was obvious from his lukewarm response that he fully intended to talk.

Sighing, Jordan pulled back, looking up at him.

"You want to talk," she said resolutely.

"We need to, Jordan," he said softly.

She nodded, not replying. She hoped he'd say whatever he had to say quickly, wanting to get past it and move on as quickly as possible.

"What's going on with the tour?" Joe asked.

Jordan shrugged. "Tom's having a fit. He wants me back there—he's had to cancel four shows, and three promoters are threatening to sue."

"So we need to get back there," Joe said evenly.

Jordan didn't say anything, her eyes searching his, trying to determine how he meant that.

"Either that or I just take my chances with getting my butt sued off," she said, grinning.

Joe didn't even crack a smile. He just nodded, blowing his breath out slowly.

"What is it, Joe?" Jordan asked, her voice reflecting her worry.

"Nothing," he said, looking away from her.

"Don't tell me that," she said, moving to catch his gaze again. "It's something—tell me what it is."

He looked at her, then shrugged. "I just don't like having to leave when Kana's not back on her feet yet. I don't like not being here for family."

"You were here, Joe," Jordan pointed out. "As soon as you heard, you dropped everything and were here."

"Normally, I'd be here while she recovered."

Jordan was silent. She knew there was nothing she could say. Joe didn't have the life he'd had before, and sometimes it became clear that he missed it. While they'd been in town, Joe had gone and spent hours and hours with his kids. Jordan had stayed at the townhouse, not wanting to interfere with that. The two of them had taken the kids out a couple of times too.

They were both silent for a while. Joe's thumb rubbed rhythmically at the curve of her waist. It told her that he still had things he wanted to say. She waited, knowing that he'd get around to it. He did.

"Jordan, look," he began, his tone somber. "This tour's over in two weeks. I think when it's over and you go back to LA, we should take some time apart to—"

"Don't!" she exclaimed, her head coming up in rebellion instantly.

"Jordan," Joe said, his tone reasoning. "We need some time."

"Why?" she asked in a plaintive whisper.

"Because," he said, reaching out to touch her cheek, "it's becoming more and more obvious to me that we need different things."

"I need you."

"No," Joe said, shaking his head. "You don't need me, babe."

"Yes, I do!" she said, her voice becoming desperate now. "I need you, Joe. I need you with me."

"You need things I can't give you, Jordan."

"I told you I don't need marriage or children—we talked about that. It's not important."

"You wouldn't have even brought it up if it wasn't, babe," he said gently. "And maybe it's not a big deal right now, but years from now, when it's too late for you to have kids, you'll resent not having them. And I'll be the reason for that."

"Damnit, Joe," she said, gritting her teeth, her eyes darkening in anger and frustration.

"Don't do it…" Joe warned.

He knew her volatile temper. She was a worse hell cat than Midnight had ever been in her younger days. Jordan's nails had sought to rake him a couple of times when he'd made her mad. After the second occurrence, he'd told her it was something he wouldn't stand for in their relationship. She'd either respect him enough not to strike out at him, or they were done. Since that time she'd curbed it, but he could sense her anger and knew she was desperate to let go.

Jordan caught the warning in his voice, and knew this was not the time to lose her temper with him. It would only prove to him that he was right. She couldn't do that.

Finally she got up out of bed, put on her bathrobe, and walked out of the room. Joe stayed in bed, knowing that she needed to think about what he'd said. He hadn't addressed any of the issues that pertained to him. Lately he'd been feeling like he'd never catch up to her. She was always on the go, always flitting from one place to another, and it was just plain exhausting. He had to be on his guard constantly. Being her boyfriend and her bodyguard was impossible. It had been hard enough keeping up with her before, but now it was just too much.

Joe found he missed his stable life in San Diego. He'd never believed that would be possible, but it was true. Life with Jordan had turned into the life he'd rejected in his youth, the life of a jet-setter. He was getting more and more jaded. At the last party they'd attended for Jordan's latest single release, he'd been offered a line of cocaine and had actually considered it for a moment, if nothing else for the energy it would give him. That had sickened him no end. Drugs? That had never been something he was into. Where was his life going? He missed his kids, his missed his job—he missed his bloody life!

The next day, preparations were made and they flew back to join the band in Tallahassee to continue the tour. Jordan had opted for icy silence. Joe made a few attempts to talk to her; she refused to talk about it, simply saying, "You've made your decision." Things went from ice to fire within three days, and they were fighting constantly. Joe put up with it for another four days, then called John Machiavelli.

"Are you free?" he asked. "I'll pay you anything you ask to get Jordan through the last of this tour."

"How much longer is the tour?" John asked.

"A week."

"Why can't you just stay? You've made it this long," John said, a grin in his voice. He knew full well what Joe was dealing with. His own wife, Cassie, was a consistent source of fire, ice, and acid.

"If I stay, I'm going to end up doing something I've never done to a woman," Joe said.

"And that is?"

"Slapping the shit out of her," Joe said, grinning.

"Ah. Yeah, man, I can take her the rest of the way," he said, glancing at his calendar. "I have a minor gig I'll have to break, but that's okay."

"Fantastic," Joe said. "How much damage will it do my bank account?"

"Consider it a favor," John said, grinning.

"Nah, man," Joe said, shaking his head. "I know your rates. Will 50K do it?"

"Joe, I don't charge friends that kind of money."

"Then name your price."

"5k and we're square."

"You're nuts," Joe said. "Send me the rest of the bill when you get done with her."

John laughed. "Where you guys at?"

"North Carolina. Raleigh."

"Show tonight?"

"No, day after tomorrow."

"I'll be there tomorrow morning."

"Thanks, man."

"No problem."

That night, Jordan started yet another fight. Joe slept on the couch in the hotel room. He was up early and packed. John arrived at the hotel at 8 a.m. Joe and John went downstairs and sat in the coffee shop, where Joe briefed him on Jordan's schedule. After that, Joe took a cab to the airport and got on the next flight back to San Diego.

He arrived at his townhouse at noon. He dropped into bed, feeling the beginnings of a cold. He'd known that night on the balcony the week before would cost him, and now it was. For the next two days he took Nyquil and slept.

CHAPTER 6

Erin watched as Kevin lit his third cigar since getting into the Durango twenty minutes before. His music was loud, and it was the aggressive, angry type he favored when he was on edge. His edge usually stemmed from his ADD.

"Kevin?" she queried when the song ended.

Kevin turned the music down, glancing over at her as he lit the cigar in his mouth. "Yeah?"

"Did you take your Adderall today?" she asked gently.

He grinned, white teeth showing. "Yeah, babe, I did."

"Then why are you chain-smoking?" she asked, canting her head to the side.

Kevin glanced at the cigar in his hand, realizing he was indeed doing just that. He shook his head. "Just on edge, babe."

"And even the Adderall isn't working to take the edge off now?" she asked, worried.

"It's this custody hearing."

Erin reached across the center console and touched his arm. "Kevin, it's going to be okay."

He nodded, not looking convinced.

"She beat your daughter—we have a professional that can prove this," she said, entreating him to listen to her. "There's no way she's going to get Emily back."

"God, I hope not," Kevin said, shaking his head. He turned to look at Erin as he stopped at a light. "You do realize if she gets her hands on Emily again, she might kill her because of what Em told us…"

"She wouldn't do that," Erin said, not totally convinced of that fact herself. "If she did, she'd lose her hold on you forever."

"I don't know that she could control herself, babe," Kevin said grimly.

Randy was fairly sure that Stacy was bipolar at best. Which meant she had horrible mood swings. Oddly enough, the same kind of mood swings that Randy's own father, John Curtis, had. So it was highly possible that Stacy was unable to control her temper. Randy had suggested that Stacy be seen professionally. That suggestion was resoundingly refused by Stacy and her lawyer. Randy had shrugged it off—as long as Emily didn't end up with Stacy again, it wasn't their concern.

"Kevin, we're going to get Emily," Erin said, confidence in her voice.

He looked over at her, staring into her eyes, drawing strength from her confidence. Taking a deep breath, he expelled it slowly, nodding.

***

"Fans were sorely disappointed last night at the Jordan Tate concert when the star refused to go on stage," reported the smiling blonde on *Entertainment Weekly*. "She was overheard screaming at her tour manager that she wanted her bodyguard back. Looks like Jordan Tate may have lost her man," the reporter finished, a satisfied smile on her face.

Randy clicked off the television. If Joe wasn't with Jordan, where was he? She called his cell phone, wanting to check on him. No answer. She called Midnight, who was splitting her time between her campaign, the department, and going to see Kana.

"Haven't seen or heard from him," Midnight said. "They said he left Jordan's tour?"

"They said Jordan was having a fit because her bodyguard was gone—who else could she have meant?"

"No, she meant Joe," Midnight said, shaking her head. "Did you try his cell?"

"First thing," Randy said. "I just don't like the idea of him disappearing…"

"I know, I know," Midnight agreed. "He wasn't real happy about having to leave last week either, said he belonged here while Kana was down."

Randy nodded, knowing how Joe thought. Kana was family to him—if she was still in the hospital, he felt like he needed to be around in case he was needed.

Midnight promised to check with everyone to see if they'd seen him. Randy said she'd head over to Joe's townhouse and see if he was there.

An hour later Randy walked into the townhouse, looking around. Sure enough, Joe's bags were in the entryway. His jacket was over a chair in the dining room, his keys on the table. Walking through the house, she noticed there were no lights on in the front room. She could see one light from the bathroom in the master suite, and to her dismay she heard coughing coming from the bedroom.

Walking into the bedroom, she saw Joe lying across the bed at an angle, like he'd simply crawled back into bed, not bothering with covers. It was cold in the room; she noted the windows were open.

"Jesus," she muttered, walking over to the windows and shutting them, then went to the bed.

"Joseph Michael Sinclair," she said, sitting down and touching him on the shoulder. "Are you trying to kill yourself?"

"Huh?" he asked, shifting on the bed to look up at her. "Am I what?"

"Trying to kill yourself?" she said, already grinning. He looked so young when he was sleepy.

He turned over onto his back, reaching up to rub his eyes and starting to cough again.

Randy got up and went into his bathroom. Coming back a few moments later, she sat down again and helped him sit up. She held the Imbuterol to his lips.

"Take a puff."

He obediently put his lips around the inhaler, and she depressed the release. He took a long, deep breath, holding it then slowly blowing it out.

"One more."

He did as she bade, then lay back down tiredly.

"How long have you been here?" she asked, searching his face.

"Dunno. What's today?"

"It's Friday."

"Two days," he said, his voice gravelly.

"You've been here sick this whole time?" she asked, shocked. "Joseph Michael, you know better than this."

Joe grinned. She was getting good at the mother tone.

"Don't you grin at me, you brat," she said, grinning herself. "What have you been taking?"

"Nyquil."

"Joe!" she exclaimed. "You know better than that! The doctor told you that Nyquil is bad, especially for you—it'll dry you out, instead of clearing out the junk in your lungs. Man, I am gonna smack you yet…" she said, giving him a narrowed look.

Joe looked wholly unconcerned. He knew she was worried about him, and she was right—he had known better about Nyquil. He just figured it was a cold, not the onset of pneumonia yet.

"How long have you been coughing?" she asked.

"Dunno," he said, shrugging.

Randy narrowed her teal-blue eyes at him. "Don't try that with me, Joseph Michael Sinclair. Not even JT gets away with that one anymore."

Joe chuckled softly, ending with a coughing fit. "'Bout ten hours or so, I guess."

"Lovely," she said, shaking her head. "And you didn't think to get the Imbuterol?"

"Who says I didn't?" he asked, raising an eyebrow at her.

"It was still in the cabinet, Joe," she said, giving him a chiding shove.

"Okay, you win, I didn't," he said, sighing and closing his eyes again.

"Can you walk?"

"Huh?" he asked, thrown by her change in topic.

"Can you walk?" she repeated. "I'm taking you back to the house—I don't want you here alone."

"I'm not alone. You're here now," he said tiredly.

"Yes, but our children are at the other house, and we need to get there, okay?"

Joe said nothing for a long moment, then nodded, moving to sit up and groaning as he did. Randy helped him. She found his tennis shoes and laced them up for him as he sat watching her with bleary eyes.

"Come on," she said, pulling at him to get up off the bed. She picked up the Imbuterol and went into his bathroom to see if he had any antibiotics left. He had a bottle; she checked the expiration date.

"Shit."

"What?" Joe asked as he walked into the bathroom.

She held the bottle up. "Out of date."

"Oh," he said, leaning against the doorjamb, looking tired again already.

"I'll call the doctor in the morning. She may want to come give you a breathing treatment anyway. Let's go," Randy said, gently pushing him off the doorjamb and taking his hand to lead him out of the townhouse, grabbing his jacket on the way out and having him put it on.

Two hours later she had him settled in the bed they'd shared for years, since no other bed in the house would accommodate his six foot, two inch frame comfortably. JT and Kat were thrilled to see their father. Susan helped Randy explain to the children that their daddy was sick and he needed to rest. Joe did his best to hug both of the kids, but it was obvious he was still extremely tired, and unwell.

Randy asked if he'd eaten; he shook his head. "Not hungry."

Randy nodded. "Okay, but you need to drink something. Lay down. I'll bring you some tea in a bit, okay?"

Joe nodded tiredly and lay down in the bed. He was asleep ten minutes later when she checked on him. She stood looking down at him. This man that had been her husband for fifteen years... He still looked so handsome to her, sleeping in their bed, his arm thrown up over his head, his dark blond lashes against his skin.

She had to admit he looked even better now than he had before they'd gotten divorced, or was it that she hadn't noticed before? The arm over his head was well muscled and defined, and his chest was too. His hair, just past his shoulders, was very straight now, whereas before the ends that reached a good five inches past his shoulders had curled. She noticed the diamond studs in both ears, and of course she'd already seen the world-famous tattoo of a fragmented British flag in a tribal pattern, designed by Jordan Tate. He just seemed like a wilder version of the man he'd been when they were married. She wasn't sure how she felt about that.

It was two days before Joe was back to normal. His cough never got really bad, but his cold definitely was. He sheepishly admitted that he'd sat out on his balcony with wet hair the evening before he and Jordan had left to go back to the tour.

"Dork," Randy said, grinning.

"Yeah, yeah," Joe said, shaking his head.

They were sitting in the living room. The family was watching a movie, and the kids were all over Joe. JT was sitting on Joe's lap, and Kat had gone back to her habit of acting like her nickname, draping herself around Joe's shoulders as she lay on the back of the couch.

"Katherine Renee Sinclair," Randy said, giving her daughter a "you know better" look. "How many conversations have we had about you not laying on the back of the couch?"

"A lot," Kat said. "But you said I might fall, and Daddy won't let me fall."

Joe grinned, his light blue eyes twinkling, knowing full well his daughter was right back to playing the two of them against each other—she was a master at it.

"Did it occur to you that you might be hurting Daddy, laying on him like that?" Randy asked, hands on her hips.

Kat looked immediately contrite.

"She's okay, babe," Joe told Randy. "But Kat, when your mother tells you not to do something, you need to listen. She's just trying to keep you from getting hurt."

"But I'm okay now?" Kat asked meekly.

"You're fine for now," Joe assured her. "I'll let you know if it starts to hurt, okay?"

"Okay, Daddy," Kat replied, her smile bright. The sun rose and set on her father, as far as she was concerned. She was absolutely thrilled to have him home. She was wishing on every star she saw at night that he would stay home this time.

Randy watched the exchange, smiling. She knew Kat had missed Joe a lot, and so had JT. Kat was the more sensitive of the two children, though, and she was very much a daddy's girl. Randy knew that Joe had seen the children as often as he could, even bringing them on the cruise so he could spend time with them. But for children it was never enough time with someone they loved. Randy knew she couldn't tell Joe how much the kids missed him; it wouldn't be fair to him. It would just put new guilt on him that she didn't think he needed at this point.

Instead she enjoyed watching him with their children and mentally prepared for when he'd leave again. She hadn't asked him what had happened with Jordan, knowing that he'd tell her when he was ready, if he felt the need to talk about it at all. Randy was sure it was just another argument, that Jordan would probably sweep in any day and beg Joe to forgive whatever she'd done, and he'd be gone again.

Randy handed Joe a soda and sat down on the couch.

"Thanks, babe," he said, smiling at her.

"Welcome," she said, leaning back and tucking her feet under her.

They were watching *Daddy Day Care*. The kids enjoyed it thoroughly. By the time the movie was over both of them were getting tired. Randy told them to kiss Daddy goodnight, telling Joe she'd put them to bed.

"I'll help," he said, getting up and following her.

Joe spent the next half hour putting his kids to bed. Randy stood by and watched, enjoying seeing him with the kids again. He'd always been a great father, loving, kind, always supportive. By the time Joe got done, Randy was back on the couch, flipping through channels to find something to watch. She glanced up as he walked into the room, grinning at him.

"All fathered out?" she asked as he sat down heavily.

"How do you keep from letting them wear you out?"

Randy laughed. "I deal with kids all day that are so badly behaved, our kids are basically angels by comparison. They don't wear me out that much anymore."

Joe shook his head, amazed by her. Without stopping to think, he lay down on the couch, putting his head in her lap and taking the remote from her.

"Hey!" she said, laughing even as she did.

"You know you're just going to settle on some Martha Stewart 'How To Redecorate Your Closet On A Budget Of Four Million' show," he said, grinning. "I'm saving you that torture."

"You mean you're saving you that torture," she said, narrowing her eyes at him.

"Yeah, that too."

He flipped through channels, looking for something to watch.

"Stop, go back!" Randy said, having seen the name Dustin Hoffman on the opening credits for a movie.

Randy loved Dustin Hoffman, and anything he was in. Joe rolled his eyes and flipped back to the channel. The movie was *Kramer vs. Kramer*, a late seventies movie about a couple getting divorced and their custody battle over their young son. The battle became vicious at some points, with accusations flying back and forth about who was a fit parent and who wasn't. The son was played by a young boy with blond hair and wide, sweet eyes.

At one point Joe glanced up to see tears sliding down Randy's cheeks. He sat up, pulling her into his arms to comfort her. To him it was a natural reaction to seeing the woman who he'd loved and been married to for fifteen years crying. To Randy it was a testament to the kind of man Joe was. Watching the movie about a bitter divorce reminded Randy of how things could have been with Joe.

Even though she'd asked for nothing, save shared custody of the kids, he could have fought her every step of the way. He could have tried to take the children from her. With his money, his very intelligent lawyer, and all his friends, he could have done just about anything and gotten away with it. But he hadn't. Not only had he not fought for full custody of the kids, he'd given her $7,500 a month in child support and alimony. He'd given her the house they lived in free and clear, and Sinclair House, a building that had cost him over two million dollars. On top of all that he'd given her a million dollars in a lump settlement. It was beyond generous. And it said a lot about Joe.

The movie had reminded her again how hard things could have been for her, but Joe had done everything in his power to make her life easier once he was gone. Even though he'd been the one to decide to walk out, she'd been the one to file for divorce. She'd wanted to set him free, knowing that she wasn't making him happy and feeling that he needed more than she could give him. Joe had fled home to England, taking the children with him. From England she'd received his counter to her divorce decree. It had left her speechless and in tears. It had also strengthened her resolve to let him go with as little pain as possible to him.

Since that time she'd been ever supportive of him and his new relationship with Jordan Tate. There had been times when her heart had ached at seeing him, but she'd never let him see that. Instead she'd encouraged him, pointing out flaws in his thinking, helping get around any obstacles he encountered with Jordan. She knew that chances were she'd be called on again this time to do just that. She found it was getting harder and harder, that her heart and her head were starting to rebel at pushing him toward Jordan.

It wasn't that Randy didn't like Jordan—she honestly thought Jordan was a very nice woman. If she made Joe happy, that was what was important. The problem was, in the darkest, deepest part of Randy's heart, she missed Joe, and it hurt her a little bit more every time he turned to her to help him go back to another woman.

She knew at some point her self-preservation would kick in, and she'd have to turn him away when he came to her for help. She dreaded that day, because she was afraid it would mean she'd never see him, except when he picked the kids up. The idea of that haunted her every day.

They finished watching the movie and then went to bed. Randy was sleeping in the room down the hall from Joe's. He walked her to her room.

"I hate that I'm putting you out of your own bed, babe," he said.

"It's okay," she said, smiling. "I'll kick you out soon," she added with a wink.

Joe laughed. "I know, I'm wearing out my welcome, aren't I?"

"Never," she assured him, her look serious. "This is your house, Joe. You are welcome here any time, you should know that."

"That'd go over well with John…" Joe said, his grin sardonic.

"You let me worry about that," she said, her eyes narrowed.

"Uh-huh," Joe said. Leaning down, he kissed her cheek softly. "Goodnight, Randy."

"Goodnight, Joe," she said, smiling up at him.

He walked down the hall to their room. Randy stared after him for a few moments then went into her room. She changed into her blue silk night shirt. She brushed out her hair, pulling it to the side and braiding it. It still fell halfway to her waist in silken waves. Getting into bed, she found she couldn't sleep. After tossing and turning for a few minutes, she finally gave up. Reaching over, she turned the bedside lamp back on, and realized her book was in the room where Joe slept.

"Damn," she said. Thinking about it, she decided to see if she could sneak in and get it without disturbing him.

She padded down the hall and knocked lightly on the door, not wanting to walk in uninvited in case he was still awake. She was, however, surprised when she heard him call, "Come."

"You're still awake?" she asked. It had been almost a half hour since they'd gone to bed.

"Yeah," he said, grinning. "Couldn't sleep. You?"

"Nope," she said, grinning too.

He patted the bed next to him. "Come, sit."

Randy walked over. "If I roll over too, will you scratch my tummy?" she said with a wink.

Joe laughed at that. "I dunno, maybe. Only if you promise not to lick my face."

Randy wrinkled up her nose. "I don't think that'd be a problem."

Joe chuckled. Randy was doing her best not to notice that his chest was bare, and that he had indeed done a lot of working out; his muscles were well defined now, his shoulders broad and strong. He was the kind of man women dreamed of, and he was her ex-husband, and they were talking about licking faces like a dog. Unreal.

"You shaved," she noted, looking at his face to distract her from his chest.

"Yeah," he said, reaching up and rubbing his jaw. "I was feelin' a bit scruffy."

"Ah, but we like you scruffy," she said, grinning.

"Like the dog."

She laughed again, moving to lean against the headboard, her body turned toward his. His eyes moved from her face down to her nightshirt. He reached his hand out, touching the lapel of the shirt.

"This is nice," he said, his voice mellow.

She smiled. "Well, I need to have something on in case the kids need me."

"Nice something," he said, winking.

Randy smiled, shaking her head.

"What?" he asked, seeing the look in her eyes.

"You just have a way of making me feel good all the time," she said honestly.

"Do I?" he asked, actually surprised by the statement.

"Of course you do," Randy said. "You've always been like that."

Joe shrugged. "When I think a woman is beautiful, I say something—doesn't matter to me that she's supposed to be my ex-wife." He said the last with another wink.

"Yeah, yeah, I know," she said, nodding. She canted her head to the side, her look serious. "So what happened, Joe?" she asked, feeling the need to get it out of him so she could help him and get him back to Jordan before she didn't want to let him go again.

He sighed, shaking his head. He turned to her, putting his arm on the headboard.

"She started talking about kids, Randy, and getting married…" he said, trailing off as he shook his head.

"She wants kids?" Randy asked, realizing that would be fairly normal for a woman at Jordan's age that didn't have any. As far as Randy knew, Jordan was about two years younger than she was at thirty-seven.

"Yeah," Joe said, not looking happy.

"So what did you say?"

"I told her I already have two kids. Two kids I almost never see now—how would I see a third child?"

Randy nodded, agreeing with that. "How did she take that?"

Joe shook his head. "She wasn't pleased."

"And the marriage thing, what about that?" Randy asked, hoping the fact that her heart was now in her throat didn't show in her voice or her face.

Joe didn't say anything for a long moment, then shrugged. "I was married for fifteen years. I don't think I'm ready to do that again just yet."

Randy nodded, feeling relief flood through her. Jesus, this meant way too much to her now. As a doctor, she knew better than to try to advise someone when her feelings were involved, but she was doing it anyway, heedless of everything she'd learned.

"So when did this happen?"

"While we were on the cruise."

Randy nodded. "I noticed you two seemed more tense with each other at one point."

"Yeah, and it's just gotten worse and worse," Joe said, sighing. "I dunno, Randy, she's wearing my ass out, ya know?"

"In terms of what?"

"Everythin'," he said, leaning his head against the wall. "I don't feel like I have a home anymore. Every night it's a different city, different hotel… I mean, I think if I was still a young man this would be great fun, but Jesus, I can't do this at my age."

Randy made a cynical face.

"What?"

"At your age," she repeated snidely. "Joe, you're in better shape now than I've ever seen you."

"Well," he said, curling his lips derisively, "I might be on the outside, love, but inside I'm becoming a total time bomb."

"In terms of what?" she asked, not liking the term—it said way too much.

He sighed again. "I guess emotionally I feel like I'm about to snap at some points. God, Randy, a few weeks ago, at a party for Jordan's new single, someone offered me coke, and I almost took it."

"Holy shit," Randy said, shocked. Joe was the last person she'd ever expect to use drugs—it just wasn't him.

"Tell me about it."

"So what are you going to do?"

"Well, I tried to tell Jordan that when this tour is done we need to take some time to think about what we really want out of this relationship."

Randy grimaced. "She didn't like that, did she?"

"Nope," he said, dropping his head against the wall again. "In fact, she became the ice queen for a while, then started fighting with me about everything for three straight days."

Randy nodded, waiting for him to finish.

"I finally gave up," he said, shrugging. "I grabbed John Mackie and put him on her bodyguard detail and took the next plane out."

"And she threw a fit and wouldn't go on stage, because you weren't there," Randy put in.

"She what?"

"It was on the news the night I came to find you at the townhouse—that's how we knew you were back."

"Lovely," he said, shaking his head unhappily.

"So, what are you going to do?" Randy asked, sure that he would run right back out and rescue Jordan.

Joe pursed his lips, contemplating his options. Finally he shrugged. "I'm going to stay here in San Diego and get my life back."

Randy was surprised, and it showed on her face.

Joe grinned. "I shocked you?"

"Uh, yeah," she said, grinning self-consciously.

He sighed, turning to face forward again, looking up at the ceiling. "I miss our kids, Randy. I miss my job. I miss everything…" he said, trailing off as he glanced at her.

She nodded wisely. "Then I think you're making the right choice for you right now."

"Thanks, Doc," he said, grinning.

"No problem. I'll send you the bill."

Joe laughed. "Great." Then he turned to her, his eyes searching her face. "Okay, enough about me. How are you? How's the center, everything…"

They ended up talking long into the night; they even ending up lying down on the bed, both of them on their backs, staring up at the ceiling as they talked on and on about anything and everything. They laughed a lot, making jokes about Midnight's competition in the AG race, and other things. It felt good. When they both started getting tired, Randy decided she'd better let him rest.

"I better get my butt to bed," she said reluctantly as she got up.

"Mmmm…" he moaned unhappily, reaching out and grabbing her hand, pulling her back to him to hug her. She laughed, letting him hold her to him. Then laughed more when she went to move back and he held her fast, saying "Uh-uh," sounding very much like JT.

"Joseph…" she whispered, feeling him getting sleepy.

"Mmmm?" he asked, his tone so innocent.

"You need sleep, I need sleep…" she said, trailing off as she gently tried to pull away again. Joe tightened his hold on her and rolled to his other side, taking her with him. Randy laughed at the gesture. "You nut!" she said, still smiling.

"This feels too good," he said softly against her cheek.

She had to agree there—it did feel really good. What harm did it do to let him hold her? None, she realized. They were adults—if they wanted to lie in bed holding each other, it wasn't a bad thing. She relaxed in his arms, snuggling against him. She heard him sigh, and smiled to herself. They were both asleep minutes later.

The next morning the kids were beyond thrilled to find their parents asleep in their bed again. They ran in, climbing up on the bed and all over their parents, exclaiming excitedly.

Randy and Joe grinned at each other. They'd slept very soundly; it had been a good rest for both of them.

They got up, got the kids ready for school, and then took them together. Joe wanted to go and see Kana, so Randy decided to go with him. Kana had a fever; they told Joe it was being taken care of but that she wasn't feeling up to visitors at that point. Joe understood and said he'd come back later.

They left the hospital, and Joe suggested an early lunch, since they hadn't managed breakfast for themselves that morning. Randy agreed. It was a nice day out, even if it was a little chilly, so they ate out on the deck of Anthony's. They had a couple glasses of wine, and talked for an hour while they ate. Afterward, they went back to the house. They were both tired, since they'd stayed up until around 3 a.m. and the kids had come and woken them at 6 a.m.

Joe took her hand, leading her back to what used to be their room. There he kicked off his boots, took of his holster and badge, and put them on the dresser. He lay down on the bed, pulling Randy down next to him. She laughed, but snuggled against him immediately.

"You gonna sleep like that?" he asked, indicating her shoes and the slacks and blouse she wore.

"Versus?"

"Naked?" he replied with a lascivious grin.

"Joseph Michael Sinclair!" she said, laughing, even as she got up to kick off her shoes and step out of her slacks. She surprised him by reaching up under her black silk blouse and undoing her bra and pulling it off.

"Better?" she asked primly.

"Mmhmm…" he said, smiling and holding his hand out to her again.

She took his hand, and he tugged her with just enough force to tumble her into bed next to him. Propping himself up on his elbow, he looked down at her, his light blue eyes searching her face.

"Have I thanked you yet for rescuing me yet again?" Joe asked.

"You don't have to," Randy said. "I appointed myself your rescuer."

He lowered his head, his lips hovering over hers. "All the same, thank you," he said, leaning in to kiss her lips softly.

Randy inhaled sharply, excited beyond belief just by his proximity. Joe pulled back, looking at her, confusion in his eyes. He'd felt her reaction—he wasn't sure if she was shocked that he was kissing her, or... But he saw it in her eyes. She wanted him. The look in her teal-blue eyes had an instant effect on his body. He hadn't realized how much he'd missed seeing that look. Without stopping to think, he leaned in, kissing her lips again, much more forceful this time.

Randy's reaction was instant. She wrapped her arms around his neck, moaning against his lips. That reaction spurred him on. He deepened the kiss, his lips moving over hers with strength and assurance born of experience. Randy marveled at the change in him. He'd always been a good kisser, but now his lips just seemed to burn hers with their heat. They kissed for a while, savoring each other. When Joe pulled back, looking down at her, his light blue eyes heated, he was breathing heavily.

"Randy... I want to make love to you..." he said, his voice husky with excitement.

She nodded, unable to think of a reply. His lips seared her again immediately. Joe moved his mouth to her neck, kissing her, his hands caressing her through her blouse. She gasped as his thumb brushed over a hard nipple. Pressing against him, she kissed his ear.

"I want you so much, Joe," she murmured huskily.

It was like someone had just turned the heat up to maximum in his body. Hearing her say that turned him on beyond belief. It was something he felt he'd lost so long ago with her. When his lips moved to hers again, there was a very definite change in him. Randy shuddered at the intensity with which he kissed her. She clung to him, riding the wave of desire he was creating in her body. He kissed her like he hadn't made love in years, his mouth exciting her beyond words. Moving over her, caressing her, his hands sliding under the blouse without removing the garment. It felt illicitly erotic to her, the cool silk against her skin combined with the heat of his hands. This was a different man entirely that was making love to her—he was kissing her and touching her with more heat than they'd ever experienced in their fifteen years of marriage.

He pulled his clothes off, tossing them aside, finally pulling off her blouse and panties, throwing them aside too, his lips never leaving her body. Randy reveled in it, coming over and over again under his ministrations before he ever even slid inside her. When he did, she cried out, clinging to him passionately even as he rolled to his back, pulling her over him. His hands were where her upper thighs met her ass, and he was guiding her body over his. Even then, he was caressing her, touching her where their bodies met, moving to touch her in places he'd never touched before, producing waves of erotic sensations. Within minutes they were both exclaiming in their orgasm. Randy could not believe the incredible high he'd just taken her to—it was far past anything they'd ever done before. And she'd always felt they'd had a great sex life when they were married.

She lay against him, trying to catch her breath. "My God…" she gasped. "Who are you?"

Joe grinned, breathing heavily too. "I could ask you the same thing…"

"What's that mean?" she asked, moving to look down at him.

"Do you know how long it's been since you've wanted me, Randy?"

Randy tried to suppress her grin, but couldn't manage it.

"What?" he asked, narrowing his eyes suspiciously.

She pressed her lips together, rolling her eyes upward. "It hasn't been long, Joe."

"Huh?" he said, apparently confused.

Randy took a deep breath. "I need to tell you something."

Joe held her to him as he rolled to his side. "Okay, tell me," he said, his eyes searching hers.

"Well, remember way back before the divorce, when I got pregnant?" she said. Joe nodded. "Well, remember that I was on the pill when that happened, and they decided I should change birth control?"

"Yeah…" Joe said, his tone showing that he had no idea what this had to do with her statement a few minutes before about wanting him.

"Well, something they apparently neglected to tell me," Randy said, reaching out to touch his lips, "is that taking the Depo-Provera can cause a severe drop in one's libido."

Joe looked back at her for a moment, still confused. Then understanding dawned. He closed his eyes, shaking his head. "That's why you didn't want me, sexually…" he said, then looked askance at her.

"Yeah," Randy said.

"Jesus…" Joe said, shaking his head. "When did you find this out?"

"About nine or ten months ago."

"Why didn't you tell me?"

Randy looked back at him for a long moment, then shook her head. "What was I going to say, Joe? 'Oh, by the way, it wasn't that you didn't turn me on anymore, I just had a problem with some meds. Now go ahead and drop your rock star girlfriend and come jump my bones'?"

He grinned at her words. She was right—at that point it was too late to do anything, but it would have done his ego some good to have heard it hadn't been him.

"There was a lot more to our divorce than just sex, Joe," Randy said, touching his cheek.

He looked down at her for a moment, his light blue eyes searching hers. "What did happen to us, Randy?" he asked, his confusion over that clear.

"We grew apart. We were like two trees someone planted close together—we grew together, we got as close as humanly possible." She shrugged sadly. "Then we grew right past each other."

Joe contemplated what she was saying. "But other people do this and are married for a lot longer than us—how do they do it?"

Randy shrugged. "We're different people, Joe. You can't compare us to everyone else. Our situation is different, our lives are different. How many people do you know who get divorced and seem to get closer than they were before?"

"Okay, that's my point. Why is it that we got along fine once we were divorced?"

Randy thought about that, then told him the only conclusion she could come to. "I think because I let you go to find what you needed, and you did."

"What I needed?"

Randy nodded. "I think you need women like Jordan—you need someone more exciting and sexy like her, or like Stevie. I think you needed a change."

Joe grinned, shaking his head.

"What?"

"Baby, you were my change."

"What?" she asked, looking surprised.

"Who did I date before you, Randy?"

"Uh…" Randy said. "Midnight, Tasha…"

"Uh-huh," Joe said, nodding. "And you met Ros, and the women before and during her were even wilder than that."

"So I was the one that was different?" Randy asked, shocked.

"Yeah, babe, that's why I married you," he said softly.

Her mouth dropped open, reflecting her surprise at what he was telling her. It didn't go with what she'd thought. She thought that he'd gotten bored with her.

"Okay, can I ask you something else?" she said.

"Okay," he said, grinning.

"Is that," she said, indicating their bodies still together, "like you are with her?"

"Sexually?"

"Yes."

It was Joe's turn to look surprised. "Yeah, I guess so. Why?"

"Why weren't you ever like that with me when we were married?"

Joe looked contemplative, then shrugged. "I guess because you were different, I wanted to be different with you. Besides, you make love to your wife—you don't fuck her."

Randy looked back at him, shocked. "So," she said, grinning, "is that what we just did? Fuck?"

"Yes," he said, his grin lopsided.

"Why?" was all she could think of to ask.

"Because you telling me you wanted me ignited it. And I just didn't bother to pull it back this time."

"So, basically you're telling me that you held out on me for fifteen years?" she asked, raising an eyebrow at him.

Joe laughed, shaking his head. "Did you feel like our sex life was lacking?"

"No, but apparently I had no idea how good you could really be, Mr. Sinclair," she said, narrowing her eyes at him.

He smiled, his light blue eyes twinkling. "So, what's this about having wanted me recently?"

"You never miss anything, do you?"

"Not often, no."

She sighed, shaking her head. "You look incredible these days, Joe. Seeing you like that on the cruise, with that tank shirt on, your arms all muscled and tanned… or dressed up for my birthday dinner… you looked so good. It didn't help that you'd always been incredibly handsome to me, but suddenly you're my ex-husband and I can't stop thinking about you."

"You hid it awfully well," he said, narrowing her eyes.

She shrugged. "No sense in making a fool out of myself."

"And how would that be?"

"Joe, you're dating a rock star."

"Am I?"

She looked back at him, not replying. She wasn't sure what he meant, but she knew it wasn't her place to ask him to do anything different.

He pulled her close, and she snuggled against him, enjoying his warmth. They fell asleep that way. Randy wasn't sure what it meant, but she knew that she wanted him back now more than anything. It wasn't helping her situation at all.

***

"What are you doing home?" Jerry asked when Palani walked into the apartment.

Palani didn't answer, simply shaking her head as she headed for her bedroom. Once there she closed the door quietly and threw herself on the bed, giving in to the tears. Kana loved Cat—that was the thought running around in her head. The words "Where's Cat? I need to tell her, I need to tell her... She needs to know... I can't do this... I can't... I love her so much, I can't... I can't let her go" ran on a loop in her head.

Palani's heart was shattered. In the time that she'd been at the hospital, she'd seen Kana through follow-up surgery that had caused a fever. It was in that fevered state that Kana had uttered those fateful words. She loved Cat! No! It was something Palani's heart just couldn't stop thinking about. It was something she was going to need to learn to live with. After she'd heard that, she hadn't been able to stay in the hospital room she'd spent so many hours in since Kana had been shot. She felt so foolish. Had Kana been putting up with her? Cat had come to visit a few times, but had never really stayed long. Maybe Kana had been trying to make Cat jealous by letting Palani stay? Was that it? Had she been a fool all along? The thought broke her heart a little bit more. She cried herself to sleep that night. She didn't go back to the hospital—she just couldn't, knowing who Kana truly loved.

Palani was once again in her room, curled into a ball on the bed, much like she'd been for the last couple of days. Jerry was beside herself worrying about her friend. She'd checked on her frequently in the last couple of days, so Palani assumed when she heard the knock on the door that it was Jerry again. She uttered, "Come in." She was stunned when Catalina stuck her head in the door.

"Palani?" Cat queried gently.

Palani looked at her, then sat up, her eyes wide as she hugged her knees to her chest.

"You're here," she said unnecessarily.

"I know," Cat couldn't resist saying, with a grin.

"What do you want?" Palani asked softly, feeling her stomach churning. This was the woman Kana loved now. Didn't she realize she'd won—why was she here, to hurt her some more?

"I want to know why you left the hospital," Cat said, leaning against the door, her arms crossed in front of her chest.

Palani stared back at her, searching the other woman's face. Finally she shrugged. "Why does it matter?"

"It matters because K needs you."

Palani looked back at Cat, pained. "She doesn't need me," she said, feeling her insides twist some more. "I know that now."

"Now?" Cat asked, catching the word.

"Yes," Palani said simply.

"What do you mean, now? What made you decide Kana didn't need you?"

"She told me."

"She told you she doesn't need you?" Cat said disbelievingly.

"No," Palani said, her eyes dropping from Cat's.

"What *did* she tell you, Palani?" Cat asked, becoming irritated.

Palani caught it, her eyes widening as she looked back at Cat. "She told me that she loves you, that she can't let you go."

Cat looked back at her for a long moment, then gave a short, sarcastic laugh, shaking her head.

"I don't know what you were smoking, Palani," Cat said, "but Kana doesn't love me. She can't—she's never gotten over you."

"She said it."

"I don't fucking care what she said," Cat said, becoming unac-countably angry. "She doesn't love me, and she does love you. And you need to march your ass back to her bedside before she gives up again. Because if she does that, I'm going to kick your pretty little ass all the way back to Hawaii. You got it?"

Palani jumped at the venom in Cat's voice. She stared back at the blond woman, unable to think of a reply. Finally she nodded, if noth-ing else to placate Cat.

"I mean it," Cat said. "So get up and let's go."

"But…" Palani stammered.

"Now!" Cat yelled, her anger snapping.

Palani jumped off the bed and grabbed her purse, responding on a base level to Cat's command. Cat drove her back to the hospital in silence, dropping her at the front. Before Palani got out, Cat leaned over, taking her arm gently.

"Talk to her, Palani," Cat said softly. "I'm sure you heard her wrong."

Palani nodded, unable to understand Cat's motivations in this. She got out of the Blazer and watched as Cat drove away. Shrugging to herself, she walked inside.

At Kana's room, she took a deep breath and then opened the door. Kana was lying with her eyes closed. Palani walked over to the side of the bed, reaching out and touching her cheek. Kana's dark eyes opened immediately, going straight to Palani's.

"Why did you leave?" Kana asked.

Palani swallowed, trying to get past the lump in her throat. "I didn't think I belonged here anymore," she said softly.

"Why wouldn't you?" Kana asked, obviously perplexed.

Palani took a deep breath, blowing it out slowly. "While you had your fever, you said some things…"

"What did I say?" Kana asked, her eyes still searching Palani's.

Palani looked down at the blanket covering Kana. She picked at it nervously, not willing to meet her eyes. "You said you loved Cat very much and that you couldn't let her go."

She didn't see the look of utter confusion on Kana's face, or the smile that started then. She was so intent on picking at the lint on the blanket and trying to hold back tears, she didn't see anything. Kana's finger under her chin turned Palani's eyes up to hers.

"Baby girl," Kana said, "if I said that, I wasn't talking about Cat. I was talking about you."

"You were?" Palani asked, her eyes wide, her voice hopeful.

"You think I stay in this world for just anyone?" Kana asked, grinning. "Even when I have more holes in me than a piece of Swiss cheese?" She shook her head. "Only for you, babe. Just for you."

Palani cried, she was so happy. Kana shook her head, rolling her eyes heavenward, even as she held her arms out to Palani. "Dumb ass," she said as Palani moved into her arms.

"Stop," Palani said, pouting prettily.

Kana shook her head again, grinning. "Next time, stick around long enough to ask for clarification, okay?"

"Okay," Palani said, biting her lip.

Kana kissed her forehead, hugging her as best she could from the hospital bed.

CHAPTER 7

Cat lay in her bed, on her stomach, her arms outstretched above her head, her face buried in the crook of her arm. She wore a jog bra and sweats and hadn't bothered to cover up, even though it was probably only fifty-five degrees in the apartment. That was the first thing Elizabeth noticed when she walked in. Shivering, Elizabeth walked over to the thermostat and noted that the heater wasn't even on. She flipped the switch and set the thermostat at sixty-eight degrees.

She looked around, noticing that the tequila bottle stood open on the counter. Elizabeth's lips twitched at that, realizing that Cat was upset again. The woman had a tendency to handle her hurts all alone. It was a nasty habit that Elizabeth intended to break. Walking over to the counter, she put the top back on the tequila and put it away. Then she walked toward the bedroom.

She saw Cat lying on the bed and stood in the doorway watching her for a few minutes. Finally she walked over. Cat sensed her there and turned her head slightly.

"Bet," she said by way of greeting.

"Cat," Elizabeth replied in kind.

Cat turned her head back to face the bed and was quiet again. Elizabeth scowled at her, even though Cat didn't see it. Taking off her jacket and kicking off her boots, Elizabeth flopped down on the bed next to Cat. Turning to her side, she faced Cat's motionless form. Reaching out, she brushed her hair back off the side of her face.

"What happened?" Elizabeth asked gently.

Cat shook her head.

"Don't give me that," Elizabeth said. "I haven't seen you indulge in—what, a half bottle of tequila?" she guessed, pretty accurately too. "Not on a whim, Catalina. What happened?"

Cat turned her head, one blue eye peeking out from behind her arm. "I did my good fucking deed for the century," she said harshly.

Elizabeth nodded. "And what was that, love?"

Cat curled her lips in disgust. "Palani left the hospital, I got her back."

"And how did you do that?" Elizabeth asked, knowing there was a lot more to this story.

Cat didn't answer.

"Why did Palani leave? I thought she was determined to stay with Kana…"

Cat gave a short, sarcastic laugh. "That's the funny part, actually."

"What is?" Elizabeth asked.

"She left because she thought Kana was in love with me," Cat said, giving another short bark of laughter that sounded anything but humorous.

"But you convinced her differently?" Elizabeth asked, grimacing at the way that sounded.

"Oh yeah," Cat said, nodding. "Then I dragged her ass back to the hospital."

Elizabeth took a deep breath, not sure what to say at this point.

"You know what really sucks?" Cat said. "What really pisses me off?"

"What?" Elizabeth asked quietly.

"When she said it, when Palani said that Kana loves me, that she can't let me go… I wanted to fucking believe it so much…" Her voice trailed off as she scrubbed her face against her bare arm. "Damnit," she muttered, feeling her throat constrict painfully.

Elizabeth winced at the sound of her voice. She touched Cat's head, stroking her hair. "Cat..."

"I can't even cry anymore," Cat said, her tone disgusted. "I'm out. I'm all out."

Elizabeth leaned in, putting her head against Cat's, commiserating with her the best way she could think of.

"Don't..." Cat said petulantly, moving away slightly.

Elizabeth moved in again, resting her cheek against Cat's head.

"Don't," Cat said again, nudging her with her shoulder.

"I'm going to comfort you whether you like it or not," Elizabeth said firmly, but with a grin already on her lips.

Cat made a little noise in her throat, still sounding petulant.

"Catalina!" Elizabeth exclaimed. "You lie there and let me comfort you, or else..." she said, trailing off ominously.

That garnered a grin out of Cat. She turned her head to look up at Elizabeth, whose head was just above hers. "Is that like, 'You're going to have fun or I'll break every bone in your body'?"

"Yes," Elizabeth said, laughing softly. "Usually utilized on small children at Disneyland."

Cat laughed, shaking her head, tears in her eyes all the same. Elizabeth put her hand to Cat's cheek, her eyes reflecting pain at seeing her upset. Their eyes caught and held, and it seemed inevitable that they'd kiss. And they did. Cat started to pull back as soon as she realized what they were doing. Elizabeth's hand moved to the back of her head, pulling her back.

Cat gave in for a full minute, her hands moving to cup Elizabeth's face. Elizabeth moaned softly; the sound of it brought Cat back to reality. She pulled away, shaking her head.

"I can't do this," Cat said, moving back, breathing heavily.

"Why?" Elizabeth asked, surprised at Cat's sudden retreat.

Cat shook her head. "No, I can't. You're my friend. I can't…"

Elizabeth reached out, touching Cat's face, searching her eyes. "Cat, why can't you? Why can't we?"

"No," Cat said. "This isn't you—this isn't right." She sat up, pulling her knees up to her chest.

"What do you mean?" Elizabeth asked, sitting up as well, facing Cat's side.

Cat looked at her, her face serious. "What part of 'straight' don't you get?"

"What?" Elizabeth asked, her face reflecting shock.

"You're straight, Bet, I know that. I don't need comforting that bad, not enough to use you," Cat said, her lips curling in self-disgust.

"But—"

"Just stop," Cat said, cutting her off angrily. Her anger was self-directed, but Elizabeth didn't know that.

Elizabeth's chin came up, her pride kicking in. "Fine," she said softly, trying to force back the tears that threatened to come up on her. In desperation to hide them, she got up and grabbed her boots and jacket. She walked out of the room without looking back. She didn't see the look of anguish on Cat's face.

"Good, Cat, real good," Cat said to herself. "Run off your last friend." The tears came then and she lay back on the bed, letting them flow. "Fuck!" she yelled to no one.

Elizabeth strode into the hospital intent on settling the score for her friend. She went to Kana's room and encountered the nurse taking care of her. She said she needed to talk to Kana, and gained entrance a few minutes later.

She was fuming, and she was ready for a fight. Stepping into the room, she had no idea her blue eyes were blazing in her anger. She saw Palani stand up, but her attention was focused on the woman in the bed. "Elizabeth," Kana said curtly.

"I hope you're satisfied," Elizabeth said without preamble.

"With?"

"Yourself," Elizabeth spat, her blue eyes points of fire. "You've fucked Cat over pretty well. She can't even see her way out of the abysmal pit you've put her in."

Kana's head came up. Elizabeth had no idea what Kana was thinking, but she didn't care. She was bound and determined to say what she'd come to say. So she pressed on. "When you get out of here, you stay away from her. Because I swear to you," Elizabeth said, her hands clenching into fists at her side, "if you hurt her again, I'll personally…" She trailed off as she searched for the appropriate threat. "Hire someone to kill you," she said, her voice serious, as was the look on her face.

Kana nodded, not saying a word. Elizabeth stared back at her for a long moment, trying to drive her point home. Then she turned and stalked out of the room, doing her best to slam the door.

***

The hearing for custody of Emily Elmasian took place in family court. The judge, who was female, was known to side with the biological mother. Kevin spent a lot of time outside of the courthouse, smoking like smoking was going out of style. Erin did her best to assure him that everything would be okay. When they were called in, he took a deep drag on his cigar and tossed it down, stubbing it out with his shoe.

Kevin was dressed in a suit, a deep, rich blue, with a crisp white collared shirt and a tie. He wore brown suede dress shoes and a belt to match. To his belt was clipped his gold shield; he also wore a holstered gun at his side, just hidden by his jacket. He had no intention of hiding the fact that he was a cop. He looked great, but Erin didn't remind him again, knowing that was the last concern on his mind. Erin was wearing a simple blue dress, nylons, and heels, with her hair pulled back softly from her face. They looked like fine, upstanding parents.

Sitting at the plaintiff's table with their attorney, Kevin and Erin waited for Stacy to walk into court. When she did, Kevin shook his head. She was wearing white, of all colors. Her hair was pulled back severely from her face and she wore no makeup. Kevin glanced at Erin, who only rolled her eyes at him. Stacy walked to her seat next to her wormy-looking lawyer. She shot Kevin a triumphant look. He just looked back at her calmly.

The hearing began with Kevin and Erin's lawyer explaining that Kevin and his wife were petitioning the court, seeking full custody of Emily Elmasian.

"While the plaintiff acceded his rights to custody at one time, in what he felt was the best interests of his daughter, he has now come to the conclusion that his daughter is being hindered rather than helped by the custody situation. It is for that reason that Kevin and Erin Elmasian are requesting full custody of Emily."

When Stacy's lawyer got up to speak, he outlined how Kevin Elmasian had an uncontrollable temper, and that he flew into rages, often striking out at anyone near. That it was Emily's mother's "worst fear" that Kevin would lash out at "poor little Emily" one day and hurt her severely.

Erin had to hold on tight to Kevin's arm to keep him from yelling about that being a bald-faced lie.

It only got worse when Stacy gave testimony, stating that she'd come to San Diego weeks before to try and work things out with Kevin. "He asked me to come," she said, her eyes demurely lowered—she'd been well coached.

"What happened when you got here?" her lawyer asked.

"He told me that I needed to give up custody or he'd have me put away for good," Stacy said tremulously.

Kevin gritted his teeth, dying to kill her. Erin held on tight to his arm, whispering to him constantly.

"She won't win, Kevin. She won't win," she assured him constantly.

"What did you say to him?" the lawyer asked Stacy.

"I told him I wouldn't give Emily up," Stacy said, the proud mother.

"What happened then?"

Stacy lowered her eyes, her hands clasped together in her lap. "He attacked me."

Kevin was sure he was going to come unglued. The lying bitch! He could just kill her!

"Attacked you?"

"Yes. He grabbed me by the throat and tried to rape me."

Kevin sat back, shaking his head, not believing the lengths Stacy would go to just to win.

"Do you have any proof of this?" her lawyer asked.

"I have pictures of the marks on my neck," Stacy said, pointing to the folder on the defendant's table.

Kevin's mouth dropped open.

The lawyer handed the pictures to the judge. The judge looked through them, then glanced at Kevin, then at Stacy.

"Who took these pictures?" she asked Stacy.

"A friend of mine."

"You didn't go to a hospital or the police?"

"Kevin's a police officer," Stacy said, her eyes wide. "I knew he'd get off if I tried to press charges here. So I flew back to Seattle. I didn't want to go to the hospital because I was afraid they'd report it, and then Kevin would come after me."

"Jesus…" Kevin muttered, gritting his teeth.

The judge nodded, apparently accepting that excuse. Kevin felt his stomach churn. He was going to lose. He was going to lose, and Emily would be with Stacy again. He closed his eyes, feeling everything start to crash inside him.

Suddenly there was a commotion at the back of the room. Kevin opened his eyes and turned to see what was going on. He was just in time to see the double doors open, and in walked Midnight, with Joe and Kyle just behind her, the rest of the Gang fanned out behind them. They all took places in the seats behind the plaintiff's table. Randy walked in last, winking at Kevin and sitting down next to Joe.

"Excuse me," the judge said. "These are official proceedings."

Midnight stood up. "And we're here to testify on the Elmasians' behalf."

"Oh," the judge said, looking shocked. "I'm sorry, I didn't understand."

"No problem," Midnight said, smiling as she sat down.

Kevin was floored. He'd expected Randy, not the entire Gang. He knew that a few of the members of Rogue Squadron had given official statements, but he hadn't expected them to show up in person. He turned to look at Erin, who was smiling. When he turned back to look at Stacy, he saw that she'd gone quite pale. The grin that spread over his face was nothing short of malicious.

Midnight's testimony, of course, carried a great deal of weight.

"Please state your name," Jacob Berringer told her.

"Midnight Chevalier-Debenshire."

"What is your occupation?"

"I'm the Chief of Police of San Diego Police Department," Midnight said, looking straight at Stacy.

Stacy looked like she was going to choke. Midnight's eyes twinkled with subdued humor. She knew the woman was lying her ass off about Kevin, and she was about to fix that.

"So, in essence, both Kevin and Erin Elmasian work for you?" Jacob asked.

"Yes, they both work for my department, therefore for me."

"And what is your impression of Kevin Elmasian?"

"He's a good man," Midnight said, looking at Kevin. "He's where he needs to be when he needs to be there. Reliable, responsible, and extremely valuable to my department."

"And what about Erin Elmasian?"

Midnight smiled, looking at Erin. "She's about the sweetest girl I've ever met. And she's also always been there when she was needed most, willing to pitch in and do whatever it took to help out. She's very reliable, very loving, and the very best person Kevin could have married."

"Why do you say that?" Jacob asked.

"Because she brings a calming influence to his life. His work is very stressful, and Erin is a good haven for him to come home to."

"And you know this how?"

"Because Erin and Kevin are personal as well as professional friends of mine."

"Do you feel that they would be suitable parents for Emily Elmasian?"

"Suitable?" Midnight queried. "They're great parents to Steven now, and yes, I think they'd do just as well with Emily."

"Thank you, Chief," Jacob said.

"Cross examine, Mr. Keegan?" the judge asked Stacy's lawyer.

Fred Keegan stood up, nodding. He walked over to where Midnight sat. He looked her over. She stared back at him, her eyes cat-like green. Fred couldn't help but think what a hot-looking woman this was. He took an extra moment. Midnight grinned, glancing back at Rick, who narrowed his blue eyes dangerously. She did her best not to laugh as she saw Joe lean over and whisper to him. She was fairly sure Joe had just informed Rick that it wouldn't help Kevin's case if Rick beat the shit out of Stacy's lawyer for checking out his wife.

Keegan didn't notice the exchange as he paced back and forth in front of Midnight, imagining somehow that he had some kind of power here. He made his first mistake the minute he opened his mouth.

"Ms. Chevalier."

"It's Chief Chevalier or Mrs. Debenshire—pick," Midnight cut in, her eyes green points of fire. Score one for the plaintiff. Never try to put Midnight Chevalier in her place by calling her "Ms." anything.

"I'm sorry?" Keegan queried, looking confused.

"I know that," Midnight couldn't help but reply.

A chuckle ran through the Gang. It never failed. Midnight always got the lawyers that thought to get smart with her. It was never wise.

"What?" Keegan said, glancing back at the group seated behind the plaintiff's table, then back at Midnight.

"Never mind," Midnight said, shaking her head. This guy was too slow to fuck with. "It's Chief Chevalier, not Ms. Chevalier," she said succinctly.

"Oh."

"Did you have an actual question?" Midnight asked, her look innocent.

Again Keegan was taken aback. He wasn't used to witnesses that were this quick or this powerful. It had finally dawned on him that he was talking to the woman running for Attorney General for California. She was no idiot. She had a law degree too. It took Keegan a few minutes to get his train of thought back. Midnight pointedly looked at her watch, then at the judge, who was looking rather irritated as well.

"Mr. Keegan," the judge finally said. "Do you have a question for this witness or not?"

"I…" Keegan said, turning to the judge. "Yes. Yes. Chief Chevalier, you said you were a personal friend of Kevin and Erin Elmasian."

"Is that the question?" Midnight asked mildly.

Keegan was getting flabbergasted, and he could hear all those people behind him snickering repeatedly. "No, my question is, are you testifying for them as a favor for friends?"

Midnight stared back at him for a long moment, her face serious. "You think as a Chief of Police I'd perjure myself in a court of law for friends?" she asked, her tone so official that Keegan felt himself instantly chastised.

"Uh, no, Chief. I'm sorry, I didn't mean…" he said, trying to cover himself.

"Yes, you did, but no, I wouldn't."

Keegan nodded, his eyes not meeting Midnight's. "I have no further questions of this witness."

The hearing went on, with every member of the Gang testifying to Kevin and Erin's fitness as parents. The court was told that they trusted Kevin with their lives. The court was also told that Erin had been a good friend to all of them, always taking care of them when they needed it. When Dave took the stand, Jacob Berringer questioned him about the incident with Stacy.

"Do you know of the incident with Stacy Mallory, Sergeant Dibbins?" he asked.

"Yes," Dave said. "Kevin told me about it the day after it happened."

"What did he tell you?"

"That she in fact attacked him when he commented on her parenting skills."

"And how do you know he was telling the truth?"

"Because he had the claw marks on his neck, face, and chest to prove it."

"Is there any evidence of this?"

"Not physical," Dave said. "But I have five other officers in my unit that can testify to the fact, since I dragged them all into the office to see the marks."

"Why didn't you take pictures?"

"Because it would have meant Kevin would have to press charges against Ms. Mallory," Dave said, his sky-blue eyes settling on Stacy with contempt. "And regardless of what Ms. Mallory has claimed, Kevin Elmasian doesn't want her put behind bars."

Jacob nodded, glancing at the judge, who was now looking at Stacy as well.

Keegan had no questions for Dave.

"Your Honor," Jacob said, "I have written statements from the members of Kevin's unit to the effect of the testimony you just heard.

Would you rather I call each witness, or in an effort to save the court some time, would you like to take the statements as evidence?"

"I'll take the statements," the judge said. "But if I have any questions I expect the officers to be available for them."

Rogue Squadron, all sitting together in the front, nodded affirmation.

"I'd like to call Randissi Sinclair to the stand," Jacob said.

Randy walked up to the stand, taking the oath to tell the whole truth and nothing but the truth. She sat down, her eyes finding Joe again. He smiled, giving her a wink. She smiled in return. Both Midnight and Rick turned to Joe, their look speculative.

"Randy, what is your official title?"

"Doctor," Randy said. "I have a PhD in child psychology."

"Did you have occasion to examine Emily Elmasian?"

"Yes, at Kevin Elmasian's request," Randy said, nodding toward Kevin.

"Did Kevin Elmasian tell you anything about the situation?"

"No," Randy said. "In fact, he was specific in stating that he wanted me to talk to his daughter and tell me what I thought. That he didn't want to tell me anything—he wanted me to make my own determination."

"And what did you determine?"

"That Emily Elmasian is a victim of abuse," Randy said. "She exhibits all the signs of both physical and mental abuse."

"Your Honor, we have a report written by Dr. Sinclair on Emily Elmasian," Jacob said, handing it to the judge.

"So entered," the judge said, nodding.

"From what you discovered with Emily, do you feel that there is any abuse by Kevin Elmasian, as Stacy Mallory has indicated?"

"Kevin Elmasian has excellent control on his temper," Randy said. "My conclusions with Emily are that her mother, not her father, is the abuser. Emily has come to understand that her place in her mother's home is out of the way," Randy said, looking over at Stacy, her teal-blue eyes cold.

"She's lying!" Stacy screamed, standing up and clenching her fists.

"Am I?" Randy asked, her eyes on Stacy.

"You fucking bitch!" Stacy shouted, lunging around the table and then at Randy.

Joe was there in a split second, blocking her way. "I don't think so," he said, his light blue eyes staring down into Stacy's.

"Get out of my way!" Stacy screamed, reaching up in an attempt to scratch Joe.

His hands on her wrists stopped her.

"Oh no," he said, laughing. "I wouldn't let my ex-girlfriend scratch me—I'm not letting you either."

There was a lot of movement then. The court officer came and took Stacy away from Joe. Joe turned to Randy, noting her grin.

"What?" he asked.

"Ex?" Midnight asked, standing next to him.

"Something we don't know?" Rick put in.

"Shut up," Joe muttered, moving back to his seat.

"He moved awfully quick to defend Randy…" Rick said to Midnight in an aside.

"He'd protect Randy no matter what," Midnight pointed out.

"True, but he did say 'ex'…"

"Shhh!" Midnight said, grinning.

After the interruption, the court was recessed for the judge's deliberation. Stacy was placed in her seat and told in no uncertain terms to remain there or she'd be arrested for attempted assault of a peace officer. Stacy remained silent. It didn't take too long for the judge to come back with her decision. There was a loud whoop in the hearing room when she awarded custody of Emily to Kevin and Erin.

The Gang reached out, patting Kevin on the back, hugging Erin. As a group they left the courthouse and hung out in the parking lot, celebrating and discussing the case. Christian cranked the stereo in his Viper—P.O.D. was on the CD player. While they all talked, laughed, and argued good-naturedly, the song "Boom" came on. It was one the guys in Rogue Squadron liked.

The three of them started singing the words with gusto. When they realized the chorus fit the situation they sang loud. Christian leaned in and cranked the speakers. As Stacy walked by the group, the words to the chorus were sung just for her—basically calling down the "boom" and asking, "How you like me now?" It was perfect for that moment, and exactly how Kevin felt, prevailing against his ex-girlfriend.

Stacy stared Kevin down. He looked back at her impassively, but his lips curled derisively. She shook her head, eyeing the rest of the group nastily. The rest of the Gang joined in for the next chorus, then broke up laughing when Stacy hurried away.

"Well, this has been fun," Midnight said, glancing at her watch. "But I have a department to run." She reached over, hugging Erin, and surprised Kevin by hugging him too. "Congratulations, you two. It was a well-deserved victory."

"Thanks," Erin said, smiling.

Kevin took Midnight's hand, his look earnest. "Thank you, Chief, for everything you said in there," he said sincerely.

Midnight nodded. "It was the right thing for all of you."

"Still," Kevin said, wanting to repay her somehow. "If there's anything you ever need, I owe you, okay?"

Midnight nodded again, grinning this time. "How about you work on calling me Midnight, huh, Mace?"

Kevin laughed out loud at that, nodding. It was a good day.

***

Joe wasn't sure what to do about Jordan. He hadn't heard from her, but he'd heard about her antics. She'd been getting into trouble at a couple of bars, and had been getting drunk and who knew what else every night.

Randy suggested that he needed to do something; he couldn't leave things hanging with her.

"If you aren't sure about breaking things off with her, Joe, don't," Randy told him the evening of the hearing for Kevin.

Joe blew his breath out, looking out over the ocean. It was already dark. They were sitting out on the deck of the house, talking over a glass of wine.

"I know that I'll never be what she wants, Randy."

Randy nodded, understanding what he was saying.

"Are you sure it's everything she wants?"

"I'm fairly sure she's serious about kids, and that's the one thing I won't do. I have two kids I never see—I won't have more to spread myself even thinner. Besides…" he began.

"Besides what?" she asked, having been staring out at the ocean but turning toward him when she caught his voice trailing off.

Joe looked at her for a long moment, his eyes searching hers. "I think I'd like to give my marriage another shot."

Randy stared back at him for a long moment. It was obvious she was shocked by his statement. She wasn't daring to hope. And she knew she needed to be the voice of reason here.

"I'd like that," she said. "But I think you need to figure out what you're doing about Jordan first, Joe. It tends to be easier to think like this, when you don't have to face her. You never know, she might be willing to do anything for you."

Joe narrowed his eyes slightly, understanding that Randy was playing devil's advocate here.

"Do you want me back, Randy?" he asked directly.

"More than anything," she responded without stopping to think, grimacing when she realized she had. "I mean…"

"No, no," he said, grinning. "Can't take it back now."

She bit her lip, smiling at him. "I don't want to take it back, Joe. But I do feel like you need to handle this thing with Jordan first."

"I know," he said, his look serious. "She's due back in LA tomorrow. I think I'll take a drive up there."

Randy nodded, trying not to look too worried. She knew that Jordan was one woman that could sway Joe's feelings. He did love her—Randy knew that. But, Randy reasoned with herself, if Joe was meant to be with Jordan, then better that they figure that out now, before she and Joe gave their relationship another chance. It would be better in the long run on the children that if Joe wasn't going to come back, they knew that now.

The next day, Joe left for Los Angeles. He drove his Aston. Randy knew it was his way of relieving stress. She also knew that he'd probably do over a hundred all the way. She'd asked him to drive carefully. He'd given her a cavalier wink and said, "Always."

Three hours later, Joe was still waiting to try and see Jordan. He'd called her house in Malibu—no answer. He'd tried BJ's house—no answer there. Finally he'd driven to Badlands Records' offices. Walking up to the receptionist, he smiled. The girl smiled back at the handsome man with the longish dirty-blond hair and light blue eyes. She thought he looked like a rock star, and if he wasn't he should be!

"Can I help you?" she asked hopefully.

"Yeah," Joe said, leaning on the counter. "I'm looking for BJ Sparks. Is he in the office today?"

"Uh…" the receptionist hedged—did the guy really think he could just walk up and ask for a superstar like BJ Sparks?

"Look," Joe said, noting the "this guy's nuts" look on her face. "My name's Joe Sinclair. If he's here can you call him and let him know I'm here?"

"I'll check, sir," she said, thinking Joe's name sounded familiar—maybe he was a rock star after all.

A few minutes later, Joe was lounging in the lobby of the offices, smoking a cigarette.

"Joe?" Tabitha Sparks queried as she walked out into the lobby.

"Tabitha, right?" Joe asked, remembering BJ's daughter.

"Yeah, hi," Tabitha said, smiling. "Dad's in a meeting, but come on back. You can wait in his office."

"Great, thanks," Joe said, stubbing out his cigarette and pushing off the wall he'd been leaning against.

"So, how are you?" Tabitha asked as she walked through Badlands' offices.

"I'm good," Joe said, smiling. "And you? When are you and Devlin going to give BJ some grandbabies?"

"Don't you start!" Tabitha exclaimed, rolling her eyes. "Dad's been hassling me for months already. I just got married, for God's sake!"

Joe chuckled. "Your dad isn't really a patient man."

"Tell me about it," Tabitha said, laughing as she opened the doors to her father's office.

Tabitha Sparks was married to BJ's best friend, the lead guitarist of his band, Sparks. Devlin had known Tabitha since she was a baby. It had been quite a surprise when the two had fallen in love and gotten together. It had caused a lot of trouble during a tour they were on featuring Sparks, Jordan, and two other big-name bands BJ represented on his label. Things had worked themselves out, but it had made for a lot of headlines for a while.

The rock-and-roll world definitely had its share of nice people. Unfortunately, it was still a bit too fast for Joe's blood now.

"Do you want anything while you wait?" Tabitha asked.

"Nah," he said, smiling. "I'm fine. It's good seeing you again, Tabitha," he added, touching her on the arm. "You're as beautiful as ever."

"Such a charmer," she said, smiling and giving him a wink.

"Tha's me…" he said, grinning.

Joe waited twenty minutes, smoking and looking around Brenden's office. He was standing at the window when BJ walked in.

Brenden James Sparks was a self-made rock star/millionaire/record producer. He'd come from nothing, and with an incredible drive, and an even more incredible voice to back it up, he made his mark in the music world. He was Irish, standing six foot three, with long, dark auburn hair and incredible light blue-green eyes. His body was lean but well built. He had women swooning even after over two decades in the business. He was the best.

He was also Jordan's best friend. If anyone knew where she was, it would be BJ.

"Don't jump," Brenden said, grinning.

"Not likely," Joe said, laughing.

"What's goin' on, man?" Brenden asked, walking over to Joe and extending his hand.

Joe grasped it, clasping his other hand over it. "Well, you know it ain't good, right?"

BJ made a face, then nodded. "You still got yer head. That's a good thing, right?"

Joe gave a short laugh, nodding.

"Sit," BJ said, gesturing to the comfortable leather chairs on the far side of his office.

Joe did, and BJ followed suit. Both men lit cigarettes and regarded each other.

"So, what happened?" BJ asked.

Joe took a deep drag on his cigarette and blew the smoke out in a long stream. "I can't keep up with her, man."

Brenden nodded. He understood that. Jordan was a whirlwind, always on the move, always restless when she was in one place too long. She was quite exhausting as a best friend. Jordan and BJ had dated for years, so Brenden knew how much attention Jordan required constantly. She could be quite exhausting.

"So, you're done?" BJ asked, not sounding either surprised or irritated by the idea.

Joe blew his breath out, nodding.

BJ nodded too. "And you're here to tell her, right?"

"I need to try and talk to her," Joe said, taking another long drag.

"That's not always an easy thing to manage with Jordan," BJ pointed out wisely.

"I know," Joe said, nodding. "But there's things that she's never going to get from me, and I know she's going to try to tell me she doesn't want them."

"Like?"

"Like kids," Joe said, his face serious.

BJ pursed his lips, nodding. "That's something she's always wanted in her heart. She just never figured on finding someone she wanted to have them with, ya know?"

Joe rolled his eyes, blowing his breath out. "Well, she's already tried to tell me she didn't want them really."

"She's lying her ass off, man."

Joe nodded. "Thought she might be. Why else would she bring it up?"

"Exactly," Brenden said. "And you don't want any more kids?"

"I've got two I never see now."

"Good point."

"I just don't see this thing going much farther with us, ya know?" Joe said, seeking some kind of substantiation from Brenden. If Brenden could understand it, maybe he could get Jordan to understand it too.

"Well, it isn't like you haven't given it a shot, right?"

Joe said nothing, knowing that it wasn't going to be easy talking to Jordan, no matter what he did.

"Have you seen her?" Joe asked.

Brenden nodded. "She's at my house."

Joe's lips twitched. He knew that if Jordan was hiding out at Brenden's it meant she was really upset. There wasn't going to be an easy fix—he had to talk to her.

"I need to see her, man," he told Brenden.

"I know," BJ said, moving to stand. "You driving then?"

"Yeah," Joe said, nodding as he stood.

A half hour later, Joe walked into Brenden's mansion. Brenden said he'd go hunt Jordan down.

"Make yourself a drink," he added, pointing toward the bar in the study.

"Thanks," Joe said, grinning.

He was standing in the study, taking yet another shot, when Allexxiss, Brenden's movie star wife, walked in.

"Hi," she said hesitantly.

Joe had never formally met Allexxiss Ramsey. She was extremely beautiful, with golden-blond hair and rich blue eyes. He grinned guiltily.

"Hi," he said, his grin still present. "I'm Joe Sinclair. We've never actually met."

Allexxiss nodded in recognition of his name. "Ah, yes," she said, walking over to him and extending her hand. "You're here to see Jordan, I take it?"

"Yeah," Joe said, not looking pleased.

"And I assume Bren is looking for her at this point?" Allexxiss asked, smiling fondly as she said her husband's name.

"Yes, I've got him hunting her down," Joe said, grimacing.

Allexxiss laughed softly. "He has to do that a lot with Jordan," she said, smiling. She canted her head at the shot glass in Joe's hand. "And I'm guessing the conversation you're going to have with her isn't going to be pleasant?"

Joe looked unhappy, and Allexxiss nodded understandingly. She put her hand on Joe's, looking up into his eyes.

"He'd never let her fall too far, Joe," she said softly.

Joe looked back into Allexxiss' eyes for a long moment, then nodded, closing his eyes. It was what he needed to hear at that point. He needed to know that BJ wouldn't let Jordan hurt herself or get heavy into drugs again because of this breakup. He needed to know he wasn't ruining her life by taking his back.

"Thank you," he said, softly but sincerely.

Allexxiss smiled, nodding. The door to the study opened, and Jordan stood there. Allexxiss glanced at her, then back at Joe. She left the room silently, closing the door behind her. Jordan stared at Joe, not moving forward. Her look was wary. She looked beautiful, as she always did, her long dark hair framing her face. Even in jeans and a white T-shirt she looked beautiful.

After a long minute, she walked toward him. He stood on the other side of the bar. Without a word she took the bottle of tequila from his hand, pouring herself a shot and drinking it. She wouldn't look at him. She stared down at the bar.

"You're here to break up, right?" she said, her voice toneless.

Joe winced at the direct way she got right to it. It wasn't how he wanted to start the conversation, but what could he do? Lie? He nodded slowly.

"I think it's better for both of us in the long run," he said softly.

She looked at him then, gold eyes blazing. "Then why bother coming, Joe?" she asked evenly.

He looked back at her for a long moment, his eyes telling her he could tell that she was getting mad already. She lowered her eyes again, mad at herself for letting him affect her this way.

"I came to talk," he said, his tone reasoning. "I don't want to fight with you, Jordan."

She nodded, knowing it was part of the reason he was breaking up with her. They fought too much. He didn't like to fight, not with his girlfriend.

Walking around the bar, he took her hand, pulling her over to the couch and sitting down with her. He held her hand in his, staring down at her face. She wouldn't meet his eyes.

"Jordan," he began. "I love you, okay? I do, but the fact is, I can't keep up with you anymore. And it's becoming more and more obvious to me that we want totally different things in life."

"Like kids," she put in quietly.

"Like kids, yes," he said, nodding. "Jordan, you're right to want kids. You have every right to want them, to have them, and to be with a man that wants that with you. I'm not that man."

She looked at him. "But I can live without that, Joe," she said, her voice a soft plea.

"You shouldn't have to," Joe said. "That's the thing. You should have everything you want in life, not be tied to what you're stuck with because you met a man that's a lot older than you."

"But I love you," she said, her eyes searching his.

"I know you do, Jordan," he said, his eyes reflecting the sadness he was feeling. "But it doesn't mean that I'm the only man you'll ever love. I came along at a time in your life when you needed someone to love you for you. I did that, and you saw how it felt to be wanted for yourself. But the fact is, we're so much alike in a lot of ways, and totally different in others."

"Different how?"

"Well, I like my life stable. I like knowing where I'm going to be from one week to the next. You don't—you love being different places constantly. I thought I could adjust to that, but I can't, babe, I just can't," he said, his tone reflecting his chagrin.

She nodded, taking a deep breath and expelling it slowly. She wanted to beg him not to do this. She wanted to tell him she'd do anything to keep him with her, but she wouldn't do it. Brenden had already drilled her with not giving Joe a guilt trip. He'd told her that Joe was a good man, that he had a right to be happy in this relationship too, and if he wasn't, it wasn't her right to keep him in it at all costs. Basically, BJ had told her not to be selfish. That if she really loved Joe, she'd want him to be happy. It pissed her off no end, but BJ was once again right.

"Jordan," he said, taking her hands in his. "I tried, babe, I really did. I tried living in your world, and being what you needed me to be, but the fact is, I need some stability in my life. And by the very nature of what you do, you're far from a stable influence." He grinned on the last, his light blue eyes twinkling.

Jordan grinned sadly, nodding. He was right about that. She was far from the grounded home body he'd been used to for fifteen years.

She looked at him then, her gold eyes searching his.

"Tell me the truth," she said softly. "Are you getting back together with Randy?"

Joe said nothing for a moment. He knew it would hurt her to hear that he was, but he also knew that he couldn't lie to her now. Finally, he nodded slowly, his look pained.

Jordan nodded too, blinking back tears. She looked away for a few moments, trying to regain her composure. She'd always known that she'd lose Joe to his ex-wife. Randy was and had always been the true love of his life.

She took a slow, deep breath, and blew it out in a deep sigh.

"I guess," she said hesitantly, "it's better that you're going back to what you've always known than leaving me for some slut that caught your eye, right?"

Joe stared down at her for a long moment, not sure what to make of her comment. Then he saw her grin. He reached out and hugged her to him. She leaned against him and cried, allowing herself that moment of weakness with him.

"I'm not going to say I won't miss you," she said, her face still buried against his chest. "But I know that Randy's really been good to the two of us. So if you're back together now, it's for the best."

Joe said nothing, feeling a bit choked with emotion himself. Randy had been right—it was much easier to talk about breaking up with someone like Jordan than it was to do it. He couldn't believe how well she was taking it either. He wondered if he owed Brenden a debt of thanks for that.

After a few minutes, Jordan sat back, reaching up to brush her tears away with the back of her hand.

"Are you going back to the department?"

"Actually, I think I'm still going to go with the idea of the bodyguard work," he said, having discussed the idea with her a number of times.

She nodded. "So maybe if I need you some time, I can get you to guard me?" she asked hopefully.

"Free of charge," he said, winking at her.

She smiled sadly, then grimaced. "I don't think Mackie will guard me again, no matter how much I pay him."

"God, what did you do?" he asked, grinning.

She rolled her eyes. "I was a bitch—what else?"

"He's used to that, honey—remember, he's married to Cassie."

"Oh! I'm telling her you said that!" she said, laughing.

Joe laughed too. "Great, I've already lost my partner."

"Oops," she said, widening her eyes innocently.

He narrowed his eyes at her but said nothing. Then his face grew serious. He reached out, touching her cheek.

"I need to know that you're okay, Jordan," he said sincerely.

She sniffled loudly, grimacing. "Well, okay isn't exactly how I am right now," she said, putting her hand over his. "But I'll be okay eventually."

"Just promise me that if things get bad, you'll call me… okay?"

"I can't promise that," she said, shaking her head.

Joe winced, knowing he was asking too much. "Okay, how about promise me you'll call BJ, if nothing else."

"That I can promise."

Joe nodded, pulling her to him again and hugging her. He felt like shit. He knew he was doing the right thing, but it still hurt to hurt her. It was the right thing—it just wasn't something that could be made perfect right now. He just prayed that in the future, Jordan would find love again and know that he'd been right about this.

Joe got home late that night, crawling into bed with Randy and snuggling up to her back. She woke when his arms went around her. Turning over, she looked up at him.

"Everything okay?" she asked softly.

Joe didn't answer, nuzzling her head.

"Joe?" she queried, reaching up to touch his cheek. She could see even in the dim light of the bedroom that he was unhappy.

When he still didn't answer her, she moved to sit up, reaching over to turn on the bedside lamp. Turning back, she could see that he was wallowing in self-castigation.

"Oh, Joe…" she said, reaching out and taking him into her arms.

He leaned against her, his eyes closed, his face pressed against her neck.

"I feel like such a bastard," he whispered, his voice choked with tears.

"You're not a bastard," Randy said firmly. "You did what you felt was the best thing. It doesn't mean it's not going to hurt, either you or Jordan."

He shook his head, his arms sliding around her waist, taking comfort in her hold on him.

"Joe, don't do this to yourself," she whispered.

Randy leaned back against the headboard, and he rested his head against her stomach. She stroked his hair. She knew there wasn't much she could say at this point to make him feel better. She didn't want to belabor the reasons he'd decided to break it off with Jordan—he knew those reasons even better than she did. It tore at her heart to see him so upset. Randy knew better than anyone how seriously Joe took his relationships. He hated worse than anything to feel like he was letting someone down.

They lay together for a long while, not talking. Randy continued stroking his hair. She glanced down frequently to see how he was doing. When she saw his eyelids growing heavy, she turned off the light. She smoothed his hair until he fell asleep.

Randy woke the next morning to the feel of his hands touching hers. She flexed her fingers, squeezing his hand gently. Joe sat up, his light blue eyes looking into hers. Without a word he leaned in to kiss her softly. Pulling back, he looked into her eyes again.

"I love you," he said softly.

Randy smiled, staring back into his eyes. "I love you too, Joe."

He hugged her to him, then moved to get out of bed.

"Where are you going?"

"I think I'll go to the office and brave my desk," he said, grinning.

She laughed. "Oh, you are feeling confident today."

He rolled his eyes, shaking his head.

Four hours later Rick stuck his head around Joe's door. The music in Joe's office was blasting. A raucous round of Metallica, a new acquisition for Joe since his time with Jordan. The song playing was "Until it Sleeps," with the lyrics that talked about things on the inside being angry and violent. It was a commentary on how Joe felt at that moment.

Rick raised an eyebrow at his choice of music, but said nothing.

"You're back," he said instead, with an ever-present grin.

"Yeah," Joe said, scanning the computer screen in front of him, even as he picked up the remote for his radio and turned it down.

"Having fun yet?" Rick asked, his smile bright as he leaned against Joe's doorjamb.

"I'm working on budgets," Joe replied, his smile wintery. "Apparently, while I was gone everyone decided that their budgets had doubled…"

Rick's smile didn't waver, his blue eyes twinkling with mischief. "So that's a no on the fun question?"

"Fuck you, Debenshire," Joe said, throwing a pen in Rick's direction.

Rick ducked the flying object, laughing. "So you'll be up for a drink around lunch time?"

"And then some."

"Back in an hour."

Joe nodded, going back to work.

Joe worked steadily until Rick wandered back to his office. Rick noted that Metallica still blared. It didn't bode well for Joe's mood.

"Do you realize that FORS is about $12,000 over budget?" Joe asked as they knocked back shots at the back of The Pit, where they wouldn't be seen.

"No fuckin' way," Rick said, shaking his head.

"Way, man. You been letting Manny handle the shit while you're gone?" Joe asked, raising an eyebrow.

Rick's deep blue eyes narrowed. "I'll fuckin' kill him myself…"

It was Joe's turn to laugh. "Not so bloody funny now, is it?"

"You've developed a mean streak, Sinclair," Rick said, pouring himself another shot.

"Hey, it's your wife that's gonna be down my throat when we're out of cash two months before the end of fiscal."

"True enough," Rick said, brightening. "But she loves me."

"Not that much," Joe said, grinning.

"Guess we should manage some food while we're here," Rick said, knocking back another shot.

"Why?" Joe queried, pouring himself another too.

In the end, they had Tom send burgers back to them, and ate while talking about Kana's recovery. Kana was doing much better and was expected to get out of the hospital the following day. Everyone was jubilant.

That evening, Randy made dinner while the kids happily told their father all about their day. Randy couldn't help but smile at how happy the kids were that Joe was home. She only hoped they could work things out between them so he wouldn't leave again. She felt like they could, but knew that it might take some work.

When they sat down to dinner, Joe told Randy about the out-of-control budget situation. Randy told him funny stories about some of the kids at the center. The kids put their two cents' worth in every so often. It was a nice dinner. Afterward, Randy ordered the kids to their rooms to do their homework. There was the usual moaning and groaning, but they went. Joe picked up the bottle of wine they'd started and gestured to Randy to accompany him into the living room.

They sat on the couch, drinking wine and talking. When the kids finished their homework, it was bath time. Afterward the four of them watched a half hour of TV. Randy was going to read them a story before bed, so Joe said he'd take a shower. He kissed each of the kids goodnight, assuring them once again that yes, he'd be there tomorrow morning too.

He wondered mildly as he got into the shower how long it would take his own kids to stop wondering when their father was leaving again. It bothered him no end. It was one of the reasons he'd wanted to be home again. His kids needed him, and frankly, he needed them too. He needed to feel grounded again. Randy and the kids were home for him.

When he finished his shower, he towel-dried his hair and then put on black sweats and a steel-gray shirt he didn't bother to button. He was sitting on the bed, reading over a report, the radio on in the background, when Randy walked in a few minutes later. She stood in the doorway, looking at him. There was no denying the sexual pull she felt for him now. His hair just brushed his shoulders and fell forward as he bent his head to read. His tanned chest and strong, tanned arms... his long, strong frame... sitting so casually on the bed. Even his bare feet were sexy to her at this point. It was such a visual feast she couldn't help but stare.

He glanced up, sensing her presence in the doorway. He stared back at her in amusement.

"You buying, or just shopping?" he asked with a grin.

Randy laughed softly, walking forward to take the report out of his hands and set it aside. His light blue eyes watched her, his grin still in place. Getting on the bed, Randy slid her hands up his chest, pushing the shirt off his shoulders. Leaning forward, she kissed the scar on his right shoulder where he'd been shot many years before. She moved her lips down his chest, hearing his breath quicken. His hands were in her hair, guiding her head as she continued to kiss his skin.

After a while he couldn't take anymore, pulling her up to him and kissing her lips fervently, his hands moving to remove her clothing. There was an urgency in him now that excited her every time he touched her. Once again he took her to extreme heights, making her bite her lip to keep from screaming out loud in her release. She could only imagine what their children would think if they heard that. The house was big, but not big enough to keep them from hearing enough.

They lay together, panting to catch their breath. Metallica, Joe's latest new choice, was on the stereo at that point, and a new song had just started. Joe lay on his back, caressing Randy's shoulder as she lay half over him. The song playing was "Nothing Else Matters"—it was actually a ballad with a beautiful guitar intro.

By the end of the song, Randy had tears in her eyes. She knew it was his way of telling her that he thought they'd make it now. That they had their own way of doing things. No matter what people thought, no matter what had happened. Nothing else mattered but that they loved and trusted each other enough to try again.

Without a word, she lowered her head to his, kissing his lips softly. His arms encircled her, his hand gentle on the back of her head, holding her to him as he deepened the kiss. It wasn't passion this time, but a sense of love and understanding that passed between them. Randy fell asleep that night feeling as if she could conquer the entire world. Joe fell asleep feeling much the same way. It was a good feeling. He knew he'd made the right choice for him and his family.

CHAPTER 8

"So, are you coming back or not?" Midnight asked Joe as she looked up at him from across her desk.

"Temporarily."

"What the hell does that mean?" she asked, grinning at her long-time partner and friend.

"That means I'm going to take retirement here soon and start my own business."

"Ohhh…" Midnight said. "You're going entrepreneur on me?"

"Sort of," Joe said, leaning back comfortably and placing a booted foot up on the other side of Midnight's desk.

It was a testament to the casual relationship they had. She was the Chief of Police; he was only a captain by department standards. But he had been with Midnight the longest, and was her best friend in the whole world.

"Explain 'sort of' to me," Midnight said, leaning back and steepling her fingers, her cat-like green eyes narrowing.

"Well, believe it or not, I'm going to start a personal protection business," he said, grinning.

Midnight looked back at him for a long moment, confusion clear on her face.

"Wait, are you or are you not broken up with Jordan?"

Joe grimaced. "I am."

"But you don't expect to be for long?"

"No, it's permanent," Joe said, still looking uncomfortable about the topic. "Randy and I are reconciling."

"Well…" Midnight said, both surprised and pleased. "How did that happen?"

Joe dropped his head against the back of his chair, his light blue eyes on his best friend. "I guess you've kinda been out of the loop on this one, huh?"

"Kinda," Midnight agreed.

"All that AG shit and all…" Joe put in, his look wry.

"Yeah, yeah," Midnight said, waving her hand in dismissal. "So give me the low down."

Joe proceeded to tell Midnight about everything. It was a rare moment when Midnight wasn't busy, so she had time to catch up with him. She was glad she could; she never liked being too far out of touch with people she considered her family. She'd been out of touch with Joe far more than she'd liked for over a year now.

When he finished, Midnight nodded understandingly.

"So, then why are you going ahead with the business?" Midnight asked. "If you were originally starting it so it would free you up to be with Jordan more…"

"Well, no, I was doing it to achieve something else, actually," Joe said, his look pensive.

"And what was that?"

"Uh…" Joe said, grinning. "Getting away from the boredom level I was achieving here."

"Oh, nice," Midnight said, laughing. She did understand him though. "Our jobs have always been about action, haven't they?"

"Yeah," Joe said. "I tend to think it was part of my problem. Feeling like I wasn't making any kind of difference anymore, ya know? I mean, unless you count the deforestation of Earth that I was achieving on a monthly basis with all my bloody paperwork."

Midnight laughed.

"At least you were doing the chief thing," Joe said. "You were making changes here. I just felt like I was standing still, ya know?"

Midnight nodded. "But bodyguard work?" she asked skeptically. "That doesn't really seem like it's going to be your kind of thing. I thought you couldn't stand ego-hyped stars..."

"Well, that's the thing," Joe said. "I'm starting the business with another guy, John Machiavelli—he's been doing this for a few years. He'll handle the star part, and I'm going to concentrate on private-citizen protection."

"How will that go?" Midnight asked, canting her head to the side.

"Well, I'm going on the domestic violence angle—the regular people out there that need protection from attackers that aren't after stars, ya know?"

Midnight narrowed her eyes in thought, then nodded. "But how will these people afford to pay a bodyguard? You're talking housewives, secretaries, not rock stars..."

"And when have I ever been about the money?"

"True," Midnight said. "So you'll be reasonable for people like that?"

"Obviously. It'll depend on what they can afford to pay. Hell, if I think it merits it, I'll do it for free."

Midnight shook her head. "Only you, Joe," she said, grinning, "would start a business with the thought in mind of giving free service."

Joe laughed. "I figure the star end of it will more than cover any pro-bono stuff I do, so it'll be cool."

"And your partner in this business doesn't mind that part?"

"Mackie left NYPD because he got tired of not making any real difference, with the justice system in the state it's in. So yeah, he'll be okay with it."

"NYPD?"

"Yeah. He used to work for Kyle. Remember that call you got way back from BJ asking about someone to help one of his artists?"

"Yeah," Midnight said, nodding.

"Well, Mackie's who Kyle recommended to BJ. In fact, Mackie ended up marrying the girl he was hired to protect," Joe said with a grin.

"Well, well…" Midnight murmured, a twinkle in her eye. "So when you planning on retiring?"

"I'm thinking at the end of the month," Joe said, knowing he was going to stress her out with this news.

"Wow, I'm getting two weeks' notice, huh?" Midnight asked, grinning.

Joe winked. "More than you were getting before that, love."

"True." She looked at him for a long moment, her eyes sad, dejected. "Won't be the same around here, knowing you're not coming back…"

"Night, you probably won't be here after the first of the year, either," Joe pointed out.

She rolled her eyes, knowing he was referring to the election which was just over a month away now.

***

Cat was overdoing it. Everyone could see it, but no one could get her to slow down. She was in the office before everyone in the morning, and stayed late on the nights when they didn't have a raid. Christian also got it from a reliable source that Cat was out most nights too. It was becoming a chief concern for everyone in the unit. They were worried that Cat would either burn herself out or make a mistake during a raid and one of the team would get hurt. They'd just gotten Kana back on her feet; they were damned if they'd take a chance at losing another member of their family.

Stevie was the one to finally break the silence one day, right before a raid. She asked Cat directly if she felt she was overdoing it a bit.

"Why do you ask?" Cat replied defensively, her blue eyes closed off.

Stevie looked back at her, her emerald-green eyes narrowing. "Because it might be my husband that gets shot when you can't hack it, that's why," she said, her voice tight with reined-in anger.

Cat's chin came up an inch as she caught the implication. She stared back at Stevie for a long moment, then nodded. Turning, she walked away, pulling the slide back on her gun. That day it was Cat that took the punishment when she blocked a punch that was meant for Donovan. The force of the block threw her back into a wall. Donovan turned in time to grab the guy before he had a chance to do any further damage. Kevin moved to help Cat up off the floor. Cat stood up, nodding to Kevin for the assistance even as she shrugged off his hands. She then continued working the scene.

As they were readying to leave, Cat caught Stevie's eye.

"Happy? No one got shot," Cat said icily. "Least of all your man."

With that Cat turned and walked out of the house and to her vehicle. Starting it with a roar, she drove off, reaching for a cigarette as she did.

Stevie stared at Cat's retreating car in shock.

"Nice teamwork," Christian muttered to his wife.

"Shut up," Stevie said, giving him a narrowed look.

She knew she'd said what everyone was thinking. She also knew Christian was kidding, but Cat's barb had struck home.

Cat's aggressive display to prove she wasn't overdoing it continued, garnering her a number of bruises and cuts and a sprained wrist. Everyone on the team was at the end of a barbed comment or two when they made the mistake of telling her to slow down, or to be careful. She wasn't acting like herself at all, and it bothered everyone.

It bothered Cat too. She knew she was being a bitch, but she couldn't seem to help it. It was the only defense she had at this point to keep from breaking down. Elizabeth hadn't returned to Cat's apartment; she hadn't in fact called or talked to Cat at all since the night Cat had pushed her away. It bothered Cat much more than she wanted to admit even to herself. She pushed herself harder, wanting nothing more than to fall into bed in the early hours of the morning and sleep like the dead until she dragged herself up to do it all again.

Kana heard about Cat's actions the weekend the Gang got together to celebrate her release from the hospital. She'd been out a week and a half by that time. During the course of the party, which Cat didn't attend, Kana heard comments about her pushing her limits beyond belief.

"What's going on?" Kana asked when she caught Dave, Donovan, and Christian talking about Cat again.

Dave glanced at Christian and Donovan. They both nodded to him, agreeing that they should tell Kana. Cat had, after all, been with her—maybe she could talk some sense into the girl.

"Cat's been way overdoing it lately," Dave said, shaking his head.

"Overdoing it how?" Kana asked, her look darkening.

"She's in the office before the sun is even up."

"And she never leaves till long after the rest of us have packed it in," Donovan added.

"And I've heard when she's not working, she's out closing down the bar," Christian finished.

Kana's lips tightened in a grimace. Cat was indeed overdoing it. Kana knew she'd been totally remiss in not talking to her about everything that had happened. Palani had confided in her that it had been Cat who had prompted her return to the hospital after Kana's fever. She'd told Kana the whole story. Kana had known that she needed to talk to Cat about what had happened, she just hadn't worked up the right words yet.

"Do you think you could talk to her, K?" Dave asked, his concern for Cat obvious.

Kana looked pensive. "I think I'm about the last person she's gonna listen to at this point," she said, sounding chagrined at the thought.

Glancing around, Kana caught sight of Susan talking to Midnight.

"Susan," she called.

Susan turned her head and walked over to join them. "Yes?" she queried, her English accent still as sophisticated as ever.

"Where's your sister these days?" Kana asked without preamble.

Susan looked surprised by the question. "Elizabeth?"

Kana nodded.

"She's in England," Susan said, sounding as perplexed by the question as she looked.

"How long has she been there?"

Susan thought for a moment. "About two weeks, I'd say."

Kana nodded. "When's she coming back?"

"I'm not sure, really…" Susan replied, a question in her tone.

Again Kana nodded. "Next time you talk to her, and make it soon, have her call me."

"Alright…" Susan said, still looking confused. She noticed, however, that Dave had started to nod.

Kana looked at him. "If she steps it up, let me know," she said, glancing down at Palani, who'd come over to stand next to her. "I'll intercede if it comes to that," she told Dave. He nodded, as did Christian and Donovan.

Elizabeth called Kana the following day. She'd been out the whole night before, and had received a message from her sister upon returning to her London flat that morning at eight. Susan's message was simple.

"Kana wants you to contact her, Elizabeth," Susan had said, her sophisticated voice making her sound more uptight. "Do it, it's quite important."

Elizabeth had rolled her eyes at her sister's tone, but had called Kana all the same, having to contact Midnight to get the number.

"Kana," Elizabeth said. "It's Elizabeth Endicott. My sister said you wanted me to call you."

"Do you care about Cat?" Kana asked without preamble.

Elizabeth was surprised by the question. "Yes, I care about her. Why? Has something happened?" she added worriedly.

"Not yet," Kana said. "But if you don't get your ass back here soon, something could."

"What's going on, Kana?" Elizabeth asked, not liking the tone of this conversation at all.

"She's working herself into the ground. And getting herself pretty beat up in the process. She's burying herself, and I think you might know how to help her."

"Is it possible it's because of you?" Elizabeth couldn't help but snap.

"It's possible," Kana agreed evenly. "But I don't think she'll listen to me. I think she will listen to you."

"Why do you think that?"

"You know why I think that."

Elizabeth was silent, knowing she couldn't answer that. Finally she sighed. She couldn't risk something happening to Cat if there was any chance she could help.

"I'll get back there as soon as I can."

"Good," Kana said, nodding. "And Elizabeth?"

"Yes?" Elizabeth queried, her mind already racing as to the fastest way to get back to San Diego.

"Thank you," Kana said somberly.

Elizabeth was surprised to hear the big woman expressing gratitude. She was fairly sure Kana had always written her off as a twit, like many of her aunt's friends had. Having Kana thank her now was surprising.

"Don't thank me yet," she said. "I have no idea what I'm going to say to Cat."

"You'll think of something," Kana said, grinning.

Elizabeth sighed. "I'll have to, won't I?"

Cat was asleep when she heard her name called softly. She stirred, and looked up at Elizabeth, not realizing how terrible she looked at that moment. "Good Lord…" Elizabeth said, reaching up to touch the bruise on Cat's cheek.

"I didn't think you were even talking to me anymore," Cat said simply.

Elizabeth made a face, shaking her head. "Nonsense," she said, her English accent making her sound very proper. "I value our friendship much more than that, Catalina."

Cat said nothing, only looking back at Elizabeth for a long minute.

"I thought you were in England," she said eventually.

"I was, this morning," Elizabeth said. "I just got back, and came here."

"Why?" Cat asked, her eyes narrowing. She suspected she knew why.

"Because I needed to know something," Elizabeth said, her tone changing slightly.

"What did you need to know?" Cat asked, surprised by the statement but curious all the same.

Cat was stunned when Elizabeth leaned in and kissed her. She tensed at first, unsure what was happening, but when Elizabeth touched her shoulder, Cat couldn't help but deepen the kiss.

Before long they were making love, and Cat forgot to worry about the fact that Elizabeth wasn't gay. She simply enjoyed the closeness with the other woman.

Afterward, they lay together. Cat had her lips pressed to Elizabeth's neck—the woman smelled damned good.

"Is that what you needed to know?" Cat asked softly.

"Yes," Elizabeth said, still breathless.

"Even this doesn't make you gay, you know," Cat said, grinning.

"What doesn't?" Elizabeth asked, furrowing her eyebrows.

"Enjoying sex with a woman." Cat knew that Elizabeth was trying to prove something, but she wasn't sure if it was to her or to herself.

Elizabeth was quiet for a long moment. "Well, perhaps that doesn't make me gay," she said amiably, "but I'm fairly sure being in love with you does."

Cat didn't move for a few moments, Elizabeth's words sinking in slowly. She lifted her head when they did, however, shocked.

"You what?" Cat asked disbelievingly.

"Love you," Elizabeth replied confidently.

Cat's mouth dropped open as she stared down at Elizabeth. She closed it and started to shake her head.

"Don't you dare," Elizabeth said, narrowing her eyes at Cat. "Don't you dare try and tell me I don't know how I feel about you. I know exactly how I feel about you. My heart has loved you for the longest time. My soul belongs to you. I just needed to know if my body could too. And it does."

Cat blinked a few times, trying to assimilate what she was hearing. She'd purposely avoided her deeper feelings for Elizabeth all this time, because the girl was as straight as straight got. Regardless of Cat's theory about every woman being capable of being bisexual, she'd never thought Elizabeth was the type.

"Say something," Elizabeth begged, her eyes showing worry now.

Cat stared down at her for a long moment, then a slow smile spread over her face. She laughed softly, shaking her head again. "You definitely know how to shock the hell out of someone."

Elizabeth laughed too. "I've become quite accomplished at that over the years," she said, then reached up to touch Cat's cheek. "But I'm not trying to shock you. I'm telling you the truth."

"That's what's so shocking, babe," Cat said. Leaning down, she kissed Elizabeth's lips. Pulling back, she looked into her eyes. "And I love you."

It was Elizabeth's turn to be shocked, her eyes widened dramatically. "You do?"

"Thought you were alone, honey?"

Elizabeth said nothing for a moment. "I—Well, I didn't..." she stammered. "I thought you were still in love with Kana..."

"I was never in love with Kana," Cat said. "I love her, and it hurt a lot feeling like second best. But you were someone I was never going to have, so I never even considered it." She lowered her head, kissing Elizabeth's shoulder. "But I fell in love with the little girl that had to scream to be heard."

"And I fell in love with the first person who ever listened to me when I whispered," Elizabeth said as tears clouded her eyes.

***

Christian, Stevie, and Kevin stared openmouthed at Dave. Impossible!

"No fuckin' way..." Christian said, trailing off ominously.

"You've got to be kidding."

"You're kidding, right?" Kevin echoed.

"I wish I was," Dave said, sounding defeated.

Sergei had been let off on a technicality. He'd all but raped Stevie, and they had him on various drug charges, but he'd slipped through anyway.

"Well, I need a drink," Christian said, his lips twisting in a disgusted grimace.

"I'll join you," Stevie said.

"Just be careful," Dave cautioned. "He's out there now."

"Oh, let him come near me..." Christian said.

"Just make sure he comes to you," Dave said, his blue eyes serious.

Christian nodded, grabbing his wife's hand and leading her out of Dave's office. Kevin stood up, looking fairly displeased as well. He left Dave's office without a word and went out to his vehicle. He got into the Durango, starting it with a roar. He drove off, cranking his stereo and smoking. Dave sat in his office, shaking his head. He hated this aspect of the job, but it was part of it. Unfortunately, the justice system protected the criminal far more than it protected the public. He called Cat in to see him, his eyes trailing Christian and Stevie through the office as they prepared to leave.

"Yeah?" Cat asked, back to her normal amiable self.

"Need you to follow Blue and Stevie. I want to make sure they're okay."

"What happened?"

"Sergei got off."

"Shit…" Cat said, her eyes going to the couple as they left. "I'm on it," she assured Dave, striding to her desk and picking up her keys.

She caught up to Christian and Stevie in the parking lot.

"So where are we drinking?" Cat asked, as if she'd been included all along.

Christian narrowed his eyes as he glanced toward the office. He knew without a doubt that Dave had sicked Cat on them. He turned back to Cat, who stared at him unwaveringly.

"Don't think you're going to want to be involved in this one, Cat," Christian said, glancing at Stevie, who nodded in agreement.

"It's not going to be official," Stevie said. She'd known without even talking about it with Christian that he wanted revenge on Sergei. She'd been hoping to avoid this confrontation, but it was obvious there was no way to do that.

Cat raised an eyebrow, her grin wry. "How about you let me decide that, huh?"

Christian glanced at Stevie. She looked back at him, shrugging.

"We could use your help…" Christian said, trailing off hesitantly.

"Name it," Cat replied without hesitation.

"We know where Sergei hangs out, but he already knows Stevie. We need to get him out of the bar."

"You got it," Cat said, again without hesitation.

Twenty minutes later they pulled up to the hole-in-the-wall bar Sergei hung out in. It was a place that catered to Russians. Cat got out, nodding to Stevie and Christian as she passed the Viper and walked into the bar.

"You stay in here," Christian told Stevie.

"Like hell," Stevie replied, moving to get out as Christian did the same.

"Steve…"

"Bullshit!" she said sharply. "If you're going to do this, so am I."

He narrowed his light blue eyes at her, but could easily see that she was quite determined. He knew his wife well enough to know that arguing with her now was pointless. If he'd wanted her to stay out of it, he'd needed to leave her at the department.

"Just be careful, please?" he asked gently.

"You too," she said, her voice softening.

Five minutes later, Cat came outside, walking directly toward the Viper. Christian stood leaning against the car, and Stevie sat casually on the hood. A minute later, Sergei and three of his guys walked out. By that time Cat was sitting on the hood of the car, just in front of Stevie. Stevie's arm was draped casually over Cat's shoulder.

Sergei's eyes found Cat, and widened when he saw Stevie. His stare then skipped to Christian, who straightened from the Viper. There was no mistaking the dangerous look to Christian. He didn't look like a cop—he looked dangerous. *More dangerous than the guy Stevie had been with before...* Sergei thought.

"New boyfriend?" he asked, his tone confident, as he looked at Stevie.

"Old husband," Stevie replied, her green eyes cool.

"Husband, eh?" Sergei said, his eyes measuring Christian again.

"You attempted to take something that belonged to me, Sergei," Christian said, his tone informational. "That was a mistake."

Sergei shrugged, unconcerned. "The charges were dropped—you can't touch me."

"Wanna bet?" Christian said, taking a step forward, his look challenging.

Sergei's head came up as he sensed that this was not an official visit by San Diego PD. He looked at Stevie, sneering. "I'll get you fired."

"For what?" Stevie asked, grinning. "Sitting on my husband's car?"

Sergei looked at Christian, trying to gauge the man. Was he serious? Or was he just bluffing? But why come here to bluff? Sergei glanced back at his men, nodding to them. They pulled out their weapons, to show Christian that he wouldn't get far.

That's when Stevie and Cat went into motion. Moving off the car with surprising agility, they both drew their weapons and showed their badges.

"No guns, boys," Cat said, smiling. "This is street time."

"You?" Sergei asked Cat, surprised. Was there no end to the beautiful women on the payroll at San Diego PD?

"Me, honey," Cat said, grinning maliciously.

"Put the guns down, now!" Stevie commanded the men, who were hesitating.

"Do it, or you'll be oh so sorry you didn't," Cat said, smiling.

When the guns were down, Cat and Stevie took up positions on opposite sides of the group. Stevie was damned if her husband was going to get shot by one of these assholes. She already knew they were all risking their careers, but she was willing to lose that—but not Christian.

Christian gestured for Sergei to bring it on. Sergei hesitated, but then resigned himself to the fight. He went for a punch, thrown high and wide. Christian merely moved back at the last second, bringing his fist back through, hitting Sergei in the face. Sergei staggered back, but shook off the punch. Christian waited. Sergei faked another punch at Christian's face, an upper cut, but then slammed his other fist into Christian's mid-section at the last moment. Christian coughed but didn't allow himself to double over, knowing that the Russian would only knee him in the face if he did. He doubled just slightly, and at the same time, launched himself at Sergei, catching him in the mid-section and knocking him to the ground.

The punches were flying then. Stevie watched the fight worriedly, while Cat kept her full attention on Sergei's men. Eventually it was Christian who staggered to his feet. Sergei lay bleeding on the ground. Christian turned to look down at him.

"Never lay your hands on someone else's property," Christian said, his light blue eyes narrowed. "Especially not mine." With that he walked toward Stevie. She reached up, dabbing at the blood at his lip. He grinned at her, giving her a wink. She just shook her head.

Cat made her way to the couple, keeping her eyes on the other men, who were now helping up their leader.

"Time to go, kids," she said with a grin.

Christian glanced back at Sergei, noting the dangerous look to the men with him. "Indeed," he said, and gestured to their cars.

They got in and drove away without hesitation. Cat followed them to a bar in Pacific Beach where Christian knew the bartender. The three of them spent the better part of an hour drinking. Cat left Stevie and Christian there and made her way back to her apartment.

Still at the bar in Pacific Beach, Stevie and Christian had drunk just enough to get into a serious discussion about what they'd just done.

"What if he reports it?" Stevie asked.

"What's he gonna report?" Christian asked. "He doesn't even know I'm a cop too."

"Won't take much to find out, babe," she said, shaking her head.

"Okay," Christian acceded. "So what?"

"So what if we get put on report?"

"What's the worst that can happen on that?" Christian asked mildly.

"We could get fired, Christian."

Christian contemplated that, then shrugged. "So? We go into a new line of work," he said, sounding drunk.

"And what will we do?" Stevie asked, grinning. She knew her husband was plowed, but was glad that he wasn't worried about any of this too. If he wasn't, she wouldn't be.

"Dunno," he said, leaning back, his elbows on the bar behind him, his long legs extended before him casually. "Maybe we could become bums…"

"Right," Stevie said. "Or alcoholics—we're headed there already…"

"Nah," Christian said, even as he held his shot glass up to Tara, the bartender.

Tara chuckled, shaking her head. Christian didn't bother to put the glass down on the bar; he simply held it over his head so Tara had to climb on the bar to pour the shot.

"Pain," Tara said.

"And?" Christian said, dropping his head back onto the bar and looking at his long-time friend.

Tara leaned over, kissing him on the forehead. "And I love ya anyway," she said, laughing and winking at Stevie.

Christian had known Tara for years, even before he and Susan had ever gotten together. They'd had a sexual relationship for a while, but he'd found that he enjoyed her friendship too. She wasn't clingy, nor did she ever expect anything from him. She was there when he needed a warm body to sleep next to, or someone to pour him drink after drink and not judge him. Stevie knew about Tara and genuinely liked the woman too.

"You know," Christian said after drinking the shot Tara had just poured him, "we could get into bodyguard work with Joe."

"Bodyguard work?" Stevie asked, her look cynical.

"You did it for Tiempo," Christian pointed out.

"Tiempo was a slime. And I had a purpose, remember?"

"Yeah, I know," Christian said. She'd become the drug dealer's bodyguard to try and kill him. "And half the people we'd probably work for as bodyguards would be slimes—what's the diff?"

Stevie rolled her eyes, shaking her head. "I think we need to go."

"Now?"

"At least."

"But…" Christian hedged, looking at his glass forlornly.

"Christian Joseph Collins…"

"Gad, you sound like my mother," he said, making a face.

"Your mother doesn't kiss like this," Stevie said, straddling his lap as he sat on the barstool, wrapping her arms around his neck and kissing him deeply. He dropped the shot glass and wound his arms around her, kissing her back. Many heads in the bar turned; there were some cat calls and a few comments. Tara looked on with a grin.

Tara had seen Christian through a few women, and she knew that Stevie was hands down the best woman for him. She kept him on his toes constantly, and it was exactly what he needed.

She saw the two of them into a cab, assuring Christian—"London," as she called him—that she'd have his Viper at her apartment in her garage space when he was sober. He kissed her on the cheek before climbing into the car with his wife. Tara stared after the cab, smiling to herself.

CHAPTER 9

Two days before the election, Midnight was on edge. Rick sensed it easily, as did Mikeyla and Ricardo. The three of them made a point of being very quiet and as little trouble as humanly possible to her. Of course, Midnight figured it out quickly.

"Okay, knock it the hell off, all three of you," she said, glaring at them in turn, even the giggling Ricardo. "Go back to your complicated, difficult, needy selves, or else!"

"Whew!" Rick said, grinning as he walked over to her, taking her in his arms and kissing her softly on the lips. "I was tired of playing the self-sufficient husband."

"Oh yeah, I'm sure," Midnight said, grinning up at him.

"Mama?" Ricardo said, walking over to Midnight.

"What, Ricky?" she asked, kneeling in front of him.

"What will you be the general of?" he asked, his eyes bright.

"The general of?"

"The Army? The Navy?" Ricardo asked hopefully.

"Ohhh…" Midnight said, catching on, and laughed. "No, honey. If I'm elected, I'll be Attorney General," she said, trying to think of a way to put it so Ricardo would understand. "Okay, you know how Grandpa Debenshire is a lawyer?"

Ricardo stared back at her, still looking confused.

Midnight glanced up at Rick. He shrugged, not sure how to explain it either.

"Okay," Midnight said, moving to sit on the chair behind her and pulling Ricardo onto her lap. "When someone is in trouble, they need what's called a lawyer to defend them."

"From what?" Ricardo asked.

"From being put in jail," Midnight said. "Or sometimes there is a lawyer that fights for what is called the people's rights."

"The people's rights?"

"When someone does something bad, there is a lawyer to defend them. There is also a lawyer to speak on behalf of the people, meaning all the people in California, or wherever."

"Why can't people defend themselves?"

"Well…" Midnight said, glancing at Rick and seeing the grin on his lips. Ricardo was a very quick learner, and Midnight was constantly having to keep up with trying to explain things to him. Given too much leeway, Ricardo could talk her in circles. "People actually have the right to defend themselves in a court of law, but usually lawyers know more about laws and precedents than normal citizens do."

"Precedents?" Ricardo repeated with some difficulty.

"Yes," Midnight said, smiling and marveling at her son's quick mind. "Precedents are certain established cases that kind of set a standard for laws."

"So they say what the law is?"

"No, but they set a guideline for laws—but guidelines can and should be challenged if they need to be," Midnight said, unsure why she was having this conversation but enjoying it all the same.

Ricardo looked like he was digesting what she was saying. Midnight waited, interested in what he'd come up with.

"So who are you a lawyer for then?" he asked after a few minutes.

"If I make Attorney General, I'm a lawyer for the people of the state of California."

"That's a lot of people!" Ricardo said. "How will they all fit in the court?"

Midnight laughed outright at that. "They don't have to—that's why I represent them."

"Oh," Ricardo said, looking impressed. "Will we be rich?"

"Uh…" Midnight stammered, not sure where that had come from. "Why do you ask that?"

"Don't lawyers make a lot of money?"

"Not civil servants," Rick put in with a grin.

"Civil servants?" Ricardo asked, turning to him.

"Ohhh, you went there, Richard—you handle this one. I'm going to change," Midnight said, moving to get up.

"Midnight!" Rick called after her. Ricardo stared up at him, wide-eyed with curiosity.

Rick looked at Mikeyla. She held her hands up, grinning and shaking her head. "Don't look at me, Dad. I don't do well in government."

"You better start," Rick said, narrowing his eyes at his daughter's grin.

"She's going to win, isn't she?" Mikeyla asked, not sounding like she minded the idea at all.

"If you could vote, would you vote for her?"

"Yep."

"Why?" Rick asked, curious as to what she'd say.

"Because she's smart, strong, and willing to listen to people."

Rick nodded, liking her answer. "I think a lot of people are going to agree with you, and yes, I'm fairly sure she's going to win."

Mikeyla nodded. "Do you want her to?"

"I want her to have what makes her happy."

"Will this?" Mikeyla asked, not sure.

"I think at first it will be difficult for her," Rick said, sitting in the chair Midnight had vacated. Ricardo climbed up on his lap. "Your mother is used to knowing everything there is to know about her job. This will be an all new arena for her. It's law enforcement, but it's also law, and that's not something she's as comfortable with."

Mikeyla nodded. "You're saying she'll need our support."

"Definitely," Rick said. "She'll also need our patience, because she's bound to be stressed out."

Mikeyla pressed her lips together. "So you're saying now's not the time to move out?"

Rick narrowed his eyes at her. "You aren't moving anywhere, young lady, at least until you turn twenty-one, and even then…"

"Daddy!" Mikeyla exclaimed, before she saw the grin playing at his lips.

Laughing, she walked over and hugged him, then kissed Ricardo on the cheek.

"Ricky, a civil servant is someone that works for the government, or a branch of the government. She works for the people, because the government is for the people, by the people," Mikeyla said, winking at her father.

Rick grinned. "Not doing well in government, huh?"

"Eh, just a B-plus," she said with a shrug.

"God forbid…"

Mikeyla was definitely Midnight's daughter—an over-achiever, smart, beautiful, and brilliant.

Midnight Chevalier-Debenshire was elected the first female Attorney General for California in history. She won by a landslide of 72% of the overall vote. She was, to say the least, stunned. She'd never been convinced she'd win. Her acceptance speech reflected that shock.

Her smile could have lit up a room as she stood for the press conference, surrounded by her friends and family. Rick stood by, wearing a dark suit, looking extremely dashing but still the wild-child man she'd married, with his long hair. Mikeyla was in a dark blue dress, and Ricardo wore a dark suit, looking so handsome Midnight hugged him repeatedly. The members of the Gang were present, although the undercover group kept a lower profile while the press was present.

"I..." Midnight stammered as the cameras rolled and clicked away. "I have no idea what to say," she said, grinning engagingly. "This is something rather unexpected, but I also think it's a statement of the citizens of California. They're saying they want to see some changes. I'm more than willing and able to make those changes. I'd like to think that everyone will like what I do, but one thing I've learned as the Chief of Police is that you never can please everyone. I'll do my best to make changes that will affect the lives of the everyday, normal people. I want to make this state strong where it counts, understanding where it needs to be, and safe for people who know right from wrong and conduct themselves accordingly." She stared right into the cameras then, her look pointed. "So, if you're a bad guy that doesn't get that, it's my advice to you that you move, *soon.*" With that she gave the reporters a cavalier wink. Many of them grinned, and a few chuckled; they were for the most part spellbound by the new Attorney General.

The reception for Midnight's victory party was held at Elizabeth's new restaurant, Catalina's, so named for the woman that had come to mean so much to her, and who'd inspired her to do something different with her life. It was the night before it opened officially to the public. Everyone was quite impressed with the combination of elegant and hip style. As usual, Elizabeth's taste was exquisite, but her sense of style was evident everywhere. The food, made by the best chefs from Paris, Rome, and Switzerland, was fantastic, as was the service. The serving people were the best in the business, all dressed in perfectly tailored pants and crisp white collared shirts.

"Good job, babe," Cat said, moving to stand just behind Elizabeth, her hand gentle on Elizabeth's waist.

"You think so?" Elizabeth asked, her eyes shining brightly as she turned to look at Cat.

"Definitely."

"So, Madam Attorney General," Rick said, his lips pressed to Midnight's temple as they danced. "How do you feel?"

Midnight raised her head, looking up into his eyes. "Scared to fucking death," she replied. A quick grin followed.

Rick threw his head back and laughed, a warm rumble going through his chest. "I suspect you'll be just fine, love," he said, lowering his lips to hers. "I'm very proud of you," he added, kissing her softly.

Midnight looked up into his eyes. The world fell away for a minute. "I'd never be where I am without you, Rick—you know that, don't you?"

"You'd be here," Rick said confidently. "But I'm glad I'm here with you."

Midnight slid her hand through his hair, pulling his head down to hers, kissing him deeply. "I love you, Richard Joshua Debenshire."

"And I you, Midnight Katherine Debenshire," he replied, putting his hand to her cheek.

"Get a room!" Joe said from the side.

"Shaddup," Rick said, narrowing his eyes but grinning just the same.

Joe leaned over, still holding Randy in his arms, and kissed Midnight on the cheek. "Let me take this opportunity to congratulate you, Night."

"Congrats, Midnight," Randy added, smiling.

"Thanks," Midnight said. "Don't thank me yet, though. I may have to steal your man if I don't like what I have to work with."

"Not gonna happen," Joe said, giving her a narrowed look.

"Yeah, yeah, bullshit," Rick said, grinning. "If she beckons, you'll come—you know it."

"Shaddup," Joe said, giving him a vile look.

Rick chuckled.

Joe and Randy moved away. Rick looked down at Midnight. "Are you going to keep the people the previous AG had?"

"It depends," Midnight said. "If I think I can trust them, I might. If I don't, you know me…"

"Uh-huh," Rick said, grinning. "A few people will be jobless, I'm thinkin'."

Midnight sighed, shaking her head. "I just hope I can do this, Rick. I mean, I'm totally confident about the law-enforcement aspect—it's the attorney aspect that's scaring the hell out of me. I've never tried a case."

"I'm betting that won't matter, love. You have people under you for that, remember?"

"Yeah, but how much confidence are they going to have in me if I've never done what they do?" she asked, her true concern coming out.

Rick grinned, shaking his head. "You are amazing, Midnight," he said, his blue eyes reflecting his sincerity. "They'll respect you for all you've accomplished. And I know that you'll knock yourself out until you're the best trial lawyer in history, if that's what it takes."

Midnight sighed, putting her forehead to his shoulder, hoping to God he was right.

CHAPTER 10

Two weeks after being elected, Midnight Chevalier-Debenshire walked into the lobby of the San Diego branch of the Office of the Attorney General. The security guard at the front desk didn't even look up. Midnight narrowed her eyes, making a mental note that the guard wasn't even armed. "Great security so far," she murmured to herself as she waited for the elevator.

As she stood in the lobby, two women and a man walked up to wait with her. The man was older, probably nearing his mid-fifties, in jeans and a plaid shirt. He wore glasses and kept his eyes on the floor. One of the women was wearing a business suit, looking like she was in her late thirties. *More than likely an attorney*, Midnight thought. She didn't even glance at Midnight. The other woman was more likely clerical, since she was dressed much more casually and in her mid-twenties.

It was the younger woman that glanced at Midnight, her eyes widening as Midnight smiled at her.

"You're the new Attorney General," the girl said just as the elevator arrived, clearly awed.

Midnight extended her hand, nodding. "Yes, I am. And maybe you can help me."

The young woman shook Midnight's hand with barely contained reverence. "Yes, ma'am. What can I help you with?" she asked as they walked toward the elevator.

The other woman was staring dumbfounded at Midnight. The man obviously hadn't heard anything, since he was shuffling toward the open elevator.

"Well…" Midnight grinned. "I don't know where my office is," she said, laughing.

"Oh!" the girl exclaimed. "I'll take you up there," she said, looking very happy to be of assistance.

The older woman had barely made it on the elevator as the younger woman hit the button for the sixth floor. The older woman gave the younger one a condescending look as she moved past her to hit the button for the seventh floor. Midnight's lips curled as she concluded her assumption about the older woman had been correct— definitely an attorney, one with an attitude, apparently.

They rode in the elevator in silence. The younger woman had obviously been intimidated by the attorney. Midnight pointedly turned around, looking at the attorney's building badge; it ready *Marilyn Hatch*. She made a mental note of the name. On the sixth floor, Midnight and the younger woman got out; the man and Ms. Hatch proceeded up in the elevator.

"Your offices are this way," the younger woman said.

"What is your name?" Midnight asked.

"Chris Isenagle, ma'am."

"I'm Midnight, Chris. What do you do here?" Midnight asked as she followed her toward a door off to the right.

"Actually," Chris said, smiling, "I work right there." She pointed to the glass reception booth they stepped past.

"Oh, you're a receptionist?"

Chris nodded. "Yeah. You're through here," she said, leading Midnight down the hall and into a side door. "This is your secretaries' offices." She pointed to the outer office, where there were three desks." Midnight thought, *How many secretaries can one person have?* "This is the kitchen, and this," Chris said, opening another door, "is your office. You have a bathroom and shower back there," she finished, pointing to the far end of the room.

The office was huge, and done all in redwood. *At least the last guy had good taste*, Midnight thought with a grin.

"Thank you so much, Chris," she said, turning to the younger woman. "It would have been really embarrassing wandering the halls looking for my office," she added with a wink.

Chris laughed softly. "You're very welcome, ma'am. I'm glad I could help."

With that, Chris turned and left, closing the door quietly.

Midnight walked around and went to the windows. It was a beautiful office, with a great view of the bay. She leaned back against her new desk and looked out at the view, trying to gather the mental strength to face this day. All she wanted to do was run out of the building and back to her office at the PD. But Kyle was the Acting Chief of Police for San Diego PD now. She felt a sudden sense of loss and unfounded terror.

Her cell phone rang. Pulling it out of her pocket, she noticed it was Rick calling her from his office. She smiled to herself. He always knew somehow when she needed him.

"Hi," she said, answering the phone.

"What ya doin?" he asked, his voice smooth and warm.

"Looking at my new view," she replied with a smile.

"And?"

"And I'm scared as hell, Rick."

"Don't be, love."

"I can't do this, Rick, I can't," Midnight said, a flash of insecurity showing through her usually confident facade. "I don't even have a clue where to start."

"Just take it one step at a time, baby," Rick said. "You can do this, I know you can. I love you."

Midnight smiled, feeling a lump in her throat. "I love you too," she whispered, sincerity thick in her voice. "So much."

"I'll come take you to lunch. I'll see you at noon."

"I'll be waiting," she replied, grinning.

They hung up a moment later. Midnight suddenly sensed someone in the room, and turned around. Chris stood there, looking guilty.

She'd come in while Midnight was on the phone and didn't want to interrupt. She hadn't been able to keep from hearing what Midnight was saying. She'd heard Midnight confess to being afraid, and it had made Chris feel for the woman that seemed to have everything. Chris had voted for Midnight Chevalier, admiring all that she'd accomplished. She had also, like many in San Diego, fallen in love with the Debenshire romance. Having just overheard Midnight's conversation, she felt even more determined to be as much assistance to her as possible.

"Um, ma'am," Chris said, grimacing at having been caught eavesdropping, "I just… I came to tell you that there's a café downstairs on three if you're interested." She looked apologetic. "I'm sorry, I didn't mean to eavesdrop."

Midnight smiled at the young woman. She reminded her a lot of Erin. She seemed very sweet, and very earnest, and Midnight liked her already.

"Just keep that 'scared as hell' comment between you and me," she said, chuckling, "and we're all set."

"Yes, ma'am," Chris assured her with a smile.

"Now, you say there's coffee to be had here?"

Chris nodded. "On the third floor."

"What time do you start?" Midnight asked, glancing at her watch; it was 7:15 a.m.

"Not until eight, ma'am," Chris assured her, thinking Midnight was trying to tell her to get to work. "My boyfriend drops me off before he goes to work, so I get here really early."

"Good. Then you can show me where this café is," Midnight said with a smile. "I'll buy," she added as she gestured for Chris to precede her out of the office.

In the café, many people recognized Midnight and murmured a "Good morning, ma'am" to her. Midnight was already getting tired of being called "ma'am"—she felt old!

The café owner greeted her effusively. "It's an honor to have you here, ma'am," the black man said, smiling broadly. "I was really glad to hear you won the election. You had that Longelo beat from the word go."

Midnight laughed. "Well, I'm glad someone thought so."

"He was a grade-A, number-one jackass," the man went on. "Always thinking he was too good for anyone, never even paid for his coffee."

"Well, I can assure you, I pay for whatever I get," Midnight said, pulling out her wallet.

His hand on hers stopped her. "No, ma'am, you will not pay here. You, I like—you don't have to pay."

Midnight smiled, liking him already and not because he was giving her free coffee. "Thank you, but at least let me pay for my friend's coffee, then," she said, winking. "I promised."

233

He looked considering, then nodded, accepting her money for Chris' coffee.

"Thank you, ma'am," Chris said as they found a table near the window.

"Chris." Midnight gave the girl a pointed look. "You can thank me by calling me Midnight instead of 'ma'am,'" she said, making a face.

"But you're the Attorney General, ma'am—I can't do that," Chris said, her eyes wide.

"Okay," Midnight said. "If I'm the Attorney General, then I call the shots, right?"

"Right."

"Then it's my edict that you call me Midnight," she said, smiling.

Chris laughed, nodding.

Midnight grimaced. "'Ma'am' just sounds too old."

"But you're not old, ma—I mean, Midnight."

"Chris," Midnight said, giving the younger woman a direct look, "forty-two is old in any country."

"You're forty-two?" Chris squeaked, then put her hand to her mouth as she realized what she'd said.

Midnight laughed, nodding.

"I thought you were like thirty-five or something."

"Ohhh… I'm promoting you to my press agent."

Chris laughed. She couldn't believe she was sitting here with the Attorney General, having a conversation like she would with any of her girlfriends. Midnight Chevalier-Debenshire was definitely down to earth.

"Okay, so," Midnight said, taking a sip of her coffee and then setting her cup down, "tell me, what was the deal with the woman in the elevator this morning."

"She's an attorney with the civil division," Chris said with a shrug.

"So that gave her the right to be a bitch?" Midnight asked, grimacing at her use of profanity.

Chris gave a snort of laughter, then shrugged again. "That's pretty much how most attorneys are—I mean, around here, anyway... I didn't mean you, though," Chris qualified, realizing she might have just insulted Midnight.

"It's okay," Midnight said. "I'm not an attorney."

"You're not?" Chris asked, surprised.

"No," Midnight said, shaking her head. "I have a law degree, and I'm a member of the bar, but I've never tried a case. Law enforcement is my specialty—it's the court law that scares me about this job."

"Why?" Chris asked, unable to fathom why a woman like Midnight would be afraid of anything.

Midnight shrugged. "They're attorneys."

Chris nodded, realizing how very human Midnight really was. It was amazing—this woman seemed to have it all, yet she could be afraid, just like everyone else.

"But you're their boss," Chris said simply.

"That doesn't automatically earn me their respect, Chris," Midnight said, her main concern coming to bear.

Chris nodded slowly. She realized then and there that Midnight wasn't going to be like any politician that had ever held the office of Attorney General. She wasn't a politician; she honestly meant what she'd said during her campaign. She wanted to make a difference. She was also afraid of not being respected by attorneys, and that would affect her ability to make a difference.

Later in the morning, Midnight called a meeting of the heads of each division. She also had the special agents in charge for the Bureau of

Narcotic Enforcement and Bureau of Investigations come in, as well as the heads of the San Diego offices of the Western States Information Network, Medi-Cal Fraud and Elder Abuse, and Bureau of Gambling Control. The meeting included the heads of the Crime and Violence Prevention Center and public rights divisions, as well as legal support.

They all gathered in the conference room while Midnight held a last-minute meeting in her office with the office manager.

"But, ma'am," the woman, Heidi Davidson, began again, "Chris is only an office assistant—I can't make her your assistant. I have an entire pool of well-qualified legal secretaries—they're better suited to the job," she said, her tone and the look on her face indicating to Midnight that she didn't think much of regular clericals.

"Look," Midnight said evenly, striving to remain pleasant, "at this point in the game, I don't need a legal secretary. I'm not going to be doing any sort of legal work. I have my own secretary from the department coming in tomorrow to work with me. In the meantime, I'd like to utilize Chris for minor needs. I'd like your permission for this," Midnight added, her look pointed, "but I don't really need it."

Heidi straightened her spine. She was fifty-eight years old, and here was this younger woman telling her what to do! Who ever heard of a female Attorney General? It was ridiculous, really! And she wanted to use some low-level clerical as an assistant? Good Lord, what was this constitutional office coming to?

"Yes, ma'am," Heidi finally said, her voice very controlled.

"Thank you," Midnight said, smiling brightly, thinking this woman needed to retire in a hurry. The last thing Midnight wanted to deal with was attitude from her office manager.

Midnight walked into the meeting. Every eye in the place inspected her as everyone moved to stand. She wore black slacks and a perfectly tailored silk suit jacket, as usual nipped in at the waist. Under the jacket she wore an emerald-green collared silk shirt. She wore black calf-skin dress boots. She refused to deviate greatly from the style she'd adopted as Chief of Police. She had no intention of becoming a woman dressing like she thought a man would dress if he were a woman. She was proud that she was a woman with a nice body, and while she never considered herself beautiful, she refused to become some stoic, stereotypical buttoned-up suit. It wasn't in her to do that.

Her long copper-blond hair was held back from her face with a black clip, the rest flowing down her back. Her makeup was light, but as usual, effective in accentuating her delicate features and beautiful gold-green eyes. Her diamond and emerald wedding rings sparkled in the conference room lights as she gestured for everyone to sit down. She got right to the point.

"As I'm sure all of you know, I'm Midnight Chevalier-Debenshire. The citizens of the state of California saw fit to elect me to this office, and it's my full intention to accomplish every single thing I promised during my campaign. I'll tell you here and now, I'm not a politician. I'm not in this position to go for governor next, I'm not here to shake hands, or kiss babies. I'm here to do a job, and I'm hoping you all are here for that same purpose.

"You may or may not agree with my opinions or my policies, nor will I ever require you to. What I will require and will endeavor to earn is your respect, trust, and loyalty. I don't expect you to give me that here and now, but I do expect you to reserve any and all complaints, comments, or suggestions for an appointment with me in my office. I'm sure you've all heard of the cliché 'open-door policy,' but for me, it isn't a cliché—it's how I operate. I want suggestions from people who know the job—you are, presumably, those people.

"It is my intention to learn this department from the ground up. I want to understand the daily workings of the office. Unfortunately, I don't have years and years to work at this—I believe the term is four years, so I have to hurry," she said, grinning engagingly. Many of the faces in the room responded with either grins of their own or soft chuckles. Midnight took note of the few faces that remained blank and unmoved.

"What I'd like from all of you is a quick summary of what your division or office is responsible for. Within the week, I'd like a two-to-four-page summary of caseloads, hot cases, and the people working under you."

A hand went up.

"Yes?" Midnight asked, looking at the older gentleman, one of the men who had chuckled earlier.

"Hot cases?" he queried.

"You are?"

"Jeffrey Cook," he said, inclining his head to her. "Head of the criminal division."

"Thank you, Mr. Cook," Midnight said, inclining her head to him, then looking around the room again. "I've worked in law enforcement for over twenty years now, so I tend to use that jargon when I talk," she said apologetically. "A hot case is basically any case that may be or may become highly publicized. This will be particularly true in the case of your division, Mr. Cook," she said, smiling at him. "I understand the criminal division handles cases such as the capital appeals?"

"Yes, ma'am."

"I'll be particularly interested in your summary report, Mr. Cook," she said, giving him a grin. "Better make yours closer to four pages."

He laughed, nodding.

They spent the next hour and a half going around the table. Each person told Midnight what all they did. Some were very eloquent in their speech, others sounded like they were reading off a script. And then there was Mr. Weiskoff, one of the people whose faces had remained unchanged the entire meeting. Midnight wasn't too surprised to hear he was head of the civil division. He spoke to her like she was a child. Midnight had to contain herself to keep from cutting him off.

"My civil division is responsible for protecting the civil rights of the citizens of the state. We settle anti-trust cases, as well as civil litigation. We were primary in tobacco litigation, heralding the end of deceitful advertising and illegal marketing of tobacco products aimed at children."

His manner was both condescending and overly boastful. Midnight found herself wanting to thank him for personally stamping out crime. Her unmoved expression was enough to have a few of the other division heads grinning behind their hands. Weiskoff had always been a major windbag. All talk. Midnight pursed her lips, her expression bordering on amusement. Then she looked at the next person at the table, waiting for her summary without commenting on Weiskoff's declaration of eminent domain. The next person identified herself as Madeline Muñoz, the head of the Crime and Violence Prevention Center.

She outlined the current programs her office had going on. Midnight was deeply interested in one particular program, and it showed.

"I've made no secret about my desire to combat domestic violence, in particular violence against women," Midnight stated when Madeline finished. "I'd like to meet with you later this week if you have the time, Mrs. Muñoz," she said, noting the wedding rings on the older woman's hands.

"Any time, ma'am," Madeline said, sensing that Midnight was very sincere in her desire to make changes in this area.

Midnight nodded, smiling at the woman, already liking her as well.

Finally she got to the special agents in charge of narcotic enforcement and investigations—now she was on familiar territory.

"Good morning, Midnight," Mike Buffington said; he'd known her for years.

She'd met him over fifteen years before, during a case with a gang called the Scorpions. Mike had been a special agent supervisor then. He'd become SAC in San Diego a few years before, when her good friend Phil Griffin had made chief of BNE and eventually director of the Division of Law Enforcement for the Office of the Attorney General. Phil had found it endlessly amusing that Midnight was now his boss. Midnight had threatened to come see him in Sacramento "soon."

"Morning, Mike. I already know what you do," she said with a grin. "But I'd like you to tell everyone here what BNE does, so we can all be on the same page."

Mike did as she requested, keeping it brief but interesting.

"Thanks, Mike," Midnight said, smiling at him. She turned then to Bob Forrester, the special agent in charge of the Bureau of Investigation.

"Good morning, Chief," he said, nodding to her, then grimaced. "I mean, uh, AG?" he queried with a grin.

"Midnight'll work, Bob," she said, grinning. "Give us the run-down."

Bob did as she asked. She'd first met him a couple of years before, when he'd been running a task force for the Bureau of Narcotic Enforcement. Stevie had worked for him at the task force for a while when she'd come back to the department. She liked him as well.

When the meeting wrapped up, Midnight once again asked that everyone get her their summaries to her no later than the end of the week. She felt she'd already gained a better understanding of the divisions. There was a lot to this AG stuff, she realized. But she was already formulating ideas for new missions, some based on current programs, others totally new.

When she got back to her office, Chris was sitting at one of the desks in the outer office, looking basically totally awestruck.

"I wasn't sure what you wanted me to do," she began, standing when Midnight walked in.

"I want you to relax a bit," Midnight said, grinning. "And come into my office. Do you have a pad of paper?"

"Yes, ma'am," Chris said, then grimaced as Midnight gave her a pointed look. "I mean Midnight."

She followed Midnight into her offices and took up a position at the small conference table. To her surprise, Midnight sat down at the same table.

"Okay, first of all, I need some things," Midnight said. "Do you have access to office supplies? Or do I have to go pander myself to that office manager person again?" she asked with a grimace.

Chris laughed. "I can get you whatever you need."

"Okay, well, get me everything normal—you know, pens, pencils, staples, all the good stuff. And we're going to need lots of pads of

241

paper," Midnight said, rolling her eyes. "I have a habit of scribbling notes about everything that occurs to me. And I'm on overload right now."

"Okay…" Chris said, starting to list out all the things she thought Midnight would need.

"And who do I have to beg for a computer?" Midnight asked.

"That would be TAC, ma'am," Chris said, grimacing again.

Midnight waved her hand in dismissal of her slip. "How long will that take?"

"A day or so, I'm guessing, but I'm sure you'll be priority number one."

Midnight nodded, picking up her cell phone and dialing a number. Chris waited, continuing to make notes on her pad. She could only hear one side of the conversation, but it was definitely interesting, even though she tried not to listen.

"Heya, Blue, whatcha up to?" Midnight asked. "Oh yeah, sitting here trying to figure out what to do with myself now that I got elected," she said, laughing. "Look, I need a favor from my best and favorite hacker. Yeah, I need a laptop, nothing too special, just something to use till they get me hooked up here." She rolled her eyes. "I don't need all that, Blue. Jesus, I'm not taking over the world," she said, laughing again. "Oh, you are the best. I knew I loved you for a reason." She chuckled then, shaking her head. "I won't tell Rick you said that, and you might live another week or two, or until your wife hears you." She grinned. "Great. Thanks, Blue, I owe ya." She hung up.

"So you won't need a laptop?" Chris asked carefully.

"No, I'll still need one, I'm just going to commandeer one from my old department till they get around to it here."

"Oh."

They spent the next hour with Midnight rattling off things she needed, wanted to see, or needed to find out about. Chris took diligent notes.

"Jesus, is this a bloody maze or what?" came an English-accented voice from the doorway.

Chris turned to look at whoever had walked into the office. She was sure her heart stopped. He was the most handsome man she'd ever seen, she was sure of it. He was tall, with jet black hair and the lightest blue eyes she'd ever seen. Glancing at Midnight, she saw a brilliant smile on her face.

"Blue!" Midnight said, standing up as he strode over to her. He hugged her, glancing at Chris and giving her a cavalier wink.

"Heya, Chief," Christian said, and glanced around. "Nice place."

"Yeah," Midnight said, nodding. "Makes me not miss my office too much."

"It's bigger."

"Yup," Midnight said, grinning. "Blue, this is Chris Isenagle. She's going to be my assistant. Chris, this is Christian Collins. He works for San Diego Police Department."

Christian put his hand out to Chris, smiling at her, his light blue eyes touching hers. "Good to meet you."

"Nice to meet you too," Chris squeaked.

Christian grinned, knowing how he affected women. He looked back at Midnight.

"Well, here's what you asked for," he said, unlooping the laptop case from his shoulder and putting it on the table.

"You are the best, Blue," Midnight enthused. "Thank you, thank you."

"You're welcome," he said, giving her a wink. "I'll let you know later how you can repay me."

"Let her know now, so I can just kill you and get it over with," came another English-accented voice from the doorway.

Christian didn't even bat an eyelash, his grin widening.

"Boys," Midnight said, a warning in her voice. "Don't start here."

"Start what?" Rick asked, walking over to her and leaning down to kiss her on the lips softly.

"Don't play that with me, Debenshire," Midnight said, giving him a narrowed look, then glanced over at Chris. "Chris, this is my husband, Rick. Rick, this is Chris. She's going to be working for me as my assistant."

Rick extended his hand to Chris, even as she did her best not to stare at him. She'd recognized him instantly. He was the man that loved his wife so much he'd stepped in front of a bullet for her. And my God, he was even more handsome in person! Did San Diego PD employ any ugly men?

"What about Cassandra?" Rick asked Midnight, even as he shook hands with Chris.

"She'll be here tomorrow," Midnight said. "She had a dentist appointment today."

"Oh," Rick said, grinning. "First day and she's already calling off shift, huh?"

"Stop it," Midnight said, scowling at him.

"So what's he doin' here?" Rick asked, nodding at Christian.

"Bringing me a laptop," Midnight said, giving Christian a wink.

"I see," Rick said, narrowing his eyes at Christian.

"Hey," Christian said, holding up his hands. "Your wife calls me, what can I do?"

"You can go back to yours," Rick said, smiling all the same.

Christian laughed, nodding.

"Thanks, Blue," Midnight said again, putting her hand on his arm.

"Anything for you, Chief."

He turned and left then, and Rick looked at Midnight.

"Ready for lunch?"

Midnight glanced at Chris. "I think we're at a stopping point, aren't we?"

"You're the boss," Chris said, smiling.

"Oh, I like her," Rick said, smiling at Chris.

"Anything to get me to take lunch on time, huh?" Midnight said, smiling up at him.

"On time, at all…"

"Yeah, yeah," Midnight said, laughing. "Don't start. Chris, I'll be back in an hour or so."

"I'll work on getting those supplies while you're gone."

"No," Midnight said, giving her a stern look. "You go to lunch too."

Chris smiled. "Yes, ma'am."

Midnight rolled her eyes and shook her head. The girl was never going to get used to calling her Midnight, apparently.

At lunch, Rick asked her how it was going. She told him about the meeting.

"So the guy was an asshole, huh?" Rick asked, grinning.

"He was condescending," Midnight qualified. "Which apparently is the order of the day in this place," she said, making a face.

"Well, it sounds like you put him in his place, and a lot of people enjoyed it," Rick said, taking a drink of his beer.

Midnight sighed, nodding.

"Still thinking you can't do this?" he asked, his blue eyes watching her.

Midnight looked thoughtful, then sighed. "I know I can, Rick. I guess I just hate being the new kid on the block again, you know?"

"Yeah, babe," Rick said, knowing full well that was the whole problem with her. "But just remember, you're the boss, no matter what."

Midnight grinned. "That's what Chris said too."

"So how'd you meet her?" Rick asked, guessing that Chris was the latest person Midnight was taking under her wing.

"In the elevator lobby this morning. The elevator lobby with absolutely no real security," she said, shaking her head ruefully. "Anyway, she was the only one out of three people that recognized me. She was nice, and showed me to my office. Then came to tell me about the café downstairs, so I went and had coffee with her. She's a nice kid."

Rick nodded, grinning. He knew he'd been right. "So what was she before you swept in?"

"A receptionist."

"Uh-huh. And now she's personal assistant to the Attorney General herself. Serious upward mobility there, love," he said with a wink.

"Hey," Midnight said, giving him a narrowed look, "I needed someone to help me that knows the place—who knows it better than a clerical?"

"I know, love, I know," Rick soothed. "So, what's the deal with lobby security?" he asked, never missing a thing.

It was Midnight's turn to grin. "Some old guy that doesn't even carry, and didn't even look up when I walked in."

"Oh, lovely," Rick said, not looking pleased. "Gonna fix that soon, I hope."

"Well, I have a meeting scheduled with my security team today, so I plan to."

Three hours later, Midnight sat staring at the man that was the head of her security detail, Ben Jansen. She knew she was far too used to men who were tall, fit, handsome, and virile in the extreme, and for that reason she shouldn't judge this man because he was the exact opposite of all those things. He was short, probably only about three inches taller than Midnight herself, and overweight by a good fifty pounds, with a nice, comfortable paunch going on around his middle. He was also not good-looking, quite plain with an overbite and what was dangerously close to a comb-over for a hairstyle. And *virile* was about the last adjective anyone would use to describe him.

All the same, Midnight did her best to garner the information she needed from him. Unfortunately for him, his approach was to treat her like she was an amateur, doing his best to take over from the minute he sat down.

"First of all," he said, sitting in the chair in front of her desk with the air of someone used to being listened to—Midnight immediately folded her hands in front of her on her desk and did her best not to grin condescendingly. "I was informed that you drove in this morning. That cannot be repeated. Also, I understand you went to lunch without security with you. That also cannot happen again."

"My husband took me to lunch, Mr. Jansen. He *is* a lieutenant with the police department," Midnight pointed out. "I think he's fairly qualified to protect me at lunch."

"That notwithstanding, Ms. Chevalier," he began again—of course, with the phrase Midnight hated most.

"It's Attorney General Chevalier or Mrs. Debenshire, Jansen. Pick one," Midnight all but snapped.

Jansen had the temerity to sit up straighter in the face of her apparent displeasure. "My apologies, ma'am," he said, inclining his head. "I'll need to go over your schedule with you so I can arrange a detail to be with you at all times."

"All times? Jansen, you do realize that I'm a former police chief with over twenty years' law enforcement experience, don't you? I think I'm fairly capable of taking care of myself for the most part."

"Begging your pardon, ma'am, but you are the Attorney General now, a high-profile political figure."

"I won an election, Jansen," she said, narrowing her eyes slightly. "I didn't have a lobotomy."

"Excuse me?"

"I'm fully aware of my position, and my need for security," Midnight said, doing her best to control her temper. "But I think it's going overboard to state that I need constant security."

"That's how things are done here, ma'am," Jansen said triumphantly, like he'd just found the perfect argument.

"Well, it's a new regime, Jansen," Midnight said, smiling tightly.

Ten minutes after Jansen walked out of her office, Midnight was on the phone to Kyle.

"What time's the meeting?" Palani asked Kana as she watched her putting on eyeliner.

"At eight thirty."

"And you don't know what it's about?"

"Nope," Kana said, shaking her head. "Midnight called and asked me and Tiny to come to her offices this morning at eight thirty—that's it."

Palani canted her head to the side, trying to figure it out. Finally she shrugged. "Midnight calls, you go," she said, smiling.

Kana glanced over at Palani, seeing her smile. "Guess that's true enough."

Palani noted how nicely Kana was dressed, even wearing dress boots. She sighed. "You look way too nice to be meeting with another woman," she said, grinning.

Again Kana glanced at her, then shook her head. "Babe, I'm going to walk into the Office of the Attorney General. I don't want to look like the poor relation."

"Uh-huh," Palani said. "If Midnight Chevalier ever decided to go gay, I'd lose you so fast…" she said, trailing off with a grin.

Kana narrowed her eyes at Palani. "I couldn't handle Midnight Chevalier, babe. I don't know how Rick does it every day."

"So you'll just stay with me, then, huh?" Palani said, moving up to slide her hands around Kana's waist.

"Yeah, poor me," Kana said, winking at her in the mirror.

Kana finished putting on what little makeup she wore, then turned to Palani, leaning down and kissing her softly on the lips. "You're the one I want, little one."

"Good," Palani said. "Or else."

"Or else what?" Kana asked with a grin.

Palani looked pensive for a moment, then shrugged. "Or else I'd be sad."

"Big threat," Kana said, chuckling as she pulled Palani into her arms.

"Yeah, I'm so tough," Palani said, laughing too.

On the drive to Midnight's new offices, Kana smoked. Tiny shook his head.

"I can't believe you're smoking again, K. I also can't believe the doctor said it was okay."

"Yeah, well, I didn't ask," she said, giving him a narrowed look.

"Was Palani surprised?"

"That I'm smoking now?"

"Yeah. You weren't when you two were together before, were you?"

"Nope," Kana said, shaking her head.

"And she doesn't mind?"

"You know what, Tiny, why don't you worry about yourself for a while?" Kana said, her tone mild but her eyes narrowed.

"Ma'am, yes ma'am," Tiny said, grinning all the while.

"Any ideas what this meeting is about?" Kana asked as they got to the underground parking garage for the Attorney General's office. Kana pulled out her badge; the guard in the shack opened the gate.

"I don't know," Tiny said. "But I heard that Midnight was on the phone with Kyle for over an hour yesterday afternoon."

"Ohhh…" Kana said, grimacing. "Are we in trouble again already?"

Tiny chuckled. "I don't think she can bust us for anything anymore, K."

"Good point," Kana said, grinning.

They walked into the lobby. The security guard continued to read his morning paper, uninterested in them. Kana raised an eyebrow at Tiny; he shook his head, rolling his eyes.

"Great security," Kana murmured as they walked into the elevator.

"Hope she's fixing that."

"And how," Kana said. "What floor?"

"Six."

Kana nodded, pushing the button. On the third floor a woman dressed in a business suit got onto the elevator. Glancing at Kana and

Tiny, her eyes widened significantly. Kana and Tiny looked at each other and grinned. They had that effect on most people. They called themselves the Samoan Express for that reason; they plowed the field when it came to people's reactions to them. When the woman looked at Kana again, Kana stared right back at her, her dark eyes unreadable but her face reflecting amused condescension. The woman turned back around quickly. Tiny shook his head, knowing Kana was intimidating Midnight's new staff.

He was still shaking his head when they got off the elevator on the sixth floor and headed toward the reception booth.

"What?" Kana asked.

"You're scaring the natives," Tiny said, grinning.

"Hey," Kana said. "She was rude, looking me over like I was some kind of criminal."

"Maybe she's not used to women who are twice her size."

"Bite me, Ako," Kana said as they got up to the reception booth.

"Not till you've had your shots."

Kana gave him a narrowed look. The receptionist was on the phone and apparently hadn't noticed their approach. It was obvious when she did, because she gave a startled gasp as she looked up and up and up at the two of them towering over her. It was obvious she was instantly intimidated, regardless of the two-inch-thick bulletproof glass between them and her.

"Can..." the woman squeaked. "Can I help you?"

Kana grinned. "Yeah, we're here to see the AG."

The woman's eyes widened as she swallowed convulsively. "Do... do you have an appointment?"

Kana glanced at Tiny, and then back at the woman. "No, we just wandered in off the street and thought we'd get to see her. Is she here?"

Tiny was grinning again, shouldering Kana aside and giving the already obviously intimidated woman an apologetic look. "Forgive my partner," he said politely. "She's having a bad morning. Yes, we have an appointment. You can let her know that Tiny and Kana are here."

"Yes, sir," the woman said, looking immensely relieved. "Thank you."

She got on the phone and called Midnight's secretary. Midnight came striding out of the side door a minute later.

"Tiny, Kana, hey!" she said, walking up and hugging them in turn. "Come on back," she said, nodding to the receptionist.

Midnight led them into her outer office. Cassandra, the woman that had been Midnight's secretary at San Diego PD the entire time she'd been chief, was set up at the desk closest to Midnight's office.

"Kana!" Cassandra stood up and reached out to take her extended hand. "You look great. I'm glad," she said, smiling happily.

"Thanks, Cass," Kana said.

"Hi, Tiny," Cassandra said, smiling up at the big guy.

"Hiya, Cass," Tiny said, grinning back.

"Kana, Tiny," Midnight said, turning toward a young woman who was standing as she did. "This is Chris. She's helping me out here. Chris, this is Tiny Ako and Kana Sorbinno. They're very good friends of mine."

Chris' eyes widened slightly when she looked at Kana, only because she recognized her name from the scandal about her being gay. She realized that was why Cassandra had made the comment about Kana looking great.

Chris extended her hand to Kana and smiled. "It's nice to meet you," she said warmly.

Kana nodded, having noted the girl's look. "You too."

Chris turned to Tiny then, extending her hand to him. "And it's nice to meet you too."

Tiny smiled down at Chris. "Anyone that's helping Midnight is a friend of mine."

"Always so smooth…" Kana murmured.

"That's me," Tiny said, chuckling.

Chris laughed softly, liking these two already.

"Chris, can you get us some coffee? I think I even saw Kona downstairs, if they have it. Kana takes hers black, right, K?" Midnight asked. Kana grinned, nodding. "And Tiny's cream no sugar, right?" Tiny nodded too. Midnight handed Chris a twenty. "Get some for you too if you want some."

"Did you want some too, ma'am?"

"Yeah," Midnight said. "Light with sugar?"

"Yes, ma'am," Chris said, smiling.

"Come on, you two," Midnight said, nodding to her office.

Tiny and Kana followed Midnight and were both awestruck by how nice the office was.

"Wow…" Tiny said. "Nice digs, Chief."

"And a view…" Kana said, nodding in agreement.

When they'd settled down in front of Midnight's desk, they both looked at her, their faces questioning.

"Guess you're both wondering why I asked you to come here, huh?" Midnight asked, leaning back in her chair.

Kana and Tiny both nodded.

"Well, I need your help."

"Whatever you need," Kana said immediately.

Midnight grinned. "Don't you think you should hear what I'm asking for first, K?"

"Why?" Tiny asked. "You know whatever it is, we'll do it, Midnight."

Midnight shook her head. She never could understand their unwavering loyalty. She very much appreciated it though.

"Well, here's the thing," she said, putting her hands on her desk. "I need protection."

Kana and Tiny tensed, both immediately concerned she'd received a threat already.

"Relax, you two," Midnight said, grinning. She glanced up as Chris walked in with the coffee.

"They had Kona," Chris said, smiling and handing a cup to Kana.

"Oh, heaven," Kana said, sighing. "I was drinking this stuff when I was seven."

"Really?" Chris asked as she handed Tiny his coffee.

"Yeah," Kana said. "I grew up on a plantation—my parents grow coffee beans. Coffee's like water where I'm from in Hawaii."

"Guess that story about coffee stunting your growth isn't very accurate, is it?" Chris said, grinning.

Kana laughed. "I'd have to say you're right about that."

"Actually, Kana's growth was stunted, Chris," Tiny said. "She should have been my size by now."

"Shut up, Nathan, or I'm calling your wife," Kana countered.

Tiny chuckled and shook his head. Chris laughed softly as she left the office, closing the door quietly.

Tiny looked back at Midnight. "So what's the deal with needing protection?" he asked. "Have you been threatened?"

"No," Midnight said. "Although I'm sure there's voodoo dolls of me in a lot of attorneys' offices by now. In which pins are being inserted," she added, grinning wickedly.

"Pissing off the natives already, huh?" Kana asked, making a face at Tiny as if to remind him that even Midnight intimidated the natives.

"Uh oh…" Midnight said, looking between the two of them, then shook her head. "I don't want to know. Anyway," she said, going on with a grin, "my security detail… well, let's just say they leave a lot to be desired."

"Your security downstairs sucks too, Midnight."

"I know," Midnight said. "So, what I need is the two toughest and best friends I have to take care of that kind of thing for me…"

"Why not Joe?" Tiny asked.

"Yeah, isn't he starting a business along these same lines?" Kana put in.

"Yes, he is," Midnight said. "Key there is 'starting a business,' guys. He can't dedicate the time to this that he'd need to. And yeah, I know if I asked him to, he would do it, but I won't do that to him. He's just getting his life back on track, with Randy and the kids.

"I know you'll need to talk to Palani and Jess on this. We'll be out of town some, but you know I want to keep that to a minimum, and I figure at least there aren't kids involved at this point with you two…" Her voice trailed off as she caught the look between them. "Okay, what?" she asked, narrowing her eyes.

Tiny was the only one Kana had confided in about the marriage to Palani and the fact that Palani wanted to have a baby. She wanted to wait until after she and Palani went to Hawaii the following week and talked to Palani's family before announcing their plans to her friends.

When neither of them spoke, Midnight leaned forward, her eyes narrowing further.

Kana grimaced. It was like being interrogated by a parent, having Midnight stare at her and Tiny like that.

"Well?" Midnight said.

Kana sighed. "Palani and I are getting married."

"What?" Midnight exclaimed, looking thrilled. "Oh my God, K!" she said, standing up and walking around her desk. Kana stood, accepting Midnight's hug.

"When did this happen?" Midnight asked, stepping back to lean against her desk.

"The night you won the election," Kana said, looking guilty.

"And you didn't bother to tell me?" Midnight asked, narrowing her eyes again.

"I didn't tell anyone but Tiny," Kana said. "And him only because he'll have to take over for me while I'm in Hawaii next week."

"You're not getting married there next week, are you?" Midnight asked, worried.

"No, no," Kana said. "Palani has to talk to her family, in person. They don't, um, know yet."

"Ohhh…" Midnight said, trailing off as she winced. "So why didn't you tell any of us?"

"Because I don't know for sure when it's happening yet, for one thing. Plus I need to make sure it goes okay with her family first."

"And that's not all the news she has."

"Shut up, Nathanial," Kana said, giving him a vile look.

"Tell her, K," Tiny said, a quirked grin on his lips.

"Tell me what?" Midnight asked.

Kana was silent a moment, looking hesitant. Again she sighed. "Palani wants to have a baby."

"Wait," Midnight said, putting her hand on Kana's arm. "What happened to the baby she was pregnant with when you two broke up?"

"She lost it," Kana said quietly.

"Oh God…" Midnight said, looking pained. She herself had experience with miscarriages, so she fully understand how difficult that would be. "When did she lose it?"

"In the fifth month," Kana said. "She didn't lose it naturally."

Midnight's eyes narrowed. "How did she lose it?"

"Her brother had come to talk her into staying with Matt," Kana said, her eyes narrowing as well. "Matt, who'd basically raped her while she slept to get her pregnant."

"He what?" Midnight exclaimed.

Kana nodded. "He thought it would keep her from divorcing him."

"So she didn't lie to you about sleeping with him," Midnight said, mostly to herself.

"Right," Kana said. "Anyway, her brother, a highly traditional Samoan, managed to alienate Palani to the point where she lost it. She told him in anger about me, being in love with me."

Midnight didn't react, but noticed that Tiny jerked his head to the side, grimacing.

"What?" Midnight asked, looking perplexed. "What did I miss?"

"A traditional Samoan man practices Fa'a Samoa," Tiny said gravely. "It means 'the Samoan Way.' All Samoans are to respect their family, community, and church. But family is number one. In loving a woman, a highly non-traditional, extremely non-conservative action, Palani, in her brother's eyes, disgraced her family."

"Oh God…" Midnight said, feeling her stomach tighten, then looked at Kana again. "What did he do?"

"He backhanded her," Kana said, looking sickened. "She was standing near the stop of the stairs. She stumbled and fell down them."

"Oh, Kana…" Midnight breathed, moving to kneel in front of her friend, taking Kana's hands and squeezing them.

Midnight knew how protective Kana was, and she knew that it would bother Kana no end that the woman she loved was hurt so badly when Kana wasn't there to protect her. Kana nodded, accepting Midnight's sympathy.

"But now she wants to have a baby with you?" Midnight asked hopefully.

"Yeah," Kana said. "She wants a baby. I can't deny her that."

"So how will that work?" Midnight asked. "Artificial insemination?"

"Yeah. You don't think I'm letting another guy anywhere near my girl, do you?" she said, regaining her sense of humor.

Midnight laughed. "No, I guess not."

"Thing is," Kana said, "I'm going to talk to one of my brothers about being the donor."

"Yeah?" Midnight said, looking surprised by the idea, but then she started nodding. "This way the baby has your family's DNA too, right?"

"Right."

"Pretty cool, K," Midnight said, smiling. "I'm glad things worked out so well for you and Palani."

"Me too," Kana said, smiling. "Too bad I had to get blown all to hell for it to work out."

"Yeah, well," Midnight said, "if you hadn't gone running into that house…"

"I know, I know! Sinclair's still on my ass about that."

Tiny grinned, nodding. He leaned forward then, his expression serious as he touched Kana's hand. "You know if you'd left us, I'd never have forgiven myself."

"I know," Kana said, glancing at her partner and long-time friend. "And that really pisses me off, Tiny. You know it wasn't your fault—it was mine."

He nodded, not looking convinced. Kana shook her head. Midnight smiled.

"This is exactly why I want you two. You two are dangerous on your own, but you're lethal together. That's what I want." She spread her hands. "Besides, who in their right mind would take on either of you to get to me?"

"No one prudent."

"Or sane."

"That's my point, kids," Midnight said, winking at them.

"I'll talk to Jess," Tiny said. "But I already know what she'll say."

"And what's that?" Midnight asked.

"She'll tell me that I should do what I think is right."

"And what do you think is right?"

"For me to protect you with my life," Tiny replied, so simply but with such conviction that Midnight felt tears sting the back of her eyes.

Kana nodded, agreeing with Tiny's assessment.

Midnight was speechless for a long moment. Then she looked at Kana. "What about you, K?"

"Palani already knows I'd do anything you asked. So I know she'll be totally behind me protecting you."

Midnight nodded, thanking God she had such good and loyal friends. "You two have no idea what a relief it will be to have you with me, watching my back."

"So, I take it you've already talked to Kyle about stealing us?" Tiny asked.

Midnight grinned. "Yeah, he said he'd hate to lose you two, but he understood that I wouldn't ask if I didn't need you."

Both Kana and Tiny nodded.

"Now…" Midnight said, turning to pick up two folders off her desk. "I got this together, just in case you actually said yes. Tiny, I can bring you in as a special agent supervisor, which would top you out about a thousand more than you're at now. K, I'd bring you in as a special agent in charge, which would put you up around eight K a month when you top out. But I need you at that level, because I want you to coordinate a whole new unit of security officers. Apparently they have DOJ security officers, but only up in Sacramento for some reason. Makes no sense to me. So, I want to look into putting them in all the legal offices, at least a team of two per shift.

"We can work out the details, but I want these people safe." She handed them the folders as she talked. Tiny and Kana were already grinning at each other. Midnight never stopped thinking; she never sat back and waited for things to happen—she made them happen. "And of course I want you both as my personal detail," she said, grinning as she realized she'd already accepted that they'd join her. She grimaced. "Those were yes's, weren't they? Earlier?"

"Yes," Tiny and Kana said together.

"Oh, thank God!" Midnight said, laughing.

"Would have been a hell of a speech either way, Chief," Kana said, winking at her.

That night Kana told Palani about the meeting.

"So you'll be her bodyguard?" Palani asked, settling more comfortably against Kana.

"Yeah, plus she wants me to be in charge of the security teams throughout the state, which I'm going to put together."

"Wow…" Palani said, shaking her head. "She trusts you a lot."

"With her life."

Palani nodded, ever impressed by the people Kana worked with, as well as Kana herself.

"I told her about us," Kana said.

"Us?" Palani asked, looking perplexed.

"The getting married thing, and having a baby."

"Oh! I thought you didn't want to tell anyone yet?"

"Well, if she's going to be my new boss…"

"If?" Palani said. "You didn't automatically tell her yes?"

"She wanted me to talk to you first."

"And you knew what I'd tell you."

Kana nodded. "Yeah, I did. That's why I already told her yes."

"Kana!" Palani said, nudging her shoulder. "You let me believe you were waiting for my answer."

"Yeah, but I did know what you'd say."

"And what was that?" Palani asked pertly.

"That you already knew that I'd do anything Midnight asked of me, and that you'd support me doing this."

Palani pursed her lips in a scowl, but then smiled. "And you were right."

"See?"

"Yes, I see," Palani said, laughing softly. "What did she think about us getting married?"

"She's happy for us, babe."

"And about the baby?" Palani asked, knowing it was important to Kana that her law-enforcement family approved, and Midnight was the matriarch of that family.

Kana nodded. "She thought it was a great idea to have one of my brothers be the donor."

"I think so too," Palani said, smiling. She sighed. "Now all we have to do is get through telling my parents, and we'll be all set."

"You honestly don't think Sampson went back and told them?"

"I know he didn't, Kana. For one thing, if he had he would have had to explain everything, especially how I ended up at the bottom of the stairs after telling him about you. And for another thing," she rushed on, seeing Kana wince at the picture she'd just painted, "I would have gotten a phone call from my father ordering me home, and that didn't happen."

Kana nodded. "Very traditional, aren't they?"

"Very."

"Do we have any hope of them accepting this?"

"Well," Palani said, "I know that they love us children, so I'm holding on to the hope that if they understand how much I love you, they'll accept it."

Kana nodded, doing a lot of hoping too. Family was very important to both of them; being ostracized from her family would be horrible for Palani. Kana knew it would put a pall on their relationship, and that wasn't something she wanted.

CHAPTER 11

Kana and Tiny officially started on Midnight's personal security detail. The first order of business was a trip to Sacramento to meet with some of the offices there. Sacramento was headquarters to a number of the units under Midnight's new responsibility, two of the most important of which were the Division of Law Enforcement and the California Justice Information System. Midnight wanted to meet with their heads personally to discuss changes that needed to be made. She also wanted to garner suggestions for improvements in all areas of the department. In the time that she'd been in office, Midnight had already discovered that the previous administration, who'd been in place a surprising full eight years, had changed almost nothing.

The drive through Sacramento in the fall was breathtaking. The leaves were changing, and the trees were a riot of colors ranging from golds to oranges and reds. Midnight was astounded by the beauty. Sacramento was known for all its trees, so there were thousands of them changing color and making the city come alive. It was also fairly chilly in Sacramento, especially for three San Diegans. Midnight found it amusing when Kana and even Tiny donned long, mid-thigh-length leather coats.

Midnight also quickly discovered that, much like at San Diego PD years before, the computer systems in Sacramento had never been updated to stay on par with the rest of the country. So she called together a meeting of the computer staff. She could tell they were all very surprised to be invited to a meeting with the AG herself, but one thing Midnight had learned over the years was that it was rarely the people at management level that had the great ideas. It was the everyday person, the one that did the work day in and day out, that had the idea that would work for the need.

The room being used was a training room; it had theater seating and filled up rather quickly. Everyone had canceled anything necessary to be at this particular meeting. Many were just curious about meeting the woman who'd gotten elected; Midnight's career was well known at the department. Also, her no mud-slinging, straightforward campaign had caught the interest of many more. Midnight was, to many, a celebrity. As such, her meetings were heavily attended.

Kana walked into the room, and many heads turned. Midnight walked in behind Kana, and Tiny followed Midnight in, closing the door behind him. Kana stepped to one side, allowing Midnight to walk down the stairs of the meeting room first. Kana and Tiny fell in behind her, scanning the group. There were a number of murmurs about the size of Midnight's bodyguards. Tiny and Kana were both dressed in black, with white shirts, their jackets open, exposing gold shields and fairly nasty-looking guns suspended in shoulder holsters. Midnight, dressed in navy blue and cream, the front of her copper-blond hair pulled back lightly in a braid and the rest flowing down her back, was a complete contrast to her bodyguards. She was petite and delicate-looking; Tiny and Kana presented a brick wall of danger for anyone fool enough to try to get to her.

At the bottom of the stairs, Kana and Tiny took up places at the corners of the room, their eyes watchful. Midnight walked over to the table positioned at the front. Turning, she leaned casually against the table, scanning the crowd.

"Thank you for taking the time out of your busy days to meet with me," she began, her sincere tone making people like her instantly. "I realize that meeting with me may seem pointless," she went on. "And I can't say I'd blame you if you thought it was. What you need to know is that I don't like to waste time—not mine, not my employees'. So please bear with me for a few minutes, and hopefully we can accomplish something.

"My concern here is the current computer systems this department is running. I don't know a great deal about operating systems, or networking, but the system we have… Well, quite frankly," she said, putting her hands up in a show of futility, "it sucks."

There were hoops and hollers from the audience, and a lot of nodding and "Got that right"s. Kana and Tiny grinned at each other. Leave it to Midnight to use the word *sucks* in a meeting.

"What I need to know, from all of you, is what we can do to fix it," Midnight said, looking around the room at each person. She wanted them to understand that she didn't care where the idea came from, as long as it came.

One woman put her hand up cautiously.

"Yes?" Midnight said, nodding to her. "What's your name?"

The woman stood up. She looked like she was in her late twenties, with long brown hair in a braid and wide brown eyes. "My name is Glenna Apple, ma'am."

Midnight nodded. "Hi, Glenna. What's your comment?"

"Well, ma'am," Glenna said, looking nervous, "part of the problem here is that we can't ever buy the best computers. We end up with the bid process, and that always leaves out getting anything good."

Midnight nodded, looking pensive. "Who do we buy our computers from now?"

"Small private vendors, ma'am."

"How do you manage to get consistency there?" Midnight asked, knowing that small vendors weren't likely to have a large supply of any one thing on hand.

"That's the problem, ma'am. We don't get consistency," Glenna said.

Midnight nodded. "First problem that needs to be fixed, then," she said, making a note on the pad she'd brought with her. "Thank you, Glenna." She smiled at the young woman. Glenna nodded and sat down.

A man raised his hand. Midnight nodded to him. "Your name?" she asked as he stood up.

"Jim Capps, ma'am," he said, smiling shyly.

Midnight smiled. "What's your take, Jim?"

"Well, ma'am, one of the other major problems is that we keep using consultants for the new systems, and they build these stupid programs then leave. We have no way of maintaining them, because we have no idea what the consultant did."

Midnight nodded. "Consultants always cost a fortune, too."

"Yes, ma'am."

"Do we have programmers that could be doing the job?"

Another man raised his hand, a much older man this time.

"Yes, sir?" Midnight said. "What's your name?"

"Ben Acres, ma'am," he said, standing up. "And in answer to your question, we have programmers here, myself included, but they don't pay us anywhere near what they pay these fancy consultants. People around here are almost afraid to suggest something, because they'll end up with the job but get screwed out of the pay." He grimaced at the profanity he'd used. "Excuse me, ma'am."

Midnight laughed, shaking her head. "No excuse necessary, Ben. Can you tell me how much difference we're talking between consultant pay and programmer pay?"

"A few thousand a month," Ben said, his lips curling in disgust. "And half the time the crap these consultants build doesn't work, because they have no idea who they're building the program for. We do."

Midnight nodded. "When you say a few thousand, are we talking two, three? What?"

"About three and a half, ma'am."

"Holy shit," Midnight said before she could stop herself. Her own eyes widened at her outburst. "Oops," she said, rolling her eyes. Many people in the group laughed. It was rather funny to hear the State Attorney General not only swear but actually say "oops" when she did.

"Okay," Midnight said, still grinning. "So if programmers made more, you think that the programs created would be more effective?"

Many people nodded. "The programmers that work for the department know the department better than any high-paid consultant," Ben said.

Midnight nodded. "Okay, then I'll see what I can do on my end. What I'd like from any of you that have ideas is an email to my secretary. I assure you," she said with a self-deprecating grin, "I read my emails. My husband has learned quite well to sleep with the light of the laptop next to him."

Again everyone laughed. Most people had heard about the legendary Debenshire love affair. Midnight usually referred to Rick at least once during every speech or meeting. It was just habit for her to mention the man that was her other half. Most men could only wish to be loved by such a dynamic, beautiful woman, and most women would kill to be that much in love with the man in their life.

Midnight concluded the meeting shortly after that. She, Kana, and Tiny went back to their hotel after a quick tour of the DLE/DCJIS facility. Once at the hotel, Midnight got on her phone, calling Rick and checking in at the office. Tiny settled on the couch in the suite with the TV on. Kana grabbed the ice bucket and the room key and headed out to the vending area. She got ice, and got gum for Tiny, which he was always looking for, bought Midnight dulce de leche Häagen-Dazs, her favorite, and got herself some cigarettes.

Heading back to the room, Kana noted a man coming toward her. She automatically shifted the things she was carrying to her opposite hand, to free up her gun hand if she needed it. The man's eyes connected right on level with Kana's. She nodded; he did too. He walked on; so did Kana. She made it back to the room, tossing the gum at Tiny. He caught it midair without even looking. Kana grinned and walked over to where Midnight sat at her desk, tapping away on the keys of her laptop. Kana set the ice cream down next to Midnight and, grabbing her lighter, went outside on the balcony to smoke. Midnight joined her a few minutes later.

"Thanks for this," Midnight said, holding up the ice cream.

Kana inclined her head, grinning as she continued to smoke.

"So, how did it go in Hawaii?" Midnight asked, not having had time before to ask.

"It went alright," Kana said. "Got into a fight with Palani's brother, but I expected at least that."

"The brother that hit her?"

"Yeah."

"You kick his ass?"

"It was more like a draw," Kana said, making a face.

"You'll get him next time," Midnight said, grinning.

"Uh-huh…" Kana said, rolling her eyes. "So when are we heading back?"

"Hopefully day after tomorrow."

Kana nodded.

The following day, the chiefs of the Mission Support Bureau, Bureau of Narcotic Enforcement, Bureau of Investigations, and the California Anti-Terrorism Information Center decided to take the new Attorney General on a "real" tour of their abilities. MSB took Midnight, Kana, and Tiny up in both the fixed-winged King Air aircraft as well as the Jet Ranger helicopter they'd traded a local sheriff's office some older helicopters for. The three were impressed. They were also shown any number of interesting gadgets by both CATIC and the Bureau of Investigation. Phil Griffin—"Griff," as Midnight called him—joined them late in the morning at the range as the rangemaster for MSB ran them through their paces.

At one point, Midnight was handed a shotgun. Griff walked over and took it out of her hands. The rangemaster looked at him oddly.

"Midnight has a problem with shotguns," Griff said, grinning.

"Fuck you, Griff," Midnight growled, shocking the rangemaster. She grimaced at her outburst, even as Kana and Tiny started chuckling. Griff was remembering many years before, when they had been at a meeting in Sacramento. They'd gotten the opportunities Midnight was getting now; at that time Midnight was only a sergeant working for FORS, but her record impressed everyone. Everyone wanted to help Midnight, including the chief of the Bureau of Narcotic Enforcement at that time, John Davies, the man responsible for getting Midnight to run for Attorney General. That time on the range, however, Midnight had managed to give herself a hairline fracture in her shoulder from the recoil on the shotgun.

"Joe taught me how to keep the shotgun from kicking," Midnight told Griff.

"Ah, I see," Griff said, glancing at Tiny and Kana for confirmation.

"Just give me the shotgun, ya shit," Midnight growled quietly.

Griff laughed, handing Midnight the shotgun and stepping back out of the way. Midnight shot well, not missing once or allowing the recoil to kick her too hard. Griff ended with a round of applause.

"You never cease to amaze me, Midnight," he said, shaking his head.

"Good," Midnight said, grinning.

Later that afternoon they went over to the agent academy. During the course of introductions, Midnight's extraordinary hand-to-hand combat abilities were brought up by someone that had grown up in San Diego.

"I always wanted to be you when I grew up," the young woman said, an awestruck look on her face.

"Okay, that," Midnight said, grinning, "made me feel really old!"

"Oh, ma'am, I'm sorry!" the woman exclaimed, wide-eyed.

Griff was hiding his grin behind his hand when Midnight turned on him. She narrowed her eyes. "Watch it, Griffin, or I'll take you down in front of all these kids."

That, of course, inspired cheers for Midnight to do it. Griff looked around the room, his expression serious and threatening. "Don't make me fire any of you."

There was a moment of stunned silence, then Griff grinned again and the room broke up into laughter.

"Come on, old man," Midnight cajoled. "Think you can take me?"

"I know I can," Griff replied flippantly, rolling his eyes. "I wouldn't want to hurt ya though…"

"Come on, let's go," Midnight said, narrowing her eyes.

Once again, Midnight found herself in a gym with the mats laid out and the academy attendees cheering for her. She felt like it was déjà vu; she'd had this same thing happen many years before, including between her and Randy when Randy was in the academy. The situation had been much different then—this was for fun, not revenge.

Midnight had been given a pair of academy sweats and a T-shirt with *Chevalier* printed across the back. She'd changed into those. She stood barefoot on the mat, waiting for Griff to make his first move.

"Now, you have told the Samoan Express this is just for fun, right?" Griff asked, grinning as he nodded toward Kana and Tiny, who stood not far away.

Midnight laughed, nodding. "Quit stalling, Griffin, and make your move." She stood with her feet shoulder-width apart and her hands down at her sides, her fingers working. It was her fighter's stance; she'd never fought like a cop.

Griff went to throw a punch. Midnight blocked it and brought her other arm up, shoving him back. Griff stepped in, grabbing her arm that was still extended, and went to flip her over his back. Instead of letting him turn to put his back into her stomach, she brought her foot up and shoved him away from her. He still held her arm, and turned quickly, so his chest was to her back, bringing his other arm around to get her in a sleeper hold. As he started to bring his other arm around, she elbowed him in the stomach, making him loosen his hold. She turned in his grasp and, bending down, stepped back, bringing her arms up through his hold and breaking it. Moving quickly, she stepped in and dropped him to the mat with a well-placed foot behind his knee. She came down with one knee on his chest, her fist stopping a hair's breadth from his face.

A cheer erupted from the crowd, which had stood mesmerized by the display. There had been a couple of moments when they were sure Griff had Midnight, but she'd pulled it out in the end. They could tell by the way that both Midnight and Griff were breathing that they'd both been playing to win. Midnight got up, and Kana moved to help Griff up as Midnight turned to the group.

"As you can see," she said, grinning, "if you learn good skills, you keep them forever."

The class cheered louder. Midnight turned to Griff, extending her hand to him. He took it, nodding and smiling at her.

"Still don't like to get beat, do you?" he said.

"Nope," Midnight replied with a grin of her own.

That night, they stayed in a hotel cabin, arranged by Griff. Midnight had asked for a chance to see the mountains, so he'd arranged a log-style cabin for the three of them. It was in an area called Kyburz. It was very rustic, with a fireplace in the bedroom set aside for Midnight. Unfortunately, Midnight wasn't in a position to appreciate it as she would normally, since she was sincerely wishing she'd never even considered doing the exercise with Griff. She was aching from head to toe. Kana handed her a bottle.

"Use five drops of this in your bath," she said. "It'll help."

Midnight opened the bottle and smelled it. "What is it?"

"Juniper oil," Kana said, holding up a bag that held a number of bottles, all with different herbs marked on them. Kana shrugged. "Palani bought it for me—she knows how I am with holistic medicine, so she knew I'd love this."

272

"Well, I'll let you know," Midnight said with a grin as she walked into the bathroom.

A half hour later, Kana knocked on the bathroom door.

"Yes?" Midnight called.

"Chief?"

"Open the door, Kana. It's okay."

Kana opened the door to see that the shower curtain was pulled far enough forward to cover Midnight except for her legs. She grinned. "Everything okay in here?"

"Oh, Kana, I think I'm in love with your girlfriend..." Midnight sighed dreamily.

Kana chuckled. "It's good stuff, huh?"

"Oh yeah..." Midnight said, sounding thoroughly satisfied.

"I'll let her know you like it. Chances are good you'll end up with a set in your Christmas stocking."

"You got yourself a good woman, K."

"Don't I know it."

Later in the evening, Kana, Tiny, and Midnight had grouped in Midnight's bedroom, watching TV together. It was getting colder by the minute, and the heater in the room wasn't keeping up. Midnight flipped through the channels and found the weather. The report wasn't good. A storm was headed for Sacramento, and it was expected to bring strong winds and drop heavy snow where they were, along with a temperature drop of about forty degrees.

"Nice," Midnight said, rolling her eyes. "Wanna bet our flight's not leaving in the morning?"

"Shit," Kana said as she reached for the phone to call Palani. Midnight picked up her cell, as did Tiny. They all called their loved ones to warn them of the possible delay in returning home.

Just as Midnight was hanging up with Rick, there was a knock on the cabin door. Kana got up and answered it; she came back looking grim.

"What?" Midnight asked, worried instantly.

"Nothing really bad, Chief, relax," Kana assured her with a grin. "But we're apparently going to get a bit colder here pretty quick."

"Why?" Tiny asked.

"That was one of the hotel people. Their furnace is blown, and they can't get it fixed tonight. So what do you want to do, Chief?"

"What are our options?" Midnight asked.

"Well," Kana said, "it's the day before Thanksgiving… Chances are real good there won't be anything available anywhere else. But… we could use the fact that you're the AG…" Kana knew the answer before Midnight even said it.

"No way," Midnight said, shaking her head. "I'm not going to put someone else out of a room just so I can be comfortable. Not my style, K."

"I know," Kana said, grinning, glad that Midnight hadn't changed at all in the twenty years she'd known her. "I just thought I'd put it out there."

"Now, if you and Tiny want to get a room with heat, I can certainly put in a call," Midnight offered.

"We're your security," Tiny said.

"And we sleep where you sleep," Kana finished.

Midnight blew her breath out, nodding. "Okay," she said, getting up and looking around. "We've got the fireplace in here." She grinned. "One perk to being AG, huh? It looks wood-burning—let's confirm that and get out and grab some wood, or Duraflames or something, for the night. If we all stay in here, we can keep the door closed and stay warm."

"Whose idea was this mountain retreat thing anyway?" Tiny asked.

Kana widened her eyes, even as Midnight looked heavenward with attempted innocence.

"Oops," Midnight said, grinning.

"Uh-huh."

Later that night, Tiny was happily asleep in front of the fire on the floor on a mattress brought over by the hotel management. Kana and Midnight were in the queen-sized bed, under two down comforters. Midnight was wearing her sweats from the academy as well as thick wool socks. Kana was wearing her usual sweatpants with a tank top; she'd already shed her sweatshirt because it was too hot for her in the room.

Kana lay listening to the wind whistle outside, wondering how high the snow was going to be in the morning. The hotel manager had told her that the valley was getting hit hard with rain and hail too. Turning over on her side, Kana noticed that Midnight was shivering. The covers had slipped off her shoulders. Kana reached over, pulling the covers back up. She closed her eyes then, forcing herself to go to sleep, knowing that she needed to be fully recharged in the morning in case they had to dig out of the snow, or anything else.

During the course of the night, Midnight was sure she was freezing to death. She gravitated toward the only other heat source in the bed. In the wee hours of the morning, she came to the realization that she was curled up in Kana's arms. She grinned to herself, thinking, *Oh, here's one to tell Rick about.* She had to admit to herself, it did feel very secure lying there. Kana had the same kind of power to protect her that Rick did, but she had the gentleness of a woman.

Midnight had never had a problem with gay people, so she didn't worry that Kana was making a pass at her or anything. Kana was warm; Midnight knew she'd moved toward that in the middle of the night. Kana had more than likely done what was totally natural for her. Midnight moved her head to look up at Kana. This woman had become one of her most trusted friends over the years. Now she was Midnight's own protection from harm. Midnight was fairly sure Kana had no idea how much it meant that she was willing to protect her with her life. It meant everything to Midnight. It was the ultimate show of loyalty, and Midnight valued that more than anything in the world.

Kana had felt Midnight stir. She opened her eyes, looking down at her and realizing with a start where Midnight was lying and that she had her arms wrapped around her.

"Oh, shit, Chief, I'm sorry…" Kana said, starting to pull back.

"Relax, K," Midnight said quietly. "We've been friends for a long time. I trust you, implicitly."

Kana smiled. "That means a lot, Midnight," she said softly.

"You being my protection means a lot, K."

"A long time ago, you gave me my life back, Midnight," Kana said, saying what all of them thought. "For that, I'm willing to lay it down for you."

Midnight smiled, unable to think of a suitable reply. Instead she leaned forward, hugging Kana. Kana hugged her back, smiling fondly.

"Should I leave the room?" Tiny asked from his mattress.

"Go back to sleep, Ako," Kana said, throwing a pillow at him.

Tiny chuckled quietly and turned back over on his stomach.

Midnight and Kana went back to sleep as well, sleeping for another three hours. When they got up, Tiny had stoked the fire, adding wood to it to keep the room warm. Kana got on the phone to check the status of their flight. Predictably, it was canceled.

"Anything going out today at all?" Kana asked. "Okay, well, I guess I'll keep calling. Thanks."

She hung up the cell phone, tossing it on the bed. "Nothing," she said, shaking her head.

"Better still," Midnight said, grimacing, "this storm is building, and it's headed for home now too."

"Damn…" Kana said, grimacing. "I'm calling Palani—I don't want her home alone."

"Have her go to Joe's," Midnight said. "She's closest to them, and they have the room."

Kana nodded. "You might want to call your niece and Cat, tell them to get off the beach."

"That's right, they haven't moved yet. I'll call them."

"Think Joe'll mind if I send Jess over there too?" Tiny asked.

"No, he won't mind. Do it," Midnight said. "Everyone was headed over there for Thanksgiving anyway. Maybe they should just stay there?"

An hour later they had made their calls, and it had been decided that everyone would stay at Joe's house, because the part of the storm that had hit them the night before would hit San Diego right about five in the afternoon.

"Now, can we get off this mountain?" Kana asked. "I don't think we should take the chance of staying here again tonight." They'd been informed that a second and third wave were headed for them. It wasn't snowing at that point.

"Where do we go, though?" Midnight asked.

"Griff's?" Kana said.

"No," Tiny said, shaking his head, even as he started dialing again. "Jess's family lives here—I'll ask her."

Five hours later, Midnight, Kana, and Tiny were welcomed with open arms by Jess's family. They had set three extra places at their Thanksgiving table for them. Jess's mother had set them up in bedrooms and assured them that the heat in the family home was working just fine. Midnight called Rick to let him know they'd made it to the house and that everything was fine. She could hear the relief in his voice.

"I miss you," he said softly.

Midnight smiled. "I miss you too, babe, trust me on that. Just be safe today, okay? Stay at Joe's with the kids."

"I plan to, babe. If nothing else, Joe'll need help getting everyone settled and making sure the house is secure. Don't worry, me and the kids will be safe," he assured her, knowing that was her chief concern.

"That's exactly what I needed to hear," she said, knowing he knew her well enough to know that.

"Joe and I will take care of our family, babe," Rick said. "You just stay there and be safe too."

"I will. Jess's mom is already talking about dessert—I think I'm going to gain about twenty pounds in this house today alone."

Rick laughed. "Well, eat and be content, love."

"I love you," she said, feeling a tug at her heart.

"And I love you, baby," he said, his tone softening again.

They hung up a few minutes later, and Rick finished getting things together for him, Mikeyla, and Ricardo to stay over at Joe's for the night.

Joe had called everyone in the Gang and informed them that they were to bring provisions to stay. They were told in no uncertain terms that this was not a request, but an order. Joe even told Kyle this; Kyle laughed. He knew Joe was relaying what Midnight wanted. He had learned enough about this extended family to know that keeping everyone safe was Midnight's main concern. She worried about hurt feelings much later on in the scheme of things. Midnight's attitude was, "As long as you're alive to be pissed at me, that's fine with me."

Everyone arrived at Joe's around 1:00 in the afternoon. Randy, Rhiannon, Stevie, Jeanie, Tammy, and Erin got to work in the kitchen, making the final preparations for dinner. Joe wanted to eat by no later than three, so they had time to get everyone settled into guest rooms. There were only five actual guest rooms, so Joe and Randy were taking the kids in with them and making other adjustments as necessary. They turned their family room into a makeshift room, as well as Randy's office, utilizing the pull-out couch in there for a bed. Fortunately, everyone in the family got along, so people were happy to double up to accommodate.

While most of the girls cooked, the boys got the stereo going. Def Leppard's *Pyromania* was first up. Joe, Rick, Christian, Kevin, and Spider made general nuisances of themselves, singing their little hearts out as they wandered in and out of the kitchen stealing whatever they could from the cutting board or counter. Dave, Susan, Deborah—Susan and Elizabeth's mother—and Allison, their aunt, were last to arrive. Susan looked very uncomfortable and very pregnant. She was due in two weeks. Dave made a point of getting her settled in a comfortable chair with her feet up. She wasn't happy about not being allowed to help prepare dinner, but Dave insisted she rest. She'd had no more trouble with false labor, but Dave wasn't taking any chances at this point. Deborah and Allison went to the kitchen to see what they could do to help.

After getting his wife settled, Dave noted that the children kept making their way over to Susan to offer her anything she wanted—toys, coloring books, cars. He grinned at that last one. JT and Steven were twin souls when it came to the cars thing. They were always dragging their sizable collections of Matchbox cars to every function so they could sit for hours and build tracks and race. Spider's sons, Joseph and Ngao, as well as Brenden, Kyle's youngest son, joined in the lively car play as well that afternoon. The girls, Kat, Emily, and Spider's youngest child and only daughter, Sheree, sat in the play-room discussing the merits of Barbie versus the return of the Care Bear craze. The children were happily occupied.

Mikeyla and Nick were hanging around with Cat, Elizabeth, and Palani. Jess and Tiny were caught up in a discussion with Kyle about law-enforcement ethics, always a passion for them. Darrell found himself moving from group to group, finally settling with his brother as Donovan talked to Joe and Spider.

The meal was, as always, an event, everyone joking and laughing as they ate. Joe made a toast to their absentee matriarch with a comment about Midnight always getting out of the hard work. Everyone laughed at that, knowing Midnight worked harder than any of them. They ate dinner and discussed the oncoming storm; the skies were already darkening threateningly.

"I think you'd be best to board up those, Joe," Rick said, nodding toward the windows that faced the ocean.

"I don't think it'll be a problem," Joe said, shaking his head. "We're pretty far inland here."

"For now," Rick put in.

Another discussion ensued as to whether or not the windows should be boarded up. It was decided that maybe it would be a good idea. After dinner, the men headed outside to do it, while the women cleaned up and got the children settled with dessert. An hour later the men came in soaked to the bone from the rain dumping out of the sky.

"Okay, all of you, out of those wet clothes," Randy ordered. "Joe, you take a shower in our bathroom. Rick, you go into the guest bath at the end of the hallway. Kyle, you get the third bathroom down here. The rest of you, get warm and wait your turn for a hot shower."

The men all grinned at each other, noting that Randy's tone left no room for argument. She was taking over where Midnight would have begun if she'd been there.

"You heard her," Joe said, nodding at the men. "Get to it."

Two hours later, everyone was in warm, dry clothes and lying or sitting in the large family room with a roaring fire and dessert. They talked, laughed, and joked while the storm raged outside. The children intermingled with their parents and the people they'd known as relatives for their entire lives. It was a nice day. At one point the lights went out; fortunately, Joe had a backup generator and it kicked on a few minutes later. The lights were more dim, but at least they still had power.

Later in the evening, everyone was settled in their rooms. Joe and Randy had their kids in with them. Rick, Ricardo, Mikeyla, and Nick all stayed in the same room, and Spider and Tammy and their three kids stayed together. Palani, Jess, Cat, and Elizabeth were in another room. Kyle, Rhiannon, Stevie, and Christian stayed together. Erin, Kevin, Emily, and Steven slept in JT's room, and Dave and Susan had Kat's room to themselves. Kat's bed was a full-sized antique, so it was big enough for Dave and Susan to sleep in. Susan had been tired all evening, so Dave wanted to ensure she'd get some rest that night. Donovan, Jeanie, Darrell, Deborah, and Allison were all in the den downstairs.

"How's your back, honey?" Dave asked Susan as he lay down next to her.

"It's still a bit achy," Susan said. "But I'm alright, David."

Dave leaned down, kissing her forehead. "Maybe if you turned over on your side, it would shift the baby just a bit."

Susan nodded and turned over, moaning softly as she did.

"Honey, I'll be right back, okay?" Dave said, feeling his sixth sense tingling. Something wasn't right here.

He got up, leaving the room and walking downstairs to the den, where Deborah was sleeping. Kneeling next to her, he touched her gently on the shoulder. "Deborah," he whispered.

"Hmm?" she murmured sleepily.

"Deborah, I think Susan might be going into labor. I might need your help."

"What?" Deborah exclaimed loudly as she sat up.

"I don't know it for sure," Dave said, glancing around at the others, who were now looking at him. "But her back's been aching all day, and it doesn't seem to be letting up."

Deborah took a deep breath, even as a crack of thunder rolled outside. "What about trying to get her to a hospital?"

"In this?" Donovan said, shaking his head.

"Donovan's right," Dave said. "I won't take a chance on getting both her and the baby killed trying to negotiate this storm."

Deborah nodded. "Well, if she is in labor it can take hours, so perhaps we'll be able to make it to a hospital once the storm breaks."

Dave glanced at Donovan, who only grinned. Deborah was basically thinking wishfully at this point. If Susan was in labor, there was no way that by the time this storm blew itself out she'd be in any condition to travel to a hospital.

"Look, Deborah," Dave said calmly, even if inwardly he was shaking like a leaf. "I need you to go up and stay with her for a few minutes. I'm going to go talk to Joe and let him know what's going on."

"Alright," Deborah said, sounding relieved to have something to do. She got up, put on her bathrobe, and headed upstairs.

Dave looked at Donovan and Jeanie. "We've got a lot of cops in this house. I just hope most of us remember all the first aid we took."

Dave went up to talk to Joe next. He knocked lightly, and heard Joe stir and call out, "Come."

Dave opened the door, seeing Joe and Randy lying in the center of the bed with the kids on either side of them.

"What's up, Dave?" Joe asked.

"Well," Dave said, leaning against the doorjamb, "here's the thing. I think my wife might be in labor."

"What?" Joe exclaimed, looking stunned.

"She's not due for two weeks," Dave said, shaking his head, as if wanting to deny the possibility.

"That's a give or take due date, Dave," Randy put in.

"Give or take what?"

"Two weeks," Randy said with a grin.

"Shit," Dave muttered.

Joe grinned this time. "Not to worry, man. We've got very capable people under this roof. We'll take care of everything."

Dave nodded. "Well, I'll let you know if she gets worse. I just wanted to kind of give you a heads-up at this point. I could be totally wrong."

Joe nodded, thinking it wasn't likely that Dave was wrong. Besides the fact that Dave's instincts were usually right on, Susan had been having back pain all day. Randy had even commented to Joe earlier that it could be back labor. Joe had rolled his eyes and told her not to jinx them. Too late.

"Come get me if she gets worse," Joe said. "I don't see the point in waking anyone else up. If she's in labor, it could be a long night—let them sleep as long as they can."

Dave nodded, agreeing completely with Joe's point. "You got it, man. Thanks."

"No problem," Joe said with a grin.

Dave went back to the room he was staying in with Susan. Deborah was on the bed, sitting behind Susan, rubbing her back. Dave watched for a moment.

"What are you doing?" he asked softly.

"Massaging her back," Deborah replied, glancing back at him.

Dave walked over to the bed. "Show me how," he said, sitting beside Deborah.

Deborah smiled, pleased to see that Dave was willing to do anything to make Susan feel better. She'd observed all evening how Dave catered to her daughter's every wish. He was very attentive and very loving. They were very good qualities. Deborah showed Dave how to massage Susan's back in a circular pattern. Susan moaned softly. Deborah moved off the bed, letting Dave lie down behind Susan to keep massaging her.

"You okay, honey?" he asked solicitously. "Does that help?"

"Mmhmm…" she murmured.

"Try to rest. You need to save your strength."

"Hmm?"

"I think you might be in labor, honey," Dave said gently. "Don't worry, okay? Don't worry, I'm here. I won't let anything happen to you, okay?" His voice was soothing, and Susan trusted him with everything she had. "Just rest," he said, his voice dropping to a rhythmic cadence. "You need to relax. Concentrate on my hand. Feel the heat of my hand on your back. You feel it, honey? Just imagine that the circles I'm making are a whirlpool, with the center being the outlet for all your tension. Take a slow, deep breath, nice and deep... now, as you blow it out, let the tension go with it. Start with your arms, draw in all that tension with your breath, and as you blow it out, feel that tension swirl down and out of this whirlpool at your back. Good girl... now in again, honey... let the tension in your shoulders go... good, good. Now your back, let it all go. Good, good. Now your neck, let it ease right out... good girl... good, honey... keep breathing nice and deep."

A few minutes later, Susan was asleep, and Deborah was once again astounded by her son-in-law's depth of abilities. There didn't seem to be anything Dave Dibbins couldn't achieve where Susan was concerned. Dave glanced up, realizing that Deborah was still in the room.

"Do you think she's in labor?" he asked, his blue eyes begging Deborah to tell him she didn't think so.

Deborah's eyes went to Susan, then back to Dave. She nodded slowly. "It's very possible. I was early with both girls."

"How early?"

"Two weeks with Susan, three with Elizabeth."

Dave took a deep breath, expelling it as he nodded slowly.

"You should get some rest too, Dave," Deborah said. "It could be a long night."

Dave nodded, not looking happy about the idea of his wife being in labor during the worst rainstorm in decades. Dave wanted, above all else, for Susan to be safe. If she had to give birth here, with no medical personnel available, it would be dangerous. Dave didn't like the idea of that at all.

In the end, he didn't sleep much, dozing off a couple of times. The last time he was awakened by Susan's cry.

"What is it, honey? What is it?" he asked, touching her face gently.

"Oh God, David, I think that was a contraction," she said, her voice fearful.

"Okay, honey, okay," he soothed. "I'm here, I'll take care of you, okay? You trust me?"

"Yes, David," she said.

"Good," he said, kissing her forehead. "We're going to sit here and time these contractions. It'll give us an idea of how long we've got. Don't worry, honey, we've got a house full of cops—there's no safer place to be if you can't be in a hospital, okay?"

Susan nodded, looking less fearful now. She trusted Dave and her entire extended family. She knew they'd take care of her.

Within an hour, Susan's contractions were seven minutes apart. Everyone was awake; the kids had been moved to a room down the hall. They'd moved Susan to Joe and Randy's bed, wanting to give her all the room she needed to be comfortable. Spider and Palani were hard at work in the kitchen, putting together herbs to soothe and relax Susan. Palani had brought a few things with her, always needing help relaxing when Kana wasn't there. Spider found a few useful things in Randy's cupboards. They put together an essence from the peel of an orange and some lavender oil Randy had. They cooked up some chamomile and sweet balm for relaxation and soothing. Palani also put together some juniper and chamomile and added it to some lotion.

Inside the room, Dave was sitting behind Susan, her back against his chest, his legs on either side of her as he leaned against the headboard. It was obvious to everyone that Susan's contractions were becoming more painful. Dave was talking to her constantly, massaging her back gently. Elizabeth, Cat, and Randy were helping Susan breathe through the pains. Tammy was at Susan's feet, massaging them, trying to help relax her. Palani and Spider came in and set up a couple of simmering potpourri pots. Palani put a third pot next to the bed, making sure the scent was drifting toward Susan.

"Susan," she said softly. "You need to breathe in deep through your nose now. Take this scent in, let it relax you."

Susan did as she was told, closing her eyes and breathing deep through her nose over and over again. She felt a sense of well-being settle over her. Her family was with her; she couldn't be safer anywhere in the world. They would take care of her, she knew that. They loved her, they'd take care of her. Was that in her head? Or had Dave just said that? It didn't matter—she knew it was true.

"Dave?" Palani said, holding out the bottle of lotion.

"What's that?" he asked curiously.

"It'll help soothe her," Palani said, smiling. "I've added herbs to it."

Dave nodded, understanding completely. Palani, like Dave, Kana, and Spider, believed in holistic medicine, which meant she understood the properties of certain herbs. If she said this lotion would soothe Susan, Dave believed her. He held his hands out to her and she poured a bit onto his palms. He rubbed his hands together vigorously, warming the lotion, then slid them back down onto Susan's back. She sighed in relief, resting her head against his shoulder. He smiled at Palani in gratitude.

They spent the next few hours taking turns trying to distract Susan from her pain. Kyle checked her three hours in; she was dilated to five centimeters, as best he could figure. Everyone stepped up the encouragement. Deborah rubbed ice over Susan's lips, while Cat and Elizabeth continued to help her breathe through the pains. Rick had taken over for Dave, whose back had begun to ache from supporting her weight and being so tense. Randy ushered Dave to her shower and told him to soak his back, that he needed to be up for this. He complied gratefully.

Rick sat behind Susan, supporting her weight and talking to her soothingly. He told her over and over again that she was doing so well, that Midnight would be so proud of her right now. Mikeyla agreed with her father; she and Nick had awakened when Rick was summoned. Mikeyla had been the one to take Ricardo into the room where the kids were sleeping, and had then joined the rest of the family in helping Susan out. Tammy and Erin lent their more recent expertise on breathing techniques. Jeanie and Stevie did their best not to totally change their minds about ever giving birth to a child. Everyone pitched in one way or the other. There were frequent checks on the children. Joe and Rick were taking turns checking the downstairs windows to ensure they were intact and holding against the wind and rain.

Randy, Erin, Tammy, and Rhiannon kept coffee and tea coming, ignoring the surreptitious trips to the bar for shots of tequila for fortification.

It had been seven hours since Susan's labor had begun; it was seven in the morning by that time. Everyone was exhausted, but no one talked about sleeping. Randy goaded a few of them out of the room, saying it was too hot in there with all the body heat. Dave, Deborah, Joe, Rick, Randy, and Allison stayed. Everyone else took turns to check on Susan and see if anyone in the room needed anything.

At one point Kyle checked Susan's progress again, grimacing. "She's still at nine," he said—she'd been at nine centimeters for two hours. The pains were getting worse and worse, and Susan was doing her best not to cry out. She'd been breathing through the ungodly urge to push for two hours now. She couldn't push until she was dilated to ten.

Dave changed places with Joe, who had been supporting Susan. Getting behind his wife, Dave lowered his head to her ear. "I know this hurts, honey, I know it hurts. Scream if you have to—do it, it'll let out some of your tension. You've got to relax…" Susan gave in for a moment and cried out; Dave winced at the sound of it, and everyone in the room saw it. "That's good, honey, just do that if you feel like it, okay?" His voice was shaking, and everyone heard it. Dave kept his head down by her ear. "I love you, Susan, I love you. My life is so much more than it would ever have been without you. You can do this. I know you can."

Dave had tears running down his cheeks as he talked to her, and he didn't care if everyone in the room saw it. He was worried to death about his wife. She was everything to him, and if something happened to take her away from him, he had no idea how he'd go on. Suddenly Rick's devastation over losing Midnight when they'd thought she was dead, Joe's leaving the force and going back to England when Randy died for a full minute in the hospital—it all made sense. These women were their lives, and if they lost them, it was over. Here was his beautiful, delicate, sweet English wife in agony, all to give him a son. It wasn't worth it—nothing was worth this. He just wanted it to stop.

"I'd give anything to take this pain away, honey… anything," he said, his voice so anguished, Susan felt it to her very core. She reached up, taking his hand in hers and squeezing it.

"I can do this, David. I love you. I want to do this for you," she said, her voice strong again.

Elizabeth walked in then. It had been passed along to everyone that Susan was stalled at nine centimeters dilated. Everyone said she needed to relax to dilate to ten.

Walking over to the bed, Elizabeth sat down, looking at her sister, amazed again at how brave she was being. Susan had always seemed like the more timid of the two of them, but Elizabeth was finding that her strength was a very dignified, quiet strength. Elizabeth found that she admired Susan's courage in the face of such a terrifying unknown as childbirth.

"Hey, Susie," Elizabeth said, using her childhood name for her sister.

Susan looked at Elizabeth, pain still clouding her deep blue eyes even as she'd decided to be brave for Dave.

"Got something I need to tell you," Elizabeth said with an impish grin.

"What's that, Elizabeth?" Susan asked, her tone halfway between impatient and pained.

"Remember that Lladró you had way back when? The one with the black kitten and the blond-haired lady in finery?"

"Yes…" Susan said, her tone cautionary. "The one that I found broken under my bed?"

"Yeah, that would be the one," Elizabeth said, far too pertly.

"What about it?" Susan asked, sensing that she was about to find out what had happened her favorite statue.

"Well," Elizabeth said, screwing up her lips in a grimace and rolling her eyes heavenward. "I kinda broke it."

"You what!" Susan screeched. "You rotten little brat. You broke it and then tossed it under my bed, letting me think one of the cats had done it. You bloody little monster!"

Dave and Kyle had been exchanging glances over Susan's head as the discussion ensued. In her anger, Susan had momentarily forgotten about the pain she was in. It had relaxed the tension in her body, and she'd just dilated to ten.

"Uh, Susan," Kyle cut in on her diatribe. "You're dilated to ten, little one, so any time you want to go ahead and push that baby out, you can."

Susan looked shocked, her mouth dropping open. Then she looked back at Elizabeth, who was smiling brilliantly now, her blue eyes twinkling excitedly.

"I didn't really break the statue, Susie," she said, giving her sister a rakish wink. "But once you've delivered my nephew, the first thing I will buy you is a hand-numbered Lladró just like that one."

Dave grinned at his sister-in-law, even as Rick came up to take his place.

"You need to be down there to deliver your son," Rick told Dave.

Dave nodded. "Liz, get your mother," he said. "Randy, will you help hold her legs?"

"Of course," Randy said, moving to one side of Susan.

"What's the breathing on this?" Rick asked, realizing he had no idea.

"Start of a contraction, deep breath in, push to a count of ten, breath out, start again, three times."

Rick nodded. "And you'll remind me again, right?"

"Right," Randy said, winking at him.

Deborah rushed in, moving to Susan's other side, and the pushing began. Rick coached Susan, along with Joe, Randy, and Elizabeth.

"You're doing great, Susan, just keep it up," Rick said, feeling his niece's body strain with the effort. "Okay, ready to go again?"

Susan nodded, even as she gasped for breath.

"One more time," Rick said. "Deep breath in… one, two, three, four, five, six, seven, eight, nine, and ten… breathe out… and relax, Susan… good… great…"

Elizabeth moved in to rub a piece of ice over her sister's lips. Susan nodded gratefully.

"You're doing great, honey," Dave said encouragingly. "We're almost there. You can do this, Susan. You can do it."

Susan nodded, taking a deep breath as she felt another contraction coming.

"Okay, ready, let's go again," Rick said, glancing at Joe; he nodded encouragingly.

It was almost another hour before the baby's head was crowning. When Dave saw it, he could hardly believe his eyes. "Oh my God, Susan, he's crowning. Hold on, babe, hold on. Don't push just yet."

Susan nodded, relaxing against her uncle, gasping for breath. Rick bent his head, kissing her forehead softly. "You're almost there, little girl. You're almost there."

"Okay, honey," Dave said, after getting Kyle over to check things out. "I need you to push, but not as hard as you have, okay? Just one push, not too hard, okay?"

Susan nodded, drawing in a deep breath.

"Okay, one, two, three, four…" Rick counted off.

"Easy, honey, easy," Dave said gently.

The baby's head came out. "Now a little more, honey." Dave twisted the baby so one shoulder slipped out, then the other. "Okay, honey, one last push and you'll be done."

Susan gave one last moan of effort, and their son was born. The look on Dave's face as his son slid out into his hands could have lit an entire city for days. He was in awe of what Susan had just done, and of what he was staring at. His son, their baby.

"Oh my God, Susan, he is so beautiful…" Dave said, his awe reflected in his voice.

Kyle moved in, tying off the cord tightly and handing Dave a knife to cut it with. Dave cut the cord with so much reverence that everyone in the room couldn't help but be moved by it. Kyle instructed him on clearing the baby's mouth and the good old smack on the butt that got the baby's lungs cleared. The baby let out a wail that could be heard throughout the house. Everyone grinned and rejoiced.

Randy took the baby and quickly cleaned him with the warm water she had on the dresser nearby. Then she swaddled him and took him to Dave. Dave walked over and placed their son on Susan's chest. He sat beside her and kissed her temple.

"I love you," he said again. "Thank you for giving me such a beautiful gift."

Susan smiled, looking exhausted but beautiful. She turned her head up to Dave, kissing his lips softly. "Thank you for giving me the chance to. I love you, David."

They smiled at each other, and no one in the room existed for a moment but them.

Randy took a picture of them, wanting to capture that particular look of complete and utter devotion. It was their first family picture, although Christian and Donovan had insisted on videotaping the entire event. Susan had early on refused any kind of close-up shots of anything below the waist. Dave had agreed with that wholeheartedly. Rick had liked the idea of videotaping it, since Midnight had missed it and he knew she'd be upset to have done so.

Randy insisted on cleaning everything up, including Susan, while only her husband remained in the room. She wanted Susan in clean, dry clothes, and sitting on clean bedding. Dave held the baby as Rick and Randy helped Susan up and then settled her back in as quickly as possible. When everyone filed in to get their first look at Dave and Susan's baby, they couldn't believe how perfect the newborn was.

"He looks like his mother," Dave said, smiling fondly.

"Thank God," Spider said, grinning.

"Stuff it, Spider," Dave said, grinning too.

After everyone had checked out the baby and congratulated Dave and Susan, they all went to bed. It was actually two in the afternoon by then, but everyone was exhausted. The storm had blown itself out by that time, but no one even noticed.

Deborah walked into the room a little while after everyone had gone. Susan was lying on the bed, propped up against many pillows, wearing a white nightgown with pink ribbons. She was the picture of glowing motherhood. Dave sat next to her, his body above hers on the bed, his arm around her, caressing his son's head as he slept against his mother. Dave's lips were pressed against Susan's forehead affectionately.

"Now, that is a picture I will always carry with me," Deborah said softly.

Walking over to the bed, she sat down carefully, reaching out to touch her grandson's soft, down-like hair. Deborah looked at Susan.

"I am so proud of you, Susan," she said sincerely. "You were so very brave this morning. You have become such a strong woman in your own right, and I am so happy for you. And Dave," she said, her eyes going to him, "if there was ever a time I doubted how much you love my daughter, the last fourteen hours would have proven it for good. You are a very strong, loving, and gentle man, Dave Dibbins, and I am very grateful that my daughter found you."

Dave smiled. "That makes two of us," he said, kissing Susan's head again.

"And you," Deborah said, leaning forward to kiss her grandson's head gently, "are a beautiful young man. With no name?" she queried, looking at Susan.

"That's going to be up to your daughter," Dave said, looking down at Susan with a smile. "She did all the work to have him—she gets to name him."

Susan's eyes widened, but then she smiled, biting her lip. "Even if I choose David Edward Dibbins?"

Dave took a deep breath, rolling his eyes, but nodded. "Even if…"

Susan's face lit up with a brilliant smile. "Then that is his name. David Edward Dibbins."

Deborah laughed softly. She left them then, and made her way back to the room she was sharing with Allison, Cat, and Elizabeth.

She saw that Cat and Elizabeth were sitting up talking. She walked over to where they sat on one bed and sat down next to her daughter.

"I must say," Deborah said, reaching out to brush Elizabeth's red hair off her shoulder, "I was very proud of you today."

"You were?" Elizabeth said quizzically.

"Yes, Elizabeth, I was," Deborah said, realizing how hard it was for her daughter to believe her when she told her she was proud of her—it wasn't something she'd done very often. "You were very strong for your sister when she needed you most. And that is something that I'm so happy to see in you. I always knew you had the strength in you, I just never got a chance to see you use it. I'm very glad I did today."

Elizabeth was speechless. She felt Cat's hand squeezing hers. Deborah could tell her daughter had no idea what to say, so she leaned forward, taking Elizabeth into her arms and hugging her. "You have done so many amazing things lately, Elizabeth. Thank you for letting me share them with you."

Elizabeth couldn't hold back the tears in her eyes anymore. She hugged her mother tight, feeling so good at that moment, and she had no idea what to do with the feeling.

Cat smiled, looking back into Elizabeth's mother's eyes. She nodded to Deborah, knowing that she had just done something she'd never done before. It was the right thing for Elizabeth at that moment. There was something new to be thankful for now.

***

Rick lay in his bed at Joe's house, staring at the ceiling. Mikeyla and Nick had taken Ricardo with them to play in the family room. The teenagers could rejuvenate quickly, whereas the adults were just plain worn out. Rick found he couldn't sleep, so he decided to call Midnight. She answered on the second ring.

"Hi," Rick said, sounding exhausted.

Midnight picked up on it instantly. "Why are you so tired? You guys party all night or what?" she asked with a grin.

"Oh yeah, big party," Rick said, grinning too. "Your niece was the main attraction."

"What?" Midnight asked, sensing something more was going on here.

"We have a new addition to the family."

"Oh my God! She had the baby?" Midnight asked, glancing at Tiny and Kana, whose heads had snapped up at the tone in Midnight's voice. She covered the mouthpiece for a moment. "Susan had the baby."

"Is she okay?" Midnight asked Rick, suddenly worried. "Oh shit, she had it there? Or did you get her to a hospital somehow?"

"Nope, she had it right here at Joe's house."

"Jesus, she's brave…" Midnight breathed.

"You would have been so proud of her, Night," Rick said, smiling. "She went through it like a trooper. And Dave, he was fantastic. He delivered their son."

"He did?" Midnight asked, looking thrilled, then made a face. "Damnit, and I missed it!"

"Well, Blue and Pony got tape on it, so not to worry."

"Oh, I love those boys!"

Midnight was still in the Harland home, sitting in a comfortable overstuffed chair. The wind was whistling by the windows. She sighed.

"God, I miss you," she said softly.

"I miss you too, babe," he said, his heart aching at the sound of her sadness.

"I'm hoping that we'll catch a break tomorrow morning and get home. I want to see that new baby."

"He is so beautiful, Night, you can't believe…"

They spent the next three hours on the phone, touching with their voices, needing to be close. Rick didn't feel like he'd experienced the night before without sharing it with Midnight.

CHAPTER 12

On Saturday morning, Midnight walked off the plane. She made her way down the gangway with long strides. Kana and Tiny grinned behind her, knowing she was anxious to see Rick again. At the end of the gangway, Rick stood waiting for her. His face lit with a brilliant smile as he saw her. She ran the last few feet straight into his arms. He grabbed her up in a hug, astounded at how happy he was to see her. She'd only been gone five days, but it felt like a lifetime.

"I missed you so much," she whispered.

"I was just thinking the same thing," Rick said, grinning against her hair.

Pulling back, Midnight looked up at him as he set her back down on her feet. He brought his hand up to her cheek, his other arm wrapped around her waist, holding her close to him. Leaning down, he kissed her lips, and she wrapped her arms around his neck, kissing him back. People around them looked on, smiling and enjoying the sight of two people so obviously in love. Many people recognized Midnight Chevalier-Debenshire and her dashing husband from all the press they'd received during the election. Midnight didn't care if people knew who she was or not—she'd never been shy about how she felt about her husband.

Mikeyla and Ricky waited, watching their parents with huge grins on their faces. It was obvious to bystanders that the children were used to seeing their parents being so openly affectionate. When Rick released Midnight, she turned to her children. She picked Ricky up and leaned over to hug Mikeyla.

"I missed you guys so much too," Midnight said, unable to stop smiling.

"Did you see snow, Mama?" Ricky asked.

"I did," Midnight said, nodding. "Way more snow than I ever want to see piled up at my front door again!"

"It was at the front door?" Ricky asked, his eyes widening.

"Yes, baby," Midnight said, smiling. "It's called a snow drift."

"Did you bring me some?"

Midnight shook her head. "Sorry, baby, snow has a bad habit of melting when you take it inside."

"Okay," Ricky said, looking glum for a moment. "Did you make snowmen?"

Midnight glanced at Rick, then over to where Tiny and Kana were talking to their spouses. "Well," Midnight said with a grin, "Tiny almost became one when we sent him out in the snow to start the vehicle. Does that count?"

Ricky laughed at the idea of the big Samoan being covered with snow.

Tiny picked Jess up in his arms, hugging her close.

"You stayed warm, didn't you?" Jessica asked, smiling at how easy it was for him to pick her up. She might as well be a rag doll.

"Yes, honey, I did," he said gently. "Your family was very good to us."

"My mom said it was great to have company. She's always liked you, Nathan, and she's met Midnight before, so I knew she'd love having her there again too. I'm glad you went there."

"I am too. It was much better than a hotel room Thanksgiving dinner—your mother is a great cook," he said, grinning. "Now I know where you get it from."

"Oh, stop it," she said, laughing. "My mother is much, much better than me."

"She isn't near as beautiful, though," Tiny said, smiling at his wife. "So you stayed safe at Joe's?"

"Yes, Nathan, I did," she said, grinning at him. "And I even watched a baby being born."

"I heard that."

"Nathan, he is so beautiful!" she said, her eyes sparkling with the memory.

Tiny looked at her for a long moment. "Our baby would be beautiful too," he said softly.

Jessica's eyes widened. "You mean… Can we? Oh, Nathan, can we?" she asked, her words running over themselves.

She and Tiny had never really talked about having a baby. They'd been married for over ten years, but whenever the subject of babies had come up, Tiny always shied away from the topic. Jessica had talked to his mother, Alea, at one point; she had told her that Tiny was worried about the size of the babies his family had. No child in his family had been born weighing less than nine pounds. Tiny was terrified it would kill tiny little Jessica to have a baby that big.

"You really want a baby, don't you?" Tiny asked, realizing for the first time that he had been remiss in dealing with this issue in their marriage.

"Yes, Nathan, I want our baby," Jess said. "And I know you're worried about how big the baby will be, but I love you and I want us to have a family together."

Tiny nodded, taking a deep breath and blowing it out. "We will talk about it tonight, okay, honey?"

"Okay, Nathan," Jess said, smiling up at him. Her husband had his own way of doing things, and she knew when not to push him. She realized she was now glad that he hadn't been there to see the birth. He would have been terrified to see Susan in so much pain. It would have kept them from having children forever.

Disregarding the people standing all around them, Kana pulled Palani into her arms, kissing her softly on the lips.

"I missed you, little one," she said softly.

"I missed you too," Palani said, smiling up at Kana. "And you missed a lot."

"I heard that," Kana said, grinning. "And when you get pregnant, you're not going to be farther than a hundred feet from a hospital for the last month of the pregnancy."

Palani laughed. "I think we did alright, all of us," she said, gesturing to Rick and Jessica. "Susan had a beautiful baby boy, and they're both perfectly happy and healthy."

"All the same," Kana said, touching Palani on the lips with her index finger, "Dave had no choice but to take that chance. I don't want to be in that position, you understand?"

Palani smiled, knowing that Kana was just worried; it was the last thing anyone wanted for someone they loved. Susan's labor and delivery had turned out alright, but it could have been very different, and everyone knew that. They were all very grateful to the powers that be that the baby and Susan were both fine. Palani nodded, knowing there was no way to assure Kana that everything would go fine with their baby. There was never any way to know.

The following week, everyone was gathered at Midnight and Rick's house for a Thanksgiving replay. Susan brought the baby, and everyone was amazed once again at what a beautiful boy David Edward Dibbins was. His blue eyes were bright and wide, and he had the lightest dusting of golden-blond hair. His tiny face was perfect. He weighed in at seven pounds, five ounces—he was a good-sized baby, and very healthy. Dave was a very proud father and handed out cigars at the party. The men hung out outside on the deck, smoking and talking. The women stayed inside and marveled at how healthy and happy Susan looked, even after her ordeal.

"It wasn't so bad," Susan said, smiling sweetly. "I had my family and the man I love with me—what more could I have wanted?"

"Drugs?" Stevie put in.

"Epidural?" Midnight offered.

"Doctors?" Kana said.

"Nurses," Cat added with a nod.

"Hell, anyone that does this for a profession would have been nice!" Randy put in with a grin.

Everyone laughed at that, agreeing wholeheartedly.

"Okay, so who's next?" Midnight asked, glancing around at the younger women in the room.

Jeanie and Stevie both held their hands up in a defensive gesture.

"Uh-uh," Stevie said.

"No way," Jeanie agreed.

"Oh, come on!" Midnight said with a grin. "You girls face bad guys with guns on a weekly basis—you're afraid of a little labor pain?"

"I'll take the guns," Stevie said, looking convinced.

"Me too," Jeanie said, nodding.

Midnight looked at Erin. "Well, I guess you already have your two, huh? Any more planned?" she asked hopefully.

"Not at this time, Midnight, sorry," Erin said, smiling.

"Damn!" Midnight said, laughing, then turned toward Cat and Elizabeth, noting the look of trepidation on both their faces. "I'm guessing that's a no, huh?"

"That's a hell no," Cat said, grinning.

"And how," Elizabeth agreed, chuckling.

Midnight sighed, shaking her head. "Rhiannon, you and Kyle are going to try again, aren't you?" she asked gently, not wanting to bring up bad memories but wanting to know that they were going to try again for the baby that Rhiannon had lost a year before.

"Yes," Rhiannon said. "We're just letting things go the way they're meant to at this point, though. We figure it'll happen when it's meant to."

Midnight nodded. "Probably the best way, right?" She canted her head at Jessica. "You and Tiny?"

Jessica bit her lip, looking pensive. "We talked about it when he got back from Sacramento, so yeah, we might try here soon."

"Oh, cool!" Midnight said. "And Palani, I'm counting on you too."

Palani smiled, glancing at Kana.

"I have to get my baby fix somehow," Midnight said, grinning. "So I have to live vicariously through all of you."

The other women in the group laughed softly, most of them nodding and understanding completely. Midnight had only been able to give birth once. Having Mikeyla had almost killed her. Subsequent pregnancies had miscarried or been terminated, due to the danger they posed to Midnight's health. It was a sensitive subject for her, but she felt comfortable with her family and knew she could allow herself to be open with them. The women that didn't know about her history would surely be filled in by the ones that did.

The men joined them a little while later, and champagne was passed around to toast the occasion.

Midnight looked around at everyone. "God, this family is just growing and growing, isn't it?" she said, both astounded and pleased.

"And branching out," Joe said, grinning as he stood next to her, his arm around Randy.

"And up," Rick added, winking at Midnight as he stood next to her on the other side.

"I don't know about that…" Midnight said, rolling her eyes.

"Always forward, never back," Dave said, smiling at her.

"The voters can't take it back now, can they?" Christian asked, winking.

"It's called recall," Donovan put in.

"You would know that," Christian countered sourly.

"Education, Blue, education," Donovan muttered with a grin.

"I got your education…" Christian replied, giving him a dirty look.

"Boys…" Stevie said.

"I swear, it's worse than dealing with the children, sometimes," Susan put in, rolling her eyes.

"Same thing," Dave said. "Only these can be sent out to the deck to freeze their butts off while we finish the toast."

"I'd rather be sent to my room," Christian said, grinning.

"No, you'd rather be sent to Stevie's room," Kyle put in, surprising everyone.

"Yeah, there," Christian said, laughing now.

Kana sighed, glancing down at Palani. "And we want a child in this midst?"

304

"Maybe our baby could teach them a thing or two," Palani said, winking at her.

Kana laughed. "Respect of elders, for one…"

"Respect for family," Tiny added, narrowing his eyes at the younger people in the crowd.

"We have respect," Christian said, looking over at Donovan.

"Yeah," Donovan said. "We're just not obvious about it."

"We're stealth," Kevin put in with a grin.

"Ah," Kana said, nodding. "Is that it?"

"That would be it," Christian said, smiling at Kevin for coming up with that one.

"Sounds like bullshit to me," Spider muttered, rolling his eyes heavenward.

"Is that what I smell?" Tiny said.

"No, I think that's the Dibbins kid," Rick said, laughing.

Everyone laughed even as the baby gurgled happily.

"You know, if you kids could just settle for a few minutes," Joe said, narrowing his eyes at all of them, "we could actually drink this champagne before it's room temperature."

"Well, do it then!" Kana said, laughing.

"To Midnight, for achieving what no other woman in this state ever has," Joe said, holding up his glass. "To Kana, for being the newest and best example I have for the proper use of body armor." He said that giving Kana a pointed look; she nodded, looking appropriately chastised. "To Erin and Kevin, for coming through the fire and winning in the end," he said, winking at the two. "To Kyle, for taking over some fairly big shoes, and from what I've heard, he hasn't dropped the ball yet," he said with a grin. Kyle rolled his eyes. "To Cat, for aiding in the straightening out and or up of the one member of our family none of us could ever get a handle on," he said with a wink to Elizabeth. "To Susan, for being the bravest member of our family for allowing a number of fairly terrified cops to deliver her son, her husband being the most frightened of all." Chuckles went up from the group for that one. "And last but by no means least, to Randy," he said, turning to her and smiling as he looked down into her eyes. "For letting me come home to rest my head and heart. And here's to hoping that she'll do me the honor of remarrying me."

With that, he handed Rick his glass and dropped to one knee as he pulled a box out of his pocket and held it up to Randy.

Randy stared at him in disbelief. They hadn't talked about getting remarried. She'd assumed he just wanted things to stay the way they were. She couldn't hold back the tears that came to her eyes instantly. Taking the box with shaking hands, she opened it.

The ring inside was a perfectly cut marquise diamond, at least a carat.

"I already have a wedding ring," she said, awed.

"Now you have another one," Joe said with a smile.

"If you say yes," Midnight put in, nudging Randy.

"Oh," Randy gasped. "Yes, of course, yes. Oh God... Joe..."

Joe stood up, taking her in his arms and kissing her deeply as everyone cheered around them.

Afterward, Midnight lifted her glass.

"To everyone's continued happiness. Thank you for being the family I can count on no matter what happens. And all this because of a little gang I started years ago..." She shook her head as she trailed off.

"To FORS," Rick put in, knowing what she was thinking.

Everyone raised their glasses. "To FORS!"

You can find more information about the author and series here:

www.sherrylhancock.com

www.facebook.com/SherrylDHancock

www.vulpine-press.com/midknight-blue-series

Also by Sherryl D. Hancock:

The *WeHo* series follows a group of women from Los Angeles as they navigate the ups and downs of love, life, work, and everything in between.

www.vulpine-press.com/we-ho

The *Wild Irish Silence* series. Escape into the world of BJ Sparks and discover how he went from the small-town boy to the world-famous rock star.

www.vulpine-press.com/wild-irish-silence-series